RUNNING
IN THE
DARK

RUNNING IN THE DARK

SAM REAVES

THOMAS & MERCER

Text copyright © 2018 by Sam Reaves
All rights reserved.

No part of this book may be reproduced, or stored in a retrieval system, or transmitted in any form or by any means, electronic, mechanical, photocopying, recording, or otherwise, without express written permission of the publisher.

Published by Thomas & Mercer, Seattle

www.apub.com

Amazon, the Amazon logo, and Thomas & Mercer are trademarks of Amazon.com, Inc., or its affiliates.

ISBN-13: 9781542048002
ISBN-10: 1542048001

Cover design by Scott Biel

Printed in the United States of America

AUTHOR'S NOTE

There are towns called Lewisburg in Pennsylvania, West Virginia, Mississippi, Tennessee, Kentucky and Ohio. As far as the author was able to determine, there is no Lewisburg, Indiana. The town, the college and the characters depicted in this novel are fictional, if suggested and informed by real communities and people. Any similarity between the characters and events of this story and any real persons and events is entirely coincidental.

1 |||||||

Abby's phone went off twice while she was running, buzzing angrily in the pouch at her waist. She ignored it. The phone was there for emergencies, not because she thought she owed it to the world to be accessible anywhere at any time. Her running time was hers and nobody else's. Anybody with anything important to say would leave a message.

The heat had eased as the sun had gone down behind the West Side monoliths, and it was a perfect evening for running, a few high cumulus tinted faintly orange in a sky going slowly deep, deep blue over Manhattan. She'd set a good pace, and if she could sustain it she had a shot at knocking off the four-mile loop in under twenty-five minutes. The path was not too crowded and Abby didn't have to weave too much to dodge the strollers, loiterers and miscellaneous humanity drifting through Central Park on a summer evening.

It was glorious to be moving, eating up ground with long smooth strides. Abby had once been able to cover six thousand meters in under twenty-three minutes, but graduate school had put an end to that; without the spur of competitive cross-country she had eased off to a fitness-maintenance level and had recently admitted to herself she would probably never claw back to top form again. But running was still her therapy, her centering technique, her refuge. What intense engagement with mathematical objects did for her mind, running did for her body.

She checked her watch and saw she was going to have to pick up the pace a bit. No matter how strong you felt, the stopwatch was ruthlessly objective, a harsh taskmaster. She dug deeper. Looping back south on the Bridle Path she skirted the reservoir, found enough strength for a bit of a kick and pushed hard to the end just past the tunnel under West Drive. Her watch read *24:53*.

Panting, sweating, wrung out, elated, Abby made her way slowly over to the park exit at Eighty-First Street. It wasn't until she was waiting for the light to change to cross Central Park West that she thought to look at her phone. Her heart sank as she saw the number.

Abby sighed and slipped the phone back into the pouch. She didn't have the energy to deal with Evan right now; she wasn't going to spoil her endorphin high. The light changed and she crossed, looking up into the darkening sky, thinking about the evening ahead. She had work to do, decisions to make, maybe even some preliminary packing. In three weeks she would be leaving for Amherst. Alone.

She reached Columbus and her gaze wandered down the avenue; she would miss all this. There was sadness in the prospect, but mostly there was a sense of freedom. A chapter was over, a new one beginning. With reluctance she reached for her phone. Deal with it now, she thought. Get it out of the way so you can enjoy your shower and supper. She tapped at her phone and put it to her ear to hear the voice mails.

"Abby, please, why aren't you answering? I need to talk to you. I know I've been a pain in the ass, but I really need to see you now. Call me. Please." Abby frowned. Evan's voice in her ear had the strained, urgent tone that always set her on edge. She brought up the second voice mail. *"Abby, I'm sorry. That's all I have to say. I'm just really sorry. Good-bye."*

That was puzzling; Abby walked for half a block with the phone in her hand, just trying to decode it. There hadn't been more than three or four minutes between the two calls, and that didn't seem like enough time for Evan to have a change of heart. But the stressed-out tone had been gone; he had sounded subdued. He had sounded . . . resigned. Abby put the phone back in her pouch.

Resigned was good. The sooner Evan accepted what was happening, the better for everyone. Abby turned a corner and looked up at the windows of her apartment as she always did and was surprised to see the living room window glowing with light. She didn't remember leaving the lamp on.

In the elevator the explanation occurred to her. Evan still had his key. She had hesitated to ask him for it, waiting for him to surrender it as a sign he accepted the new status quo. Her fears were confirmed when she pushed open the door of her apartment and saw Evan's beat-up canvas low tops sitting on the mat where he always parked them. She pushed the door gently shut behind her and sagged against it, closing her eyes. I'm really, really not in the mood for this tonight, she thought. Not tonight. "Hello? Evan?" she called out.

There was no answer. Abby opened her eyes and pushed away from the door. She listened. She could hear the hum of the fridge in the kitchen; she could hear the vast muted rumble of Manhattan outside. There was no other sound. She took three steps toward the living room and stopped. Her heart began to beat wildly.

It was only a chair, one of her four wooden dining room chairs lying on its side in the middle of her living room, and only part of it, the ladder back poking into the visual field framed by the doorway. For a moment Abby could not think why the sight of a chair knocked over on her threadbare Persian rug should send a jolt to her heart like this.

And then her mind caught up and she knew what she was going to see when she stepped into the living room. "Oh, God, no," she said out loud, and as she said it she knew that she was going to be paying for not answering her phone for a long, long time.

- - - - - - - - - - - - - - -

"I'm looking for a metaphor," said Abby. "I'm looking for a mental model to help me cope with this, a way of thinking about it that lets me function."

The therapist was squinting at her with that look that reminded Abby of nothing so much as the Orkin man peering under the sink. "Metaphors can be very helpful." The therapist was a woman of fifty or so, gray and spectral. "I've had people describe their depression as an endless amount of snow to shovel, or a tunnel where everyone but them can see the light at the end."

"Terrific," said Abby. "And this helps them how? Anyway, I'm not *depressed*. Until this happened I was always energetic, focused and happy. I'm still energetic and focused. I'm just not happy with this guilt impaling me. What I am is *traumatized*. I want to know how to recover from the trauma. It's cost me a good job already and I don't want it to cost me anything else."

The therapist nodded slowly, sinking back in her chair. Abby realized suddenly she was through with the whole thing; there was no therapist in New York or anywhere else on earth, no matter how many thousands of dollars Abby paid, who could fix her. "Injuries heal with time," the therapist said.

"Yeah." Abby saw from the clock on the desk that the therapist owed her another seventeen minutes, but she stood up anyway. "I don't want to waste your time."

"Or your money," the therapist said, achieving a genuine insight. She stood to face Abby. "Sometimes a change of scene helps," she said. "Get away, go do something different."

Abby nodded at her. "Exile," she said. "They used to exile people who had committed crimes. Then after a few years they could come back. Maybe it would help."

"Welcome to Lewisburg," said the desk clerk. He was a pale ectomorph with bad skin and colorless hair. "I hope you enjoy your stay." Judging from his tone, it was not an especially fervent hope.

"Me, too," said Abby. She then flashed him a quick smile, not wanting to sound rude. "I hope I'll just be here for a couple of nights. The college is supposed to have an apartment lined up for me soon." That was no better, she sensed, but she didn't bother with the smile this time.

The desk clerk shrugged, shoving her key card across the desk. "Stay as long as you want. You need help with your bags?"

"That would be great, yeah."

From the second-floor walkway outside her room, Abby took stock of her position, fighting the feeling of dismay that had afflicted her ever since a garrulous elderly man driving a Tippecanoe College van had met her at the Indianapolis airport and brought her deep into the Indiana countryside. She could hear her mother saying, "Indiana? What on earth is in Indiana?"

What was in Indiana was this: the Booth Tarkington Motor Inn lying three blocks from the campus where she had accepted a two-year appointment, its twin wings framing two sides of a much-patched asphalt parking lot where a half-dozen vehicles were parked, three of them pickup trucks. The streets on the open sides of the lot were lined with shabby frame houses and trees stirring listlessly in the August heat. A door was open somewhere on the lower level and languid country music floated on the evening air.

Abby wandered back into her room. It was decent, a little down at heel but clean enough, and the college functionary had been apologetic about the need to stash her here. But having stashed her he had disappeared, leaving Abby to wonder if she had the courage to go out and forage for food.

Hunger prevailed, and she braved the steps at the end of the walkway and headed toward what she hoped was the center of town. The houses got a little larger and better kept; she passed a funeral home and a church. She reached a wide commercial street and there on the corner was a gas station with a minimart. Abby looked up and down the street and saw no sign of anything that looked like a restaurant. She went into the minimart and bought two chicken-salad sandwiches encased in plastic, an energy bar and a bottle of apple juice. She walked back to the motel by a different route, passing what looked like a supermarket that had been converted to a Salvation Army store.

"Maybe you can blog about it," her mother had said. "'Dispatches from Darkest Indiana' or something."

In the motel parking lot a party was going on. The country music was louder, and three men stood at the rear of a pickup truck, drinking beer. They were beefy, sunburned, ill groomed. They stared at Abby as she passed and she flicked them a fast smile, avoiding eye contact. She went up the steps to her room, resisting the urge to run.

Back in her room, having thrown the bolt and put on the chain, Abby sat on the bed and surfed the television channels while she ate. She found all the usual cable networks and local stations in Indianapolis and a town called Lafayette. She watched CNN for a while, unmoved by the world's travails. She watched a recycled sitcom, trying not to think. She turned off the television, tried to call Samantha on her cell phone, got her voice mail, remembered the time zone difference. She texted Samantha: *In darkest Indiana. In search of intelligent life.*

Abby took a shower, lay on the bed in an oversized T-shirt, and listened to bad music and raucous laughter coming faintly through the door. Her room was close to the ice machine at the end of the walkway and two men were prolonging the noisy process of transferring ice into a cooler by holding a conclave, all too audibly, a few feet from her door.

"Gittin' kinda drunk out, ain't it?"

"Gimme a cigarette. Where's Ricky?"

"Last I saw, he was suckin' face with Crystal down in the room."

"No shit? Wait'll Cody hears about that."

"Where the fuck is Cody?"

"In the hospital with a busted head. Rolled his truck."

"Again? That sumbitch can't drive worth shit."

"Brand-new fuckin' truck, too. Hey, Kyle's out of jail, d'ja hear?"

I am on a different planet, Abby thought, marooned.

I am not going to cry, she told herself. I am an adult and I can handle a night of dislocation and loneliness. Things will be better in the morning. Somebody at the college will help me find a place to live. They will have to, they promised. Soon I will be busy and in the company of people who can read and this will turn out not to have been a hideous mistake.

Abby turned out the lamp and lay on her back, staring at the pattern of light across the ceiling. The men outside went away and now there was only the music and the outbursts of laughter, distant and muted. Tears crept down Abby's cheeks and onto the pillow.

This is my punishment, she thought. This is what I have to suffer for my guilt.

2 |||||||

"I'm a big-city girl," Abby said. "I've never lived in a town that you couldn't fly to."

"Oh, you can fly into Lewisburg," said Bill Olsen. "There's an airstrip south of town. You just have to know somebody with a small private plane." He smiled. Bill Olsen was head of the math department, bearded and imposing, tall and unkempt, the man who had brought Abby to Indiana.

Abby smiled back, a little sheepishly. Her morale had recovered with a change of surroundings, the day spent getting oriented on campus and undergoing an intense tête-à-tête with Olsen before winding up in this handsome oak-paneled room with high windows looking out onto a pleasant swatch of green. Two dozen people in the throes of a reception filled the room with the hum of conversation.

"Let me introduce you to some folks." Olsen steered Abby by the elbow to a man who had just drifted into the room and stood looking about with his hands in his pockets and a vacant but receptive look on his face. "This is Philip Herzler, in classics. You need something translated from Latin or Greek, Phil's your man. This is Abigail Markstein, from MIT. Our new recruit. She's never seen a town this small and she's feeling a little dazed." They shook hands and Olsen promptly sheered off and left them.

Herzler was tall and slightly stooped in his rumpled suit, his unruly hair and patchy beard once black but now mostly gray. "MIT, did he say?"

"Yes. And a postdoc at Columbia. And I did my undergrad at NYU, after growing up in Manhattan. So actually, Cambridge was kind of a small town for me."

Herzler threw back his head and laughed. "Oh, my. This will be a bit of an adjustment."

A portly man in a blue sport jacket, sixtyish and bald, grabbed Abby's elbow, slopping a little sherry over the rim of her glass. "You must be one of the new hires," he said.

"Um, yes, hi. I'm Abigail Markstein. Mathematics." She fumbled a little with glass and napkin, wiping sherry off her hand, before extending it to shake.

"Jerry Collins, psychology. Welcome to Tippecanoe."

"Thanks. I'm happy to be here." So much for sincerity, Abby thought. "Just trying to get my bearings."

"Well, if you can make Phil Herzler laugh, you're off to a good start." He cocked his thumb at the classicist. "Normally he's so distraught over the decline and fall of the Roman empire that he just sulks in the corner at these things."

"I don't miss the Romans," Herzler said, deadpan. "The decay of civilization started with the arrest of Socrates."

"Civilization's not all it's cracked up to be anyway. Not that we have much of it in central Indiana, right, Phil?" Collins winked at Abby.

"Actually we were just discussing the question," said Herzler. "Abigail's a New Yorker, and I was trying to offer her a ray of hope."

"You can reach New York by phone," said a woman who had appeared at Collins's elbow. "That may be the best we can do." The woman was tall, thin, somewhere past fifty, with dark-eyed looks that might once have been striking but now were severe, the face deeply lined. Her brown hair was shorn close to the skull but the effect was slightly feminized by a pair of hammered silver earrings. She sounded like a smoker. The glass she was clutching held something over ice that wasn't wine. "I'm Lisa Beth Quinton," she said, sticking out her hand.

"My better half," said Collins, beaming and putting a hand to the small of her back.

"I don't think we'll get an argument there," said Quinton. "You're Abby, is that right?"

Blinking at the notion that these two were a couple, Abby said, "That's right. I'm new in the math department."

"So we hear. Bill Olsen's been raving about you. He told me what your area is, but it meant nothing to me."

"I do combinatorics," said Abby. "I wrote my thesis on hyperplane arrangements in finite fields."

There was a brief silence, three blank looks. "Well, Bill says you're the cat's meow," said Quinton.

"Who's this who's won over the Ogre of Harrison Hall?" The man who had drifted into their orbit had been eyeing Abby from across the room, working his way steadily toward her from the table where he had filled his glass, stopping to shake hands, slap backs and banter as he came. He was no more than a couple of years older than she was, she judged, dark haired, clean shaven, not hard to look at, one of the few men present wearing a tie. She met his inquiring look and held out her hand.

"I'm Abby Markstein. Mathematics."

His smile had some wattage. "Graham Gill. Economics, if we have to be defined by what we teach."

"I had to start somewhere."

"Fair enough." He hoisted his glass to the group. "Everybody have a good summer?"

That brought murmurs, shrugs and nods. Collins said, "I thought you were off somewhere doing research, Singapore or someplace like that."

"I was. Just flew back yesterday. Jet-lagged to the max. Right now the sun's just coming up in Singapore, and I've been up all night."

Lisa Beth Quinton said to Abby, "Have you found a place to live yet?"

Abby grimaced. "Not yet. I thought I had a place lined up through the housing office, but there was some kind of mix-up. When I got here it was rented. So I'm at the motel over on Oak Street."

"The Tarkington? Oh, my God, that place is a hellhole. Are the housing people still steering people over there? Hasn't anyone told them about the meth busts and the prostitution stings?"

"Um, I haven't seen anything like that. But having spent a night there, I can't say I'm surprised. Should I be worried?"

Collins was laughing. "My wife is the authority on the seamy underbelly of Lewisburg. She's the crime reporter for the local paper."

Quinton tossed off the last of her drink, a hand on her hip. "Honey, I'm the *everything* reporter for the local paper. And no, you're not likely to be murdered in your bed at the Tarkington, though I'd check for bedbugs. But yes, the local lowlifes have been known to rent a room there on occasion to practice their low-lifery in."

Gill laughed. "Lowlifes? In Lewisburg? You amaze me."

"Where do you think you're living, sonny? Some of the people in this town make Jed Clampett look like David Niven." She turned back to Abby. "You'd be better off at the Holiday Inn out by the highway."

"Well, I don't have a car. So I'm sort of limited to places within walking distance of campus. But yeah, an upgrade would be good."

Quinton put a hand on her husband's arm. "Didn't Stan tell us Ned McLaren was looking for somebody to rent out the back of his house?"

"Yeah, hey, that's an idea." He turned to Abby. "We know a fellow who just moved back to town. His father was on the faculty here for years. The house is in a nice spot and he's converted one floor to an apartment. Might be worth a look."

"Is it furnished? I don't even have a pillow to sleep on."

"I think so. Unless he's thrown all his folks' stuff out."

Quinton said, "It's just on the other side of campus, in what passes for a ritzy neighborhood around here. A couple of professors live up there, and the odd doctor and lawyer. I'll call him, see if it's still available."

"Um, thanks." Before Abby could react, Quinton had gone striding away, digging in the bag that hung over her shoulder.

"Can I get you another drink?" said Gill, pointing at Abby's empty glass.

Abby wasn't much of a drinker, but the sherry had helped the anxiety ease a little. "Sure, thanks." Gill made off with her glass and Collins was lured away, leaving Abby alone with Philip Herzler.

"You do look a little dazed," he said.

Abby nodded. "I think I'm having culture shock."

Herzler gave her a kindly smile. "I went through the same thing when I got here, fresh out of Princeton. Where am I? But there's life here. The college gives you a tight little community of highly educated people, plenty of lectures and concerts. Town and gown relations are OK, and the local bourgeoisie is reasonably cultivated. Indianapolis is less than an hour away by car and Chicago about three. When you start to feel constricted, those are easy getaways for an evening or a weekend. My wife and I have lived here pretty happily for twenty-seven years. It doesn't have to feel like an exile."

Two years, Abby thought, as Lisa Beth Quinton rejoined them. "All right, I just talked to Ned and he says he's still looking for a tenant and he would love to show you the place. He's not home right now but he says you can come by any time tomorrow morning. It's easy to find. I'll draw you a little map. Where's a napkin?"

Gill was back with Abby's drink. "So, Abby. To coin a phrase, what's a nice girl like you doing in a place like this?"

She laughed a little. "I'm not sure yet. When I figure it out, I'll let you know."

Lisa Beth Quinton's map was schematic but clear, and Abby had no trouble finding the Hickory Lane subdivision where Ned McLaren lived. It made a pleasant walk on a summer morning to follow Jackson Avenue south past the campus down into a wooded dale, over a bridge across a stream, and turn up a drive that wound through stands of the trees that gave the place its name. The houses were a jumble of styles: a Cape Cod, a split-level colonial, a ranch, all comfortably separated and amply shaded, a little pocket of upper-middle-class respectability.

It didn't look like the type of neighborhood that would have apartments to rent, and Abby wondered if it was a wild goose chase. She looked for house numbers, and here it was, 6 Hickory Lane, the third house on the right. It was a one-story ranch style in brick with a garage linked to it by a roofed porch, not especially prepossessing. Behind it rose the woods.

A man was kneeling at the steps that led up to the porch, working mortar into a joint between bricks. He looked up as Abby came up the driveway. He wore a T-shirt, jeans and work boots, a baseball cap with a logo on it Abby didn't recognize. From under the visor he squinted at her.

"Um, hi. Is this the McLaren house?"

"Yup. You found it." He stuck the trowel into a bucket full of mortar.

"Hi, I had an appointment with Ned McLaren? To look at the apartment?"

The man got to his feet, knees cracking as he did. He was not quite six feet tall, with dark blond hair curling on the back of his neck, hazel eyes and a close-trimmed moustache and goatee, a little gray showing. He looked to be in early middle age but was lean and fit. "You must be Abigail."

"Yes. Is Mr. McLaren available?"

"I'm available." He smiled. "Excuse me for not shaking hands." He walked to a spigot set in the side of the house and turned on the water.

"Oh, I'm sorry. I . . ." She had been looking for a professor's son and not a bricklayer. "Nice to meet you."

He rinsed his hands, turned off the water, and stepped toward her, flapping his hands to dry them. "Same here. You just signed on with our little Hoosier Harvard, did you?" He spoke softly, with a midwestern drawl that to Abby's New York ear sounded almost southern.

"Um, yeah. And I need a place to live. I'm at the Tarkington right now."

He shook his head. "Well, we'll have to get you out of there before you get arrested for visiting a common nuisance."

"Excuse me?"

"That's the legal term in Indiana for getting caught on premises where people are using drugs." He gave her a disarming smile. "Let me show you the apartment."

He led her across the covered porch toward the back of the house. Abby had found it hard to imagine where an apartment could fit in a one-story ranch house; as she followed him it became clear. On the other side of the porch the ground fell away sharply. Stone steps led down the slope along the side of the house to a strip of lawn, maybe fifty feet wide, beyond which another slope plunged into the woods lining the stream she had crossed on Jackson Avenue, the glint of water just visible through the foliage. They went down the steps and turned the corner, and Abby saw that it was in reality a two-story house, the lower story invisible from the street and facing back toward the woods.

"That's some backyard," Abby said.

"Yeah, it's nice. You'll see deer down by the stream quite a bit in the evening." Pulling a ring of keys from his pocket, McLaren stepped to a door and unlocked it; Abby followed him inside. He drew the curtains that had masked a big picture window and light filled the room.

It was a big welcoming room, carpeted and paneled in wood, with a sofa along the wall opposite the door, a coffee table, armchairs, lamps, books from floor to ceiling on the far wall. Abby stepped into the room and turned toward the window to see green, nothing but trees. "Wow," she said.

"Yeah, the view's good. If you're a bird-watcher you've come to the right place. When the leaves go in the fall you can see across to the campus. Makes a nice postcard view, with the chapel and all."

"It's lovely." Abby took a few slow steps, scanning the room, her eye then drawn again to the view. "Very peaceful."

"It is dark, facing north, that's one thing. You want sun, there's no surcharge for sitting on the front lawn."

She wheeled away from the window. "It's a nice room."

"My folks never did much with it. They moved in here after I was grown up and gone. They mostly lived upstairs, and all the furniture from the old house got shoved down here. But it's all serviceable. That old sofa's the most comfortable place to nap I ever ran across."

"Your father taught at the college, is that right?" Abby wandered toward the bookshelves.

"Yup. Taught history here for thirty-some years. My mom hung on here for a few years after he died and then she passed three years ago. My sister in Indianapolis tried renting the place out, but that was a headache, so she was planning to sell it. But then last year I decided I'd had enough of what I was doing, so I said what the hell, maybe it's time for the prodigal son to come home."

Abby was looking at the books: Bertrand Russell's *An Outline of Philosophy*, Toynbee's *Civilization on Trial*, Popper's *The Logic of Scientific Discovery*. And here at the end of the shelf, *The Complete Cartoons of the New Yorker*. The books reassured her; Abby felt like a castaway reaching dry land. She turned. "OK, what else?"

"Well, you got your choice of bedrooms." He pushed open a door to the right of the bookshelves. "They used this as a study. But I can shift the furniture around however you want. I could move a bed in here."

No, thought Abby, standing in the doorway, leave it just like it is. The window here looked out onto the same sylvan view, and there was a desk in front of it. There was a couch, and more bookshelves; it instantly appealed to Abby as a perfect place to work: secluded and tranquil. "Nice. No, I think I like it as a study."

"The Wi-Fi router's in here. The connection's good. I cleared out the desk drawers. I can get rid of the books, too, if you want. You probably have your own you want to bring in."

"A few, yeah. I'm having some stuff shipped as soon as I get settled. Don't worry about it, I'll figure out where to put them." Whoa, thought Abby, slow down. "If I decide to, you know . . . I might want to look at another couple of places."

"Sure, no problem." He led her into a small tile-floored alcove with three doors opening off it. "Here's the bathroom. The plumbing's sound. Plenty of hot water. Check it out if you want."

"That's OK."

"And this is the other bedroom." He flicked a switch. "Not much light here. But the beds are OK. These are the ones my sister and I had when we were kids. Take your pick. Go ahead and flop on them. I wouldn't expect you to take my word for it." He gave her the grin again. "I'll be in the kitchen."

A little self-consciously, Abby sat on each bed in turn, finally lying down on the one closer to the single tiny window. Staring at the ceiling, she thought, Can I live here? Is this really going to be my life?

She went across the alcove to join McLaren in the kitchen. He was standing at the sink watching the water run. "The pipes are a little rusty because nobody's used the water here in a while. But it all works. I put all this stuff in new. This used to be an unfinished basement." It was all spotless and gleaming: stainless-steel fridge, stove, double sink, granite countertops with microwave, blond wood cabinets, track lighting. McLaren pushed open a door. "Laundry's through here, in the unfinished part. I put in a new washer and dryer. It's all yours. I've got my own upstairs."

Abby poked her head in for a look, then stood nodding, looking around. She could hear her father's voice telling her sternly: Look at some other places before you make a decision. She turned and walked slowly back into the big room, arms folded, the picture of a woman deep in thought. The view through the big window greeted her, leaves fluttering gently in a breeze. Behind her she heard doors closing, McLaren's step on the tiles.

"How much is the rent?" Abby said.

He came to stand beside her, hands on his hips. "Well, I'm not really in it for the money. How about four hundred a month? I think you'll find that's pretty much in line with what people pay for a one-bedroom apartment around here."

Abby gaped at him. She had known rents would be a whole lot lower than in New York, but that was ridiculous. Four hundred dollars for the short walk to campus, the new kitchen, the study, the books, the view? "Um, that sounds fine," she said. Her father would not approve, but suddenly the prospect of having a place to live, the anxiety resolved, carried the day. "When could I move in?" she said.

Ned McLaren shrugged. "What are you doing today?"

3 |||||||

What I am doing today, Abby said to herself some hours later, is being thoroughly intimidated by the demands of my new job. She sat at the desk in the study of her new apartment, looking out at the woods in the deepening twilight and feeling her spirits sink. The browser on her laptop was open to the *Tippecanoe College Faculty Handbook*; next to the laptop sat a pile of thick textbooks, a raft of insurance paperwork and several pages of handwritten notes detailing the obligations, expectations and complications connected with her status as an instructor at Tippecanoe College in Lewisburg, Indiana.

In the morning she had met with Bill Olsen, who, after showing her to her bare, cramped office under the stairs in a corner of Harrison Hall, had taken pains to impress on her the standards of teaching she would be expected to meet. "We give you small class sizes, and in return we expect a high level of engagement," he had said. "They pay a lot of money to come here, and they deserve your best effort."

Abby had nodded, queasily wondering if her imagined fondness for teaching would survive an encounter with a roomful of entitled undergrads. On Monday the term would begin. Students were trickling onto campus, in high spirits, greeting each other with hugs and laughter. Abby had eaten a hurried lunch alone in the corner of the campus snack bar and rushed off to the personnel office to deal with employment red tape. Late in the day she had finally made it back to the motel and belatedly checked out, wearily conceding that the college should be charged for an extra night. The clerk had summoned what seemed to be the only taxi in town, driven by an obese woman with thick glasses, to haul Abby and her luggage the few blocks down the way to Hickory Lane.

This is where I live now, Abby thought, gazing out at the trees. I have a job and a home and colleagues who seem friendly. So why do I still feel like crying?

She picked up her phone. No, she thought. Don't call Mom when you're in this mood. It will confirm all her dire predictions. Daddy will make you feel better. He will make you believe that things will be better as soon as classes start.

But it's Friday evening in New York and Daddy will be out somewhere with Marcia, trying out a hot new restaurant in the Village or taking in something intriguing at the Film Forum or having cocktails in Saul and Gloria's apartment high above Seventh Avenue. Daddy would talk to you but Marcia would be irked.

Abby set the phone down; her parents' divorce was another thing that made her sad, still, years after the fact, at odd times. She put her face in her hands. Call Samantha, she thought. Samantha will always talk to you; that's what Best Friends Forever do. Unless they are too harried by the demands of caring for a baby, or enjoying a rare Friday evening of liberty thanks to an expensive babysitter. Don't bother Samantha again, Abby told herself, knowing she was perilously close to feeling sorry for herself.

Once upon a time you would have called Evan.

Abby roused herself and walked into the main room of the apartment. She stood looking through the big picture window, mesmerized by the gentle riffling of leaves in the golden light of early evening. This is what you wanted, Abby thought. You wanted to be alone but you didn't bargain for the loneliness.

She was startled by a tapping at the door. When Abby pulled it open she was surprised to see Lisa Beth Quinton standing there. "Hi, Abigail. Sorry to drop in without calling, but I didn't have your number." Lisa Beth's white linen jacket and painted nails were elegant, a contrast with her short hair. "Have you had dinner yet?"

There wasn't a scrap of food in the place but anxiety had robbed Abby of appetite. "Um, no. I haven't."

"Jerry and I thought you might like to come out to dinner with us."

"Oh, thank you. That's so kind." Relief and gratitude made Abby speechless for a moment. "Let me . . . Um, please, come in." She stepped back, beckoning.

"Thank you. I'd love to see what Ned's done with the place."

"Let me get some shoes on. Can you give me a minute?"

"Take your time. Jerry's upstairs jawboning with Ned, and when he gets started it can take a while. No rush."

Abby hurried into her bedroom and changed into the short-sleeved black-and-white shift dress she had worn earlier, and after a quick session before the bathroom mirror, she rejoined Lisa Beth in the main room. The older woman said, "Very nice indeed. How much is young Ned charging you for all this?"

"Four hundred."

"Sounds like a pretty good deal. Did you sign a lease?"

"Yeah. He said it was just boilerplate off the Internet. He offered to let me have somebody review it, but I read through it and it seemed OK. I signed for a year."

Lisa Beth shrugged. "I'm sure it's fine." She wandered to the foot of a flight of stairs at the back of the room. "This goes up to the house?"

"Yeah." Abby came to stand beside her and looked up the steps to a closed door. "He seemed pretty concerned about my privacy, actually. He took me up there to show me he'd installed a bolt so there's no way he can open it from that side."

Lisa Beth smiled. "I think your virtue will be safe. The McLarens were a pretty straitlaced family." She moved away from the stairs. "Though young Ned is a bit of a mysterious story."

Abby followed her toward the door. "Really? How so?"

"Oh, I'm just retailing old gossip. Apparently he was a bit of a wild youngster. But he seems perfectly presentable now. Ready to go?"

When they went up the steps at the side of the house they found Jerry Collins and Ned McLaren sitting on canvas director's chairs on the covered porch. Collins wore his sport jacket; McLaren looked freshly showered, his curly hair still wet. He had changed into white cotton trousers and a guayabera shirt, his feet in sandals. "Did the premises pass inspection?" he said to Lisa Beth.

"Very nice," she said. "Looks like I won't have to include you in my exposé on local slumlords."

McLaren laughed softly. "You want slums, go check out some of the frat houses over on South Street." He looked at Abby. "Settling in OK?"

"Fine. I think I'll be very comfortable."

"We're taking Abigail here to the Azteca," said Jerry, rising from the chair with an effort. "Want to come along?"

Abby suddenly tensed. Was this all a setup? But McLaren shook his head. "Nah, I've got plans. I have a little card game scheduled here with some local ne'er-do-wells. Have a good time."

"I am shocked, shocked to find gambling going on here," said Lisa Beth. She laughed harshly and they went down the steps. They got into a dark-gray sedan parked at the end of the drive, Jerry behind the wheel. He snaked down the lane and turned north on Jackson. Lisa Beth twisted to talk to Abby over the seat. "There's not much in the way of fine dining around here, I'm afraid. You have to drive to Indianapolis if you want anything really upscale. But the Azteca's not bad, if you like Mexican food."

"That's fine. I wouldn't have expected to find a Mexican place here."

Jerry laughed. "Oh, we've got Mexicans. Do we ever."

Lisa Beth said, "The Midwest is changing. We've got about three thousand Mexicans in Lewisburg. Nobody knows how many there are for sure, because ninety percent of them are illegal."

"I had no idea. In New York we tend to think of the Midwest as just cornfields as far as the eye can see."

Jerry said, "We've got the steel plant, some big corporate farms. The employers like Mexicans because they don't skip work and they don't file workmen's comp. Everybody knows the IDs are fake but nobody polices it. It's too convenient for all concerned."

Abby watched residential blocks give way to a strip of commercial buildings with old brick façades, none higher than three stories, a couple of banks, a Carnegie library, a Masonic temple, a courthouse on a square with a Civil War–vintage cannon in front. "Downtown Lewisburg," said Jerry. "Don't blink or you'll miss it."

"Here's where I work," said Lisa Beth, pointing as they passed a storefront with a sign that said **HERALD GAZETTE**. "Not exactly the Gray Lady, but we try to keep the local populace informed of who's stealing their lawn mowers. Every once in a while a real story comes along."

"Like the drunken police chief," said Jerry. "Or the embezzler at the college."

"The store owner busted for tax fraud and money laundering," said Lisa Beth. "Even in Middle America, turn over a rock and you'll see nasty things squirming."

To Abby it looked like a movie set, four blocks of small-town America. They turned onto a broad commercial strip with the franchise outlets that made everywhere in the country look the same: the burger joints and the auto parts store and the chain drugstores. And then they were on a highway heading out of town past scattered gas stations and liquor stores; Abby couldn't believe how fast the town had vanished.

"Here's the Azteca," said Jerry, slowing. "Looks like a pretty good crowd. We may have to wait for a table."

It was a long low building in the middle of a gravel parking lot nearly full; a neon sign flashed the name in red and green. Inside it was aggressively air-conditioned with tinny mariachi music overhead. They were greeted by a young Mexican woman whose delight at seeing them was a bit thin but who duly led them to a table in a corner and gave them menus. Abby glanced at hers but was more interested in looking at her fellow diners, her new neighbors. She saw a couple of Mexican families: stolid parents and squirming children. And here were the Hoosiers, running the gamut from a trio of prim elderly ladies to a man with a mullet who had come out on a Friday night date in a spotless white wifebeater, tufts of underarm hair on shameless display.

Lisa Beth snapped her menu shut and laid it on the table. "The quesadillas are good. The margaritas are terrible, but tequila is tequila, and they work."

"I like the enchiladas, myself," said Jerry. "Should we get a pitcher of margaritas?" He raised an eyebrow at his wife. "That would be cheaper if you're planning to down your usual amount."

"Why not? You're driving."

"I might just have a beer," Abby said.

A waitress arrived and took their orders. Small talk occupied them until the drinks and then the food came. Mexican was not Abby's favorite cuisine, but she was hungry and the chiles rellenos went down fast. Lisa Beth worked her way steadily through a pitcher of murky green booze, eating little and tossing in the odd acerbic comment as Jerry Collins held forth, around mouthfuls of food, on the history, traditions and peculiarities of Tippecanoe College.

"Oh, my," said Lisa Beth over the rim of her glass, peering toward the entrance. "Look who's here."

Abby cast a look over her shoulder and saw a couple following the hostess down the room toward them. The man was big and broad shouldered, his polo shirt stretched by a swelling gut, an ex-jock going to seed. He had neatly groomed gray hair and a rakish goatee. The blonde walking a step behind him was still an eye-catcher but was getting to the stage of life at which cosmetics bore an increasing share of the burden.

"Looks like he's got a new one," said Lisa Beth. She set down her glass and leveled a steely glare at the man as he approached. "Hello, Jud," she said as he reached them.

"Lisa Beth." The man halted at their table, the blonde at his side, an uncertain smile on her face. "Please don't tell me you're hot on the trail of a story. Because I'm just here to have dinner. Jerry, how are you?"

"Jud," said Jerry, reaching to shake his hand. "How's that boy of yours? I understand he's got a shot at a starting spot this year."

A broad smile blossomed on the man's face. "That's what they say. We'll see. It's tough at that level, but he's hanging in there." His gaze lingered for a second or two on Abby before he gave Lisa Beth a look of mock gravity and said, "Saw your big story in the paper the other day. About the cows that got out onto the road. Cutting-edge journalism, great work." He smiled at Jerry and proceeded toward his table, the blonde trailing, her smile fading.

"Asshole," said Lisa Beth under her breath.

Jerry smiled at Abby's puzzled look. "Jud Frederick. Local real estate guy. He's got a son down at IU on a football scholarship. Terrific athlete."

Lisa Beth said, "He's bad news." She drained her glass and refilled it from the pitcher, concentrating on her hand-eye coordination. "I wasn't joking about that slumlord exposé. That's public enemy number one. He owns a trailer park and a bunch of tumbledown houses on the bad side of town. He also owns a lot of commercial property, including the Tarkington Motor Inn, so if you want to complain about the bedbugs, now's your chance. He has a reputation for playing fast and loose, flipping properties with cosmetic remodeling that hides code violations, stuff like that."

"But mostly he just bugs you because he's rich," said Jerry. He winked at Abby. "My wife the Bolshevik."

"He bugs me because of the sense of entitlement." To Abby she said, "He's part of that Alpha Male club, the Guys in Charge bunch. I'm sure you know the type. The frat guys, the jocks. I hate jocks."

Abby nodded. "Yeah. They can be a pain." She sensed it was time to lighten the mood. "Though I have to say, I was kind of a jock myself. I did cross-country in college. Just Division III, but we worked hard. We went to the NCAAs one year."

"Well, that would account for the trim figure," said Lisa Beth. She smiled. "Don't mind me, I'm just jealous. I have the nonathlete's grudge against people who are good at sports. Gym class was hell, and then I discovered cigarettes and booze."

"All I can do is run," said Abby. "Though I haven't done much recently. I need to get back to it. I'm hoping to find some good routes around here."

Jerry said, "Well, I can tell you where the college cross-country people go. They go out South Street past the frat houses and out into the country southwest of town. They run to the Hainesville bridge across Shawnee Creek and back. I think it's about five miles round trip."

"My God," said Lisa Beth. "They're all here. It's sleazeball night at the Azteca." She was looking toward the entrance again. This time it was a slender man in a blue blazer, tieless, with a head of gray hair that was just a little longer than currently fashionable and thick black eyebrows that gave his long-jawed, cleft-chinned face a fierce look. He was by himself, and he was scanning the room. When his eyes lit on Jud Frederick he waved and started toward him. "Oh, wonderful," said Lisa Beth. "They're together. They're here to scheme and plot mischief."

Abby was beginning to be entertained. "OK, who is this?" she said.

"This is Rex Lyman. Our top criminal-defense lawyer. All the burglars, drug dealers and drunk drivers in the county know his number by heart. He's the go-to guy for the local lowlifes."

"And a respected member of the local bar," said Jerry. "Everyone deserves competent counsel, right?"

"Of course. But you wonder about a lawyer who seems to enjoy rubbing elbows with his clients." Lisa Beth leaned toward Abby and lowered her voice. "Lyman owns a bar out on Lafayette Road, the kind of place where there are a lot of motorcycles parked outside and a lot of fights on a Saturday night. And the rumor is, that's the place to go if you want to get a lot of money down on the Super Bowl or March Madness. He's been running a sports book for years, but nobody's ever been able to nail him."

Jerry shook his head. "He fired a bartender for gambling a few years ago. Nobody's ever proved he profited from it."

Lisa Beth snorted. "Oh, please."

"And he gives a lot of money to the United Way and the Community Foundation, so he's fairly well viewed around here."

"Tactical charity. You know he's greasing a few of the right palms under the table as well."

Jerry rolled his eyes and winked at Abby. Lyman had to pass their table on his way to join Frederick. He made the same quick survey the other man had, giving Abby a slightly longer and more interested look, before making eye contact with Lisa Beth. "Ah, the press is here," he said with a grin. "I have no comment at this time."

"You never do," said Lisa Beth.

Lyman went on past and joined Frederick and the blonde. "The slumlord and the sleazy lawyer," said Lisa Beth. "Wonder what they're cooking up now."

"Maybe they're just having dinner," said Jerry.

"I am professionally suspicious." She gave Abby a rueful smile. "I know, it's pathetic. I dreamed of covering congressional hearings in Washington, DC, and I wound up here in Lewisburg, yawning at city council meetings."

"That's what you get for yoking yourself to me," said Jerry. "You should have taken the job in Cincinnati."

She cocked an eyebrow at him. "Believe me, I question the decision constantly." To Abby she said, "We met in grad school in Bloomington. When I got my degree I was offered a job on the *Cincinnati Enquirer*, but I was married to him by that time. So instead I followed him here."

"Much to her regret," said Jerry. He was smiling, but Abby sensed one of those encysted grievances married couples learned to live with.

Lisa Beth looked at Abby and said, "You managed to avoid romantic entanglements in graduate school, did you?"

A sudden pang took Abby's breath away. She poked at the refried beans on her plate. "Not entirely," she said. "I just ended a relationship last year, actually."

"Oh, I'm sorry. Just ignore the question. I'm professionally curious, too, and it overcomes my manners sometimes."

"No, it's all right." Abby flashed her a smile. "It wasn't meant to be. Our paths diverged, you could say."

"Well, independence has its advantages," said Lisa Beth, reaching for her glass again.

"Yes," said Abby. "That's what they say."

4 |||||||

Abby went up the steps at the side of the house, treading carefully in the dark, crossed the porch and walked to the end of the driveway, tucking her key into the waistband of her shorts. The eastern sky was just beginning to lighten and the air was cool. The gentle rustling of the trees was the only sound. She stooped to tighten the laces of her left shoe, straightened and began jogging gently down Hickory Lane, the houses on either side still dark with only a few porch lights shining.

Abby had not run in a week, and the need to work idle muscles was getting urgent. She had gone to bed early, exhausted after several anxious nights, and consequently come wide awake well before dawn. It was darker than she would have expected at five in the morning; in New York the sun would be gilding the eastern faces of the buildings, but here at the western edge of the time zone it was still dark. Finding no excuse for staying in bed, she had risen and dressed in her running clothes.

There were no cars moving on Jackson Avenue. She jogged up toward the campus at an easy warm-up pace. It was pleasant to be loping quietly through deserted streets. Abby usually ran alone, and often at odd hours. In New York or Cambridge she would not have dared to run alone in the dark, though in Cambridge she had known a man who always ran just before dawn, swearing it was the safest time because all the criminals were in bed.

She reached South Street and went left, the campus spreading out on her right, isolated lights showing through the trees. Just past the campus was a line of fraternity houses, Greek letters just visible in the glow of the streetlamps. Lights shone in a handful of isolated windows.

By the time Abby had left the frat houses behind she had broken a sweat, settling into a comfortable pace. She passed the college baseball field and was abruptly in a neighborhood of ramshackle houses, the town thinning. The street became a road, the curbs and the streetlights disappearing. The houses fell away, replaced by woods on her left and a deserted industrial plant behind a high wire fence on the right. The road curved to the south and began to dip into a hollow.

The sun was still below the horizon. The road was taking Abby down into darkness, trees looming now on either side and something massive and black rising against the sky as she descended. She slowed, suddenly uneasy, but the grade was steep and her momentum was hard to resist. The shape in front of her cut across her field of view, blotting out the sky. She was almost to the bottom of the slope when she identified it as a railway viaduct arching across the road, a solid wall of stone fifty feet high with a tunnel cut through it for the road, and a stream that converged with the road from the left and then passed under the road before flowing through the arch beside it.

Abby quelled a little flutter of alarm. She had expected the road to pass quickly into open countryside, but instead she had run blithely into a dark hollow where a dog or a rapist could jump out of the bushes at her and nobody would see or hear. And since the day Evan died she had not even considered bringing her phone with her on a run. The thought of her phone buzzing at her waist in the middle of a run terrified her.

She quickened her pace, just able to make out the road rising to high ground again at the other end of the short tunnel. Just before the viaduct, the road went across a bridge; the stream below it was invisible in the dark. Abby pressed the pace, entering the tunnel. It was a mere thirty or forty feet long, but it smelled of dank and dead things. She was nearly sprinting as she went through it.

She came out the other end unscathed and slowed as the road rose and curved west again, climbing steeply out of the hollow into a lightening sky. The hill exhausted her. She had to slow to a walk just before the crest and she rested for a hundred feet or so, walking with her hands on her hips, before breaking into a trot again.

Here was the country she had envisioned, flat tractable farmland opening out in front of her in the growing light, a line of woods in the distance and open fields and farmsteads nearer at hand. Recovered, Abby reestablished her pace. She crossed to the left side of the road, realizing that it was still dark enough that she would not be easily visible to a person at the wheel of a car.

She ran for another half mile past farms and isolated houses and stopped at a crossroads, panting, dripping with sweat. There was probably a circuit that would take her back to town, but she wanted to look at a map before she went wandering down side roads. She estimated that she had come something over two miles, so retracing her steps would make a leisurely four, not bad for a first time out after a layoff. She turned around and began to jog again, toward the sunrise. The eastern sky was an exquisite shade of pink and her spirits rose.

Behind her she heard a vehicle approaching. She cast a look over her shoulder and saw running lights coming up fast. Abby moved well off the road, almost into the ditch. As the car tore past her she caught a glimpse of a figure hunched over the wheel of a big dark sedan. Abby panted out a curse, a jogger's reaction to reckless speed on an unlit road. The car left her behind in a hurry and she saw brake lights come on a few hundred yards ahead as it approached the dip into the hollow and then disappeared.

The sound of the engine died away and there was only the scuffing of her feet on the gravel shoulder. She steadied, sustaining a respectable pace. In a couple of minutes she had reached the hollow. The road plunged and curved into deep shadow, the black wall of the viaduct came into sight, and there was a deep, muffled concussion, the trees farther down the slope abruptly lit with a strange orange glow.

Abby's momentum carried her downhill for several steps in bewilderment before the perception made sense to her. Just as she identified it as an explosion, the tunnel came into sight and the source of the glow appeared: beyond the far end of the tunnel, a car was burning.

Abby descended with jarring steps. Framed in the arched exit to the tunnel she could make out what looked like the black sedan that had passed her. It sat slewed across the road at an angle, a few feet beyond the tunnel. It was burning vigorously, billowing flames coming from every window, black smoke rising, liquid fire spreading out across the pavement beneath the vehicle.

Abby halted, horrified. The driver's side was angled away from her; she could not make out whether there was anyone at the wheel. "Oh, my God," she gasped out.

I cannot just stand and watch, Abby thought. Where is the driver?

At the mouth of the tunnel she could feel the heat but it was not so intense that she couldn't get closer. The gas tank has already exploded, she thought; that's what I heard. Abby began to run through the tunnel toward the fire. The heat increased as she went, and she had a bad moment when something in the car popped, sending sparks into the air, but when she had passed through the tunnel and was within twenty feet of the car, the heat was still bearable.

What was not bearable was the sight of the body in the driver's seat. Abby cried out and dashed past the wreck, giving it as wide a berth as she could on the shoulder of the road, seared by the heat, seared by the sight of the human form that sat behind the wheel, being consumed by fire. "Oh, my God, no." Abby put her hands to her head. The figure in the heart of the flames was already black, faceless, the skin beginning to split, fat bubbling up from beneath. As she watched, the figure moved, limbs contracting, leaning forward. "Oh *God!*" Aghast, Abby took two quick steps forward, unthinking, driven by the need to take action. The heat quickly drove her back. The figure on the driver's seat had stopped moving; it sat slumped over to the right, black and lifeless, nothing but fuel now.

I am watching a person die, Abby thought with the icy calm of shock, and then she saw the man standing at the edge of the road, on the other side of the vehicle.

Illuminated by the flames, he was gazing at her. He stood just off the road, at the end of the guardrail of the bridge. He wore cargo shorts and sneakers but was shirtless, his arms and chest bearing a scattering of tattoos. He had long dark hair combed straight back, hooked behind his ears and curling at the back of his neck. His face was gaunt and haggard, the mouth framed by a moustache that curled around to the jaw on either side. The look in his black eyes was fierce.

Abby took a step toward him. "What happened?" she cried. "Are you all right?"

The man smiled at her in the livid glow, then stepped into the brush and disappeared.

"He smiled at me."

"He smiled?" The white-haired detective frowned.

Abby nodded. "I thought he'd gotten out of the car. I was worried he was hurt. But when he smiled, I knew he was the one who had caused it, somehow. I panicked and ran." Abby shivered and pulled the blanket tighter around her shoulders. The interview room was air-conditioned and her sweat-soaked running clothes had cooled on her. A patrolman had finally brought her a blanket and a vending-machine cup of coffee but she was still cold.

The white-haired man had introduced himself as Detective Ruffner. He had blue eyes, a receding hairline and a moustache. He looked a little too young and robust to have such white hair. On the table in front of him was a small spiral notebook in which he had made occasional notes with a ballpoint pen. "You did the right thing. I wouldn't call it panic."

"It was *horrible*." Abby closed her eyes but opened them again right away because when she closed them all she could see was a man-shaped cinder in a bright-orange flame. "I'm sorry, I'm trying to keep it together."

She had been on the point of physical collapse after climbing the hill and staggering, lead legged and gasping, to the first house with a door she could pound on. The owner had not been pleased to be roused at dawn but had promptly called 911 when Abby had pointed to the column of black smoke rising from the hollow. Abby had sat on the man's front steps with her face in her hands as the sirens drew nearer, lots of them, and a small crowd gathered at the top of the hill. It had been at least half an hour before a patrolman had come up the walk and said, "You're the lady that found him?"

Now Ruffner said, "I can take you to the hospital if you need medical attention."

"No. I just need not to have seen that. But it's too late."

Ruffner nodded, a pained look on his face. "We can take a break for a while."

"I'm fine. I just want to get through this and go home." Home as in New York City, Abby thought, but she knew that was impossible.

Ruffner sat back on his chair. "OK. Did you see this man exit the car?"

"No. When I first noticed him he was standing at the end of the bridge, at the side of the road."

"So he might have been waiting there and flagged down the car."

"I guess so."

"Or he might have been just a bystander, like you."

Abby considered. "Maybe. But then what happened? And why did he smile like that?"

Ruffner grunted, reserving judgment. "All right. Can you describe this individual for me?"

"I only saw him for a few seconds. But I'll try." Abby closed her eyes and brought up the image. She recited the features, the hair, the gaunt face, the dark eyes, the moustache. The bare torso, the tattoos. "He looked . . . I don't know. He looked rough. He looked like a biker, or the guys you see in mug shots. When he smiled he scared the hell out of me."

Ruffner nodded. "Could you make out any of the tattoos? What they were? What they depicted?"

Abby shook her head. "No. I just remember he had tattoos."

Ruffner sat looking at her for a moment. "I'd like to take you back there and have you show me just where you saw him. OK?"

Abby's heart sank. "Sure."

The road into the hollow was blocked by a squad car. The crowd at the top of the hill had grown, gawkers mingling with uniforms and a cluster of officials with credentials on lanyards around their necks. Ruffner pulled up and an officer wandered over from the squad and bent down at his window. "Has the body been cleared?" said Ruffner.

"What was left of it. Car's still there. The ISP guys are going over it."

Ruffner looked at Abby and said, "OK?"

Abby nodded. "I'm fine."

"I'm gonna take our witness down there." Ruffner steered around the squad car, the officer shooing people out of the way, and eased down the hill. Abby tensed and closed her eyes; when she opened them it was all there: the hulking viaduct, the road snaking over the bridge into the tunnel, the burned-out carcass of a sedan sitting crookedly across the mouth of the tunnel. She could see through the tunnel to another roadblock on the far side, attended by a smaller crowd.

Two black SUVs with Indiana State Police markings were parked on the bridge. Officers in black uniforms and rubber gloves were peering into the wreck, various cases and items of equipment laid out on the ground to one side. Ruffner parked and they got out and approached the wreck.

It was just a burned-out car under a hot sun now, but Abby was taking deep breaths, remembering what it had looked like lighting the dawn a few hours before. Ruffner exchanged greetings with the state police technicians. "What's it look like? Any chance it's an accident?"

One of the techs, burly with a fat neck and crew cut, said, "Yeah, if you can accidentally spread accelerant all over a vehicle, including the driver, and then ignite it."

Ruffner grunted softly. "I don't think I'd sit still for that."

"Me neither. So we're thinking maybe he was already dead. Or unconscious at least."

Ruffner nodded slowly, turning to Abby. "Does that help?" he said softly.

She closed her eyes for a moment. "A little." She frowned. "So who was driving when the car went past me?"

"Maybe your guy. Did you see two people in the car?"

Abby closed her eyes. "I don't know. It went by fast, and it was dark. There could have been two, but all I saw was the driver."

Ruffner beckoned with his head. "Show me where you were when you saw him."

Abby walked slowly toward the wreck. Where the body had been there was nothing but charred metal now. "About right here."

"And he was where?"

"Right at the end of the bridge, just off the road. Where the rail ends there."

Ruffner walked to the spot, hands in his pockets, scanning the ground, his eyes going off into the brush at the side of the road and then down into the streambed. In the daylight Abby could see water rippling over pebbles, shaded by trees. "And he walked down into the stream here?"

"I think so. It was dark. I couldn't see him after he was out of the light from the flames."

Ruffner nodded and turned to the ISP officer, who had been listening. "My witness here came along right after it happened," he said. "She saw an individual go down into the streambed here. I wonder if you guys could see if there's anything in the way of tracks, or anything else that looks like evidence."

The technician shrugged. "Sure. We'll add it to the list."

"I appreciate it." Ruffner came back toward Abby, deep in thought. "I know I've put you through a lot today. If I can keep you for just a while longer I'd like you to come back to the station and look at some pictures."

"Pictures of what?"

"We keep a photo album of habitual offenders. The usual suspects. You never know, we might get lucky."

"I'm sorry," she said, scrolling down the screen. "They all start to look alike after a while."

Ruffner set a plastic cup full of coffee on the desk at her elbow. "Yeah. They do. Take your time, be sure. If you do see the guy, I think he'll jump out at you."

Mug shots were nothing new to Abby; everyone had seen mug shots online. These faces covered the spectrum, from young and defiant to old and decrepit, from sullen to brazen to bewildered. What struck Abby was how white they were. A lifetime in New York had conditioned her, fairly or unfairly, to the idea that somebody who mugged you or broke into your apartment was most likely to have dark skin. Out here in the heartland, she saw, he was most likely to be named Ryan or Wayne and to look like a Viking with his helmet knocked off.

Abby scrolled some more, reaching the end of the screen. "Any more?" she said.

"That's it. You've seen the whole roster."

"Sorry I couldn't be more helpful."

"You've been extremely helpful." He took a sip of coffee. "Whoever he is, this seems to be the guy we need to find."

Abby took a deep breath. "Can I ask you a question?"

"Sure."

"Am I in danger? I got a good look at this guy, and he got a good look at me. How worried is he going to be about me?"

Ruffner frowned, his gaze drifting across the room for a few seconds. "I think your moment of greatest danger was right then, when you saw him. If he didn't go after you then, then he probably didn't think you were a threat. In my experience there's only danger to witnesses once we get to the stage of potential testimony at trial after an arrest. But please, don't take that as any kind of guarantee. Take all the precautions you would normally take and then some. And if you see this gentleman again, anywhere, get the hell out of there and call us, fast. That's about the extent of my advice, I'm afraid."

Abby nodded. "I guess that will have to do."

5 |||||||

"Do you want me to fly out there and stay with you for a couple of days? I will if you need me to." Abby could hear the concern in her father's voice.

Yes, she thought. Get here as fast as you can. Standing with her phone to her ear, looking out through the big picture window into the trees, she took a deep breath and said, "No, that's all right. I just needed to talk about it. But thanks. The best Mom could come up with was, I should come home for a while. But I can't do that. I start a new job in two days."

"Are you going to be all right?"

"I'll be fine. I can do this."

A few seconds went by in silence. Her father said, "You've had a rough few months, sweetheart."

"Well, like Nietzsche said, or whoever it was, if it doesn't kill me it makes me strong. I'm going to be Supergirl here before too long."

"That's my girl. Hang in there. Call whenever you need to."

"I will. Thanks, Daddy. I love you."

Abby stood looking into the trees after ending the call, her throat tight with the need to weep. After a while she put her phone away and began to gather her things for the walk to campus.

I can do this, she told herself. I am Supergirl.

I will have to be, she thought, if this shit keeps up.

Abby heard footsteps coming down the long hallway and thought: Please come and talk to me.

She had been looking forward to the work. There were courses to plan, textbooks to review, syllabi to draw up. She had planned to show up early and spend the day with her laptop and books, working at a leisurely pace. Instead it had been well after noon before she had finally been able to go home, shower, call her parents, and then hurry to the campus. She had stopped at the student union to appease a raging hunger with a vending-machine sandwich and had been at her desk ever since, trying to concentrate on a mountain of work while suppressing the image of a human being going up in flames.

She had to stop and take a breath for a moment; this was not the first image she'd had to learn to suppress, and it took energy.

She saved the document on her computer and looked up as the footsteps halted at her door. "Knock, knock." Graham Gill stood there, in jeans and a khaki shirt with the sleeves rolled up. "I'm glad somebody's hard at work," he said, flashing the blinding smile. He hadn't shaved that morning, and the rugged look suited him. "Getting it all sorted out?"

"More or less," said Abby. She forced a smile. "I ought to be able to make it through the first class session."

Gill took a step into the office. "Wow, don't stand up too fast. You'll knock yourself out."

"Yeah, it's a little cramped. The new kid gets the office nobody else wants, I guess."

"The new kid needs a couple of plants and a picture or two on the walls."

"I haven't had time to acquire any frills. I think this empty Coke can brightens the place up a bit, though."

Gill laughed. "Give it time. Soon your office will be filled with junk, like mine. Hey, you have plans for this evening?"

Abby remembered Gill eyeing her from across the room at the faculty reception. She wasn't in the mood to be courted but she had a feeling she was going to need all the company she could get for a while. "My plan was to see if I can get Netflix on my computer in my apartment. I'm open to suggestions."

"Well, some of us younger faculty members are gathering for dinner and possibly some adult beverages. We thought you might like to join us."

"Thanks, I'd like that."

"I think the plan was pizza at Alberto's, and then for the true degenerates maybe drinks afterwards at one of the two bars in town where college people can drink without being hassled."

"Pizza I can probably handle. We'll see about the drinks afterward. I don't know if I'm a true degenerate."

"Well, the second half of the program is optional. You want me to pick you up?"

"That would be great. You know where Hickory Lane is?"

"Who doesn't? That's where the rich folks live."

Abby had to smile. "And me."

Alberto's was a pizza joint that appeared to have been converted from a gas station, built of white enameled brick with a canopy jutting out over the entrance, the pumps long gone. Inside it was bright and loud and full of families. The pizza was, in Abby's estimation, not up to much. The company was more interesting; besides Graham Gill there was Adam Linseth, a physicist, somewhere between thirty-five and forty, built like a fireplug with a shock of brown hair, rimless glasses and a mordant sense of humor. "Alfred North Whitehead said that ultimately matter itself was an abstraction. I found that a tremendous comfort when that great big abstraction rear-ended me at that stoplight last year." He was, apparently, a bachelor like Graham. The party was rounded out by Tina and Steven Stanley, a couple in their early thirties who were both in the biology department. They had a one-year-old at home but had finagled a babysitter for the evening.

"You'll like it here," said Tina. She was petite and doe-eyed, illuminated by contentment, happy to be who she was. "We thought, oh my God, it's so small, how can we go to a place like that, but the people are great. We met at UCLA, which is enormous, and to be somewhere where you know just about everyone on campus is amazing. And it's so easygoing, so small-town."

Her husband had a massive hipster beard. He said, "It's nice to be in a place where there's no crime to speak of."

Except for the people incinerated in cars, Abby thought.

Graham said, "There was a murder today."

Everyone looked at him, startled. "What, here? In Lewisburg?" Tina said.

"Out southwest of town."

"Was that what all the sirens were about this morning?" said Linseth.

"I heard those," said Tina. "I thought it was a fire or something."

"It was," said Graham. "They found a body in a burning car. But it wasn't an accident. The guy was murdered."

Tina gasped. "No."

Graham nodded. "One of the maintenance guys told me. He has a brother who's a cop or something."

"Oh God, that's awful."

Abby sat, looking at her plate, thinking: keep your mouth shut.

"Who got killed?" said Linseth.

"I have no idea. I don't know if the cops know. Apparently the body was pretty badly burned."

"How do they know it wasn't an accident?" said Linseth.

"Because the car was torched on purpose. With the guy inside."

"Oh, dear God." Tina put a hand to her mouth. For a moment there was silence.

"Ow," said Linseth. "That's gotta hurt."

"The police think he was already dead," said Abby.

Four people stared at her, startled. Here we go, Abby thought. She was conflicted: she wanted desperately to tell them all about it but she didn't really want the attention. "I was there," she said. "I saw it. I ran and got somebody to call the police."

She looked at them all in turn and almost laughed at the blank astonishment on their faces. Tina broke first. "Oh, Abby."

Graham frowned. "What were you doing there?"

She told them about it. "I thought it was the safest time to run. Who's out at five in the morning?"

After a couple of murmurs of sympathy and a soft but distinct obscenity from Adam Linseth, Graham said, "But wait a minute. If you came along right as it happened, heard the explosion and all, that means whoever did it was still around, right? Like, right there."

Abby nodded. She could see the man smiling at her in the flickering orange light. Careful, she thought. "Yeah. I got the hell out of there. Best workout of my life, going up that hill."

They all digested that in silence for a moment. Nobody seemed interested in the pizza anymore. Tina leaned toward her. "Are you all right?"

Grateful for the concern but determined not to crack in front of people she barely knew, Abby made herself laugh. "I'm OK. I spent the morning with the cops. That will drain the drama out of any situation."

Another few seconds went by in silence. Linseth said, "So who got killed?"

Graham said, "I believe the *Herald Gazette* has a website. Or it will be on one of the Indianapolis TV stations."

Linseth pulled out his phone. He swiped at it for a few seconds while the others watched. "Here we go. 'Top story. Local man found slain. The body of a Lewisburg man was discovered in his vehicle on County Road 200 South on Saturday, apparently the victim of foul play. The victim was identified as Rex Lyman, fifty-two.'"

"Who?" said Graham.

"Oh, my God," said Abby.

Everyone was looking at her again. "I met him," she said. "Last night. At the Azteca, with Lisa Beth Quinton and her husband."

"You are making this up," said Graham.

"I wish I was."

"You are definitely my number-one suspect," said Linseth.

"Who is he?" said Steven Stanley.

"A lawyer. Lisa Beth told me he was a lawyer. I don't think she liked him much. But it's still horrible."

Tina said, "Of course it is. My God, Abby. What a thing to go through."

"The cops told me he was dead or unconscious when the car was set on fire. That makes it a little easier. It wasn't a nice thing to see."

That thought was finally starting to sink in with her audience, Abby could see. The silence became awkward and Tina reached out and laid her hand on Abby's. "What do you need tonight?"

Bless you, thought Abby. "This," she said. "Just this. Just talk to me."

"We can do that," said Tina.

"And maybe some more adult beverages."

Linseth picked up the pitcher of beer. "I think we can probably supply those, too."

Graham Gill pulled into the driveway of 6 Hickory Lane and stopped. "Thank you so much," said Abby, undoing her seat belt. "This really helped."

"You going to be all right?" Concern showed in the handsome face.

"I'll be fine. Thanks. I really needed the company tonight." She got out of the car.

"See you at the office, then. Let me know if you need anything."

"I will." Abby shut the door, walked to the steps, waved as Graham backed the car out onto the street. She crossed the porch.

And here she stopped, looking down the slope into the night. All she had to do was walk down those steps into the darkness. Just walk down the steps and go around the corner and go into her dark house.

Abby stood rooted on the porch and told herself she was being childish. But the steps still descended into the black. She pulled her phone out of her purse and poked at it to bring up the flashlight app.

She was startled by a floodlight going on, on the corner of the roof above the steps. She squinted against the sudden brilliance. The steps were now brightly lit, along with an expanse of lawn behind the house. The door to the house opened and Ned McLaren appeared in the doorway, backlit from inside. "Is that better?"

Abby blinked at him. "Um, yeah, thanks."

McLaren stepped out onto the porch. He was in a T-shirt and jeans again, barefoot. "The switch is inside the door here. I try to remember to turn it on at night, but I never do. What I can do is install a switch out here on the porch so you can control it. Or I could make it motion sensitive. I'll try to get to that tomorrow."

Abby put her phone away. "Thank you, that would be good."

"Everything working OK down there?" The floodlight was enough to show McLaren's expression. Abby thought he looked tired.

"Yeah, so far everything's fine, thanks."

"Cool. Let me know if you need anything. I'll get that switch installed as soon as I can. G'night."

"Good night, thanks." Abby went down the steps. She halted at the bottom and looked back up at the porch for a moment. Come and talk to me, she thought, please. I can see where I'm going now, but behind that door there is still a dark, empty apartment.

6 |||||||

When Abby awoke the sun was shining; she was alive and unharmed but there was still no food in the house. The brand-new refrigerator and the freshly installed cabinets were still absolutely empty. Coffee, Abby thought. Coffee and granola, some berries and yogurt. Where can I get some?

She had no car and no idea where the closest supermarket was. The gas station with the minimart was not going to be a long-term solution but surely they would have some emergency basics, if only a bag of trail mix. She put on jeans and a tank top and set out. The morning was fresh and cool, the darkness lifted, the horror more distant by twenty-four hours. She felt a little light-headed; the world did not seem entirely real this morning.

She headed north on Jackson, crossed the stream in its little belt of woodland, went one block uphill, and here was something she had failed to notice before: a little corner store at the back of a small parking lot. The sign over the door was in Spanish: POZA RICA. There were hand-lettered signs in the window: TOMATILLOS, CHILES GUAJILLOS, JARRITOS. And here was one she knew: LECHE.

Why not? Milk was milk; they probably had coffee and would surely be happy to take her money. Abby crossed the street. She hesitated as she approached the door, daunted by the sound of rapid Spanish being spoken inside. What the hell, thought Abby. We're all foreigners here. She went in.

The conversation stopped dead as three people froze, looking at her. A short, squat woman and a grizzled old man in a straw hat stood before a counter behind which a young woman sat at a cash register. Abby blinked at them and said, "Um, hi. I was hoping I could get some milk."

She was prepared to turn tail and run at the first sign of hostility, but the young woman smiled at her and said, "Sure. Back there in the cooler."

Abby went down the aisle, scanning. There were racks of magazines with covers shouting *Quién*, *OK!*, *¡HOLA!*, bins of vegetables she didn't recognize, shelves full of cans labeled in Spanish. What was all this? *Pozole, picadillo, sofrito.* Here was the cooler, with plastic jugs of milk. Abby grabbed a half gallon and made her way back up toward the front. Here was coffee; here was a package of some kind of pastry, labeled *pan dulce.* Abby grabbed them. There wasn't going to be any yogurt or granola, she guessed.

She put her choices on the counter. "Did you find what you need?" the young woman said. She had dark eyes in a round, pleasant face, black hair pinned up loosely in back to keep it off her neck. She wore an Indianapolis Colts T-shirt but her face showed unmistakably the Iberian and Mesoamerican strains intertwined in her genome.

"Yeah, I think so, enough for breakfast anyway." Abby smiled at the elderly couple, who were staring at her wide-eyed. "I just moved in, up the street, and the cupboard is bare."

"Well, take your time, get what you need. There are baskets there by the door."

"Well . . . OK." Abby took a basket and made another pass, more slowly, gathering salad and sandwich makings, a loaf of bread improbably labeled *Bimbo*, butter, a few other staples.

Ringing them up, the girl asked, "You with the college?"

"That's right. How can you tell?"

"You don't sound like a Hoosier. And people from the town don't come in here much. Where did you move from?"

"New York City."

The girl's eyes lit up. "Oh, I always wanted to go to New York. Times Square, the Empire State Building." She laughed, and then in a burst of Spanish she addressed the couple. Abby caught the words "Nueva York." The man and woman smiled and nodded. Bagging Abby's purchases, the girl said, "What's your name? I'm Natalia."

"I'm Abby. Nice to meet you. What does 'Poza Rica' mean?"

"That's the name of the town we come from. It's in Veracruz state. Most of us here come from Veracruz. We came when I was eight."

"So you grew up here."

"Oh, yeah. Go Red Raiders, Lewisburg High, woo! I wanted to go to Tippecanoe, too, but it's too expensive. Plus, I didn't do too good on the SAT. I really blew the math part. So maybe community college in Lafayette next year, if I can save the money."

"What do you want to study?"

"I don't know. My daddy just wants me to do something girly, like cosmetology. Me, I always liked science. I thought maybe I could go into nursing. But I gotta improve my math for that."

Natalia's eyes flicked past Abby toward the door, and Abby turned to see a young Mexican man coming in. He was under six feet tall but athletic, barrel-chested and a little bowlegged in billowy oversized basketball shorts and a blue soccer jersey. His hair was cut in a fade with the shaved sides; he was handsome enough but his face wore a scowl. He had a blue tattoo on the side of his neck. He nodded a greeting to the elderly couple and then muttered something at Natalia in Spanish as he stepped behind the counter. She replied and they carried on a brief conversation as he moved past her to the register, jabbed at a key to open the drawer and took out a few bills. Natalia caught Abby's eye. "This is my brother," she said. "He thinks he's my boss. Luis, this is Abby. She just moved here, from New York."

The look Luis gave Abby was just a shade off the scowl. "Hi," he said. "There's a Kroger's at the mall out on South Jackson. That's probably where you want to get your groceries."

Natalia smacked her brother on the shoulder with the back of her hand. "That's not very friendly."

"I'm just trying to help the lady," he said, folding the bills into a wallet. "We mostly just have Mexican stuff here." He pulled a smartphone out of his pocket and started jabbing at it with his thumb.

Natalia rolled her eyes and shoved Abby's bags across the counter to her. "Come buy all the Mexican stuff you want, Abby. I'll teach you to cook Mexican. I'll teach you how to make *tamales huastecos*."

"I'd like that," Abby said. "You know, math is my field. I could tutor you if you want."

"Really? That would be awesome."

Oh, God, Abby thought, instantly regretting the impulse. "Right now I'm pretty busy, starting a new job and all. But maybe in a few weeks we could work something out. I'll be around."

"I would love that. I'm so glad to meet you." Natalia wiggled her fingers and went back to Spanish, addressing the old couple.

Abby grabbed her purchases and fled. Outside, she stood for a moment taking stock: It was good to make friends, but what had possessed her to offer to commit valuable time to somebody she didn't even know? You're desperate, she thought.

The next moment she thought: desperate or not, you need all the friends you can get.

Philip Herzler's wife Ruth was zaftig and matronly, with a reassuring smile. "This place terrified me when we first moved here," she said, nudging lumps of pickled herring into line on a plate with a knife. "I had the feeling when I walked along Courthouse Square that all the old men in overalls on the benches were pointing and saying, "Look, there goes a Jew.""

Abby laughed, uncomfortably. Terrified? I can top that one, she thought. But here in the Herzlers' kitchen she felt safe, with a glass of wine in hand, olives, cheeses, salamis and half-sliced baguettes scattered on the butcher-block tabletop in front of her and the murmur of conversation wafting back from the living room. "I'm afraid I'm a really bad Jew. As in, I got presents on Hanukkah and Christmas both."

"Well, goodness. Phil and I are hardly models of orthodoxy. Let me just say that bacon has been known to pass our lips."

Jerry Collins came into the kitchen with an empty beer bottle in his hand. "Oho! So here's where the real party is." He set the bottle on the counter and beamed at Abby. "So, are they putting you in the Witness Protection Program?"

There was a stunned silence, Ruth blinking at Jerry and then at Abby. Abby said, "I guess they'll have to, pretty soon. Is it all over town?"

"I don't know about that. Lisa Beth saw you in a squad car at the scene. But nobody would tell her why you were there."

"And I am consumed with curiosity," said Lisa Beth Quinton, who had appeared in the doorway. "But I wasn't going to be indiscreet enough to ask you about it." She shot her husband a scathing look.

Abby remembered the crowd at the top of the hill; she had been oblivious. She said, "I was out for a jog and I saw the car burning. I reported it. That's all." She met Ruth Herzler's baffled look and said, "I happened to come across that murder yesterday."

Ruth gasped. "Oh, how awful."

"It's drawing a lot of attention," said Lisa Beth. "Lawyers don't get themselves killed too often around here." She made her way past the wine bottles arrayed on the counter to where the harder stuff stood and picked up a bottle of vodka.

Abby set her glass down on the butcher block. She had been gripping it so tightly she was afraid she was going to snap the stem. "They're sure about the identification, are they?"

"Apparently. I think they got the dental records yesterday. Today they got the autopsy results from Terre Haute, and guess what? He had two deep knife wounds. One in his thigh and one right through the heart. So he didn't feel a thing, probably, when the car went up in smoke. Whoever did it drove him there and set him up behind the wheel, then torched the car."

"That's appalling," said Ruth. "Do the police have any ideas?"

"They do," said Lisa Beth. She poured vodka over ice and took a healthy swig. "They're looking very hard at Lyman's client list. He had a lot of what you could call unsavory associates."

Ruth Herzler heaved a sigh. "Well. It's horrible." Her look lingered on Abby for a moment. "How awful for you."

"I'll be all right. Nothing to do with me."

"You're very brave." Ruth's look lingered on Abby and then she reached out and patted her hand. She picked up plates and took them out to the living room, leaving Lisa Beth and Abby in the kitchen.

Lisa Beth took a sip of her drink. "You didn't just find the car, did you? You saw something else, I'm thinking. That's why nobody at the police station will talk about you."

Abby felt the blood drain from her face. She opened her mouth but nothing came out.

Lisa Beth raised a hand. "Don't tell me anything you don't want to. Forget I said anything."

"It's all right." Abby looked into her wineglass and said, "I saw a guy, that's all. I don't know if he had anything to do with it."

"OK. Don't worry. I'm not going to write about you, I promise you."

"Thanks, that's good to know."

A moment passed and Lisa Beth said, "And the cops are not talking. Do what they tell you and you'll be fine."

"I plan to," said Abby. "Believe me."

7 |||||||

"All right, then. First problem set due on Wednesday, first quiz one week from today. Be ready. See you Wednesday." Abby gave the class what she hoped was a confident, authoritative smile and closed the folder on the lectern in front of her to signal the end of the session. She busied herself with gathering papers, markers and books while the room erupted in a hum of voices and shifting chairs.

"Uh, Dr. Markstein?" The girl was blonde and pretty, hair in a topknot, track shorts and tank top showing a lot of healthy tanned limb. "I just wanted to say, that was awesome."

Abby blinked at her, unsure what feat she had accomplished. "Thank you. Sorry, the names are going to take me a while. You are . . . ?"

"Giselle. Giselle McCullers. I just think it's great to have a woman teaching calculus. I've never had a woman math teacher."

"What, never? That surprises me. We're not that exotic."

"Never. Not since like, middle school, I mean. Everyone thinks it's such a guy thing."

Abby had to smile. "It is pretty guy intensive. But not exclusively. Not at all."

Giselle beamed at her. "I want to major in math, and all my friends are like, ooh, math, you are so hard-core."

"Guess what, you are hard-core. Hold on to that thought."

Behind Giselle loomed a giant, a strapping six-plus-footer with a barrel chest stretching a gray T-shirt with TIPPECANOE FOOTBALL on it. "Hi," he said, holding out a massive hand. "Cole West. Looking forward to the class."

Abby squeezed hard against a grip that was confident but not aggressive. "Good. Me, too."

"I was wondering, I'm in a fraternity, Tau Kappa Zeta, and we do this thing every year, where we invite faculty members over for Sunday dinner, and I was wondering if you'd want to come over some time. Just to like, meet the guys, you know, and so we can get to know you and stuff." He had friendly eyes, a granite jaw and an assertive smile.

"Um . . ." Think fast, Abby told herself. Could this possibly be legit? Was this behemoth hitting on her already, on day one? "Thank you, that's very kind. Let me get back to you on that, OK? But thank you."

The behemoth went off with Giselle, and a thin, dark-eyed, vaguely Asian-looking young man who had been loitering behind him stepped up. He wore a black T-shirt with an indecipherable graphic on the front; he was good-looking in a frail, slightly brooding way. "Hi, can I talk to you for a second?"

"Sure, that's what I'm here for. Sorry, who are you?"

"Ben Larch."

"Ben, right. What's up?"

He smiled, but it was a nervous smile. "I think I might be over my head in this class. My advisor said I should take it, but I'm not sure I'm up to it. I didn't really follow everything you went through today."

Abby's smile widened, because here in front of her at last she saw her true constituency. "Well, number one, don't panic," she said. "I can help you."

Abby dropped her books on the desktop in her office and sank onto the chair, her legs suddenly giving out. She planted her elbows on the desk and put her face in her hands. Round one, she thought. Went OK, didn't embarrass myself, established the parameters. Students not hostile. Some even eager to learn. So why the stress?

Pick one, she thought. Because you have two more classes to get through. Because you are still a fish out of water here. Because after your day's work is done you will be going back to an empty apartment.

Because you saw a man being roasted like a pig on a spit.

Voices and steps sounded in the hall, cheerful voices of people who had no connection to a charred corpse in a bad crime scene. Abby took her hands from her face and sighed. A figure swung into the doorway. "How'd it go?" said Graham.

"Fine, I think. Nobody threw anything or asked to transfer to a different section."

He came a step or two into the office. "I think you'll have the opposite problem. Once word gets around, people will be clamoring to get into your section. Guys, anyway."

"Terrific. Five years of grad school and a postdoc and my looks are all that count?"

"That's what eighteen-year-old guys see first, yeah. Sorry, I don't mean to make light of your professional qualifications. I just know how it goes. It happens with me, with the girls. Younger faculty members deal with it all the time. Kids get crushes on you."

"Great, something to look forward to. Can I ask you something? One of my students invited me to dinner at his frat house. Is this legitimate? Do people do that?"

"It's legitimate. They do that a few times a year. Having faculty over for dinner gives them an excuse to clean up the house and make themselves presentable. Boy, they didn't waste any time, did they? Usually we get a few weeks into the semester before the invitations start coming. Which house is this?"

"I think he said Tau Kappa Zeta."

Graham's eyebrows rose. "No kidding? It just so happens I'm their faculty advisor."

"Aha. And are they house-trained?"

"Well, they're the jock fraternity. But they're usually on their best behavior on these occasions. Just don't let them lure you into any drinking games."

"Not bloody likely."

Graham laughed. "It happened to me once; I got invited to one of their parties. I reeled home about two in the morning and woke up a chastened man."

He lingered for another minute or so of small talk and then went on his way. Abby surveyed her desktop, thinking about all the things she had to do. She dug her phone out of her purse and turned it on, the voice-mail icon coming up. She put the phone to her ear and heard Ruffner asking her to call him.

She tapped on the screen and after a few rings the detective answered. "Thanks for getting back to me. I know you're busy."

"Please tell me you've arrested someone."

"Not yet, I'm afraid. I was wondering if you could come in and look at some more pictures. The state police are here with a roster of some of their favorite people."

Ruffner met Abby at the front desk and took her back to the office where she'd looked at mug shots before. There was another detective there, this one young and muscular, with the look of a weight-room devotee. "Joe Ross, ISP Criminal Investigation Division." He shook her hand and ushered her to a chair. "I understand you got a look at a suspect the other day."

"I don't know. I saw a guy."

"Right. We're going on that assumption. He's what we've got, until we know different. So we're gonna try and run him down. I've got some more yearbook pictures for you to take a look at here." Ross smiled. "Be glad you never went to this school."

He slid a laptop across the desk to her. "Take your time, don't feel any pressure to come up with an ID. He may not be there. Don't finger anybody unless you're sure."

Abby started scrolling, slowly. The faces were the same, defiant, dazed or defeated, but this time there was a difference: all the names were Hispanic. Some of the faces were pure Mesoamerican; some could have been Mediterranean. None was Anglo-Saxon. The Ryans and Waynes had been replaced by Pedros and Franciscos. "They're all Latino," Abby said.

"That's right," said Ross. "That is the direction our investigation is taking."

"Can I ask why?"

"Because of the nature of the crime. The Mexican cartels frequently dispose of bodies in this way. They execute the victim and then set his vehicle on fire."

She gave him an astonished look. "The Mexican cartels? Here?"

"They have a presence in the Midwest. Anywhere they run drugs. Which is pretty much everywhere now. And this is like their signature move."

Across the room Ruffner spoke up. "Plus, the victim's connections. Lyman had clients who were Mexican."

Abby paused, looking at a face. The dimensions were right, long and gaunt, with the same heavy brows. There was a moustache, but it didn't go past the corners of the mouth. The hair was shorter, too, but Abby could allow for that. It was a dead-end face, the eyes empty. It disturbed Abby in the same way the man at the end of the bridge had disturbed her. "Maybe this one," she said. "Just maybe. I'm not going, 'Yeah, him for sure.' He's just the right type. And he had this look."

Ross leaned over the desk to read the screen. "Alejandro Gómez. OK, we'll put him down as a maybe." He made a note on a sheet of paper.

"This face jumps out at me as Mexican," Abby said. "The guy I saw didn't."

The detectives exchanged a look. "All right," said Ruffner. "Understood."

"But he could have been." She looked up, flustered. "I'm sorry, I'm trying to be objective. I want to help, but I don't want to make any false accusations."

"There's no pressure," said Ruffner. "We're not here to railroad anybody."

Abby went back to looking at faces. There were only a few more, maybe twenty in all. She went back through the display, trying to summon up the face she had seen and compare it to these, but she was already feeling that it was futile. She pushed the laptop back across the desk. "I'm sorry. Just that one, and I'm not sure about him."

"That's OK," said Ross, reaching for the computer.

"You've been a great witness," said Ruffner. "We really appreciate your help."

Abby reached for her purse. "By the way, I didn't tell you before, because I didn't know who the victim was at the time, but I saw Lyman the night before he was killed."

"Did you now? That's interesting. Where?"

"At the Azteca. He was talking to another guy, I don't remember his name. I was out to dinner with a couple of people from the college: Lisa Beth Quinton and her husband. She pointed out Lyman and the other guy to me. She said they were both kind of shady. I didn't think any more about it until I heard who the victim was. But I thought you might want to know."

Ruffner nodded. "Thanks. Actually, we already knew. Mr. Frederick, the other guy, came to us as soon as we released Lyman's identity and told us about their dinner date. He said when Lyman left the restaurant that night he told him he had to go and collect some money he was owed by a client. We're working on that angle. Don't know what's there, but we're working on it."

A moment passed in silence. Abby said, "If the guy was Mexican, does that make it more or less likely that I'm in danger?"

Ruffner exchanged a look with Ross. "The most likely thing is that he's no longer around. That's how they operate, if it is a professional hit. They would bring a guy in, he does the job, he goes away again. But I can't guarantee anything."

"I understand. I just need to know if I have to be afraid."

"I would say cautious. I would be careful where I went jogging for a while, for example. But even if he is still around, what are the chances he's just going to spot you on the street or something? He got a look at you, but would he recognize you again? I would say it's unlikely."

Abby sat nodding slowly. "All right," she said. "Thank you."

"Abby, I have to go. The baby's starting to make a fuss."

Which one, Abby wanted to ask. Samantha had spent much of the call complaining about her husband and his failure to pull his weight in a household stressed by the irruption of an infant. "All right," Abby said. "Go take care of your child. Love you."

There was a brief silence. "Abby, you sure you're OK?"

"I'm fine." Abby's mouth hung open for a second as she stifled the words that really wanted to come out: I'm scared, I'm lonely, I'm in a strange place a long way from home. I called so you could make me laugh and comfort me, and instead you complained about your baby, your husband, your lack of sleep. "Say hi to Tom for me. Go feed your baby."

"I'll talk to you soon. Love you."

"Bye." Abby ended the call and stood looking down into the woods. She had come outside to make the call, for better reception and because it was pleasant to stand in the cool shaded yard with the trees rustling softly in the evening breeze, the blue of the sky deepening as the sun sank in the west.

Something moved in the twilight down by the stream. Abby tensed and strained to see. A doe and a fawn came into view, stepping daintily along the bank of the stream. Abby watched as they foraged on spindly legs, nosing through the thick ground cover.

When the deer went out of sight into a thicket, Abby turned and looked at the back of Ned McLaren's house looming above her. There was light behind drawn curtains on the top floor, and below it a lamp burned in Abby's living room, which through the window looked almost inviting.

This is my home, Abby told herself. I can do this. I can walk back in there and confront the work and the anxiety and the solitude. And the fear.

Abby laughed, a single bitter breath. She had not thought about Evan in two days.

8 |||||||

Abby labored north along Jackson Avenue under a westering sun with a full backpack and a double handful of shopping bags, shoulders aching, sweat running into her eyes. Ahead the road began to dip. The entrance to Hickory Hill was in sight, a mere three hundred yards away.

Abby had decided it was time to diversify her sources of supply and find out where the rumored mall with its supermarket actually lay. That turned out to be three-quarters of a mile south along Jackson beyond the edge of town; what had been a pleasant stroll empty-handed had turned into the Bataan Death March on the way home, burdened with her purchases.

A car horn sounded and a dark-gray car swerved to the curb. The passenger's-side window went down and as Abby drew even, Lisa Beth Quinton called to her from behind the wheel. "Honey, jump in the car. I hate to see a woman suffer."

Abby slung her bags in the back and flopped on the front seat. Rolling home in air-conditioned comfort, starting to recover, she said, "Maybe it's time to get a bicycle."

Lisa Beth made a noncommittal noise. "You could do that. Or you could throw caution to the wind and get a car. These hills can be hell on a bicycle, especially with a load of groceries. And a bicycle won't get you to Indianapolis on a Saturday night."

Abby considered. "I've never had a car. The only reason I have a license is because my father told me it was something grown-ups have."

"You're not in New York now. Out here we take the car to go three blocks for a gallon of milk."

"Yeah. I was hoping to resist that."

Lisa Beth made the turn into Hickory Lane. "A decent used car won't cost you that much. Tell you what, I'll come with you. I like shopping for cars. What are you doing on Saturday?"

Abby heaved a sigh. "Sounds like I'm buying a car."

"It's motion sensitive," said Ned McLaren. He stood on the covered porch, looking up at the light at the corner of the house. "It'll come on when you start down the steps and go off after a few seconds when you go inside. You can override it with this switch here." He stepped to a switch by the door. "Click it off and on again, fast, and it stays lit. Turn it off for ten seconds and it goes back to motion-sensor mode."

"Um . . . I probably won't mess with it too much. Thank you. I really appreciate that."

McLaren was in handyman mode again today, jeans and T-shirt and cap, with a bandage on his left little finger and dirt on his knees. He gave her an appraising look and a tentative smile. "How's the teaching going?"

"Fine. Actually, there was something I wanted to ask you about."

"Shoot."

"I was thinking about buying a car. But I didn't know where I would park it. I thought I should ask."

McLaren's eyes went to the asphalt driveway leading to the single-car garage. "Well, I guess you'd have to park it on the grass. If you left me room to get in and out, you could leave it at the side of the drive. Say under the tree there. Pull over far enough so I can get by and that can be your spot."

"OK, thanks. I'm not sure when this is happening. Maybe Saturday."

"Finally gave in to the tyranny of distance, did you?"

"Something like that."

"You got your sights on a particular car?"

"I've done a little research online. But Lisa Beth Quinton's going to come with me. She says she knows the dealers and she'll make sure I get a good deal."

McLaren grinned. "Yeah, I'd say you're probably in pretty good hands with Lisa Beth."

"OK, I can multiply the exponent by the coefficient all the way along, no problem. That's just mechanical. But I don't really get the concept. Why does the derivative work? Where does it come from?" Ben Larch was giving Abby an anguished look across the desk.

"Well, do you remember when we calculated the slopes of those secant lines in class?"

"I remember watching you do it, yeah." He laughed.

"OK, let's go back. You see that different secant lines can approximate the tangent to a curve?"

She took him through it again, pausing at each step to quiz him, then watched him puzzle it through, the olive skin of his brow wrinkled with the effort. He was a nice-looking boy, but still a boy, almost pretty. "That's right. So we started here with x squared, and we wind up here with 2x. Right? And if you work through the same process for y equals x cubed, what do you think you'll get?"

He sat back, a smile slowly spreading across his face. "OK. Sure, that makes sense."

"Math does make sense. That's the beautiful thing about it. If it doesn't make sense, that just means you missed a step somewhere. And you can always go back."

"I'm just afraid I might have missed too many steps."

"Well, you've got the fundamentals. What you need is practice. Math is like basketball. You don't get good at shooting free throws by watching LeBron do it and going, 'OK, now I can shoot free throws.' You have to get in the gym and do it, over and over. That's what the problem sets are for. They're the practice free throws."

Ben sat nodding slowly, gazing at her. "OK," he said. "That helps, thanks."

"So go back and look at that problem set again. Can you bring it to me tomorrow so I can look at it before class?"

"Yeah. OK, for sure."

"Great. Slip it under the door if I'm not here."

Ben stuffed papers and books into his backpack and stood. "Thanks, Abby. You're amazing." The boy's smile was dazzling.

She listened as his steps died away down the hall. That's Dr. Markstein to you, she thought, slightly irked at the familiarity but pleased at the compliment. There are rewards, she thought. Sometimes there are rewards.

Having located the Kroger's, Abby didn't want to drop the Poza Rica entirely; it was convenient for miscellaneous items, and any outpost with a friendly face was worth maintaining. On her way home from campus she detoured to cross Jackson Avenue, hoping Natalia and not her sullen brother would be on duty.

Nobody was on duty, apparently; when she stepped inside she saw no one behind the counter. She saw no customers, either, but voices came from the rear of the store, behind a closed door. Abby took a basket from the stack by the door and made her way down the first aisle. As she got closer to the back of the store, the voices resolved enough for her to distinguish that somebody was speaking English, and he was not happy. "I've got fucking FBI agents coming around," a man said.

As Abby lingered at the cooler, milk in hand, she was unable to hear the reply, which was much softer. Abby put the milk in her basket and made for the vegetable bins along the side wall. "I hope they throw you and your whole God damn family out of the country," the first voice said.

She reached the door in the corner just as it burst open and a man she knew came storming out. She pulled up short, and she and the man stared at each other for a couple of frozen seconds. He said, "Who are you?" in an aggressive tone.

"I'm a customer," Abby said. "Who are you?" She had just identified him as the man she had seen with the blonde at the Azteca restaurant; what was his name?

"I own this place," the man said. He was scowling at her, starting to move again, but obviously trying to place her. "You're not Mexican," he said.

Abby couldn't come up with an answer to that, and she was staring after him as he strode toward the front of the store when Natalia came through the door from the back. "Abby!"

Abby stared; Natalia's eyes were glistening with tears. "What's going on?"

Natalia shook her head, wiping tears with her fingers. "Oh, nothing. I'm glad to see you. How are you?"

At the head of the aisle the man had halted and was looking back at Abby. "You're with the paper, aren't you?" he said, pointing at her. "I saw you with Quinton."

"I'm not with the paper." Abby almost laughed.

He advanced a couple of steps back toward her. "Sure. OK, you want a story, here's the story. I was dumb enough to rent to a Mexican criminal and he's been running his rackets out of this place. But that's over now. Him and his whole criminal brood are going out on the street. Back to fucking Mexico, if I have anything to say about it. Write that." He spun and stalked toward the door, clipping a shelf with his shoulder and sending packets of rice to the floor.

Abby looked at Natalia, who exhaled heavily. "Sorry, Abby. Bad day at the office."

"I can come back some other time. I just needed a couple of things."

"No, no, no. Don't worry, we're open. Get what you need. He's just . . ." She shook her head. "Long story," she said, heading for the register. "Take your time."

A man had appeared in the doorway at the rear. He was Mexican, gray haired and balding with a salt-and-pepper moustache, in a white shirt with the sleeves rolled up. He wore a deep frown. He watched Natalia for a moment and then looked at Abby and nodded once. "Hello," he said softly, and pulled the door shut.

Abby made a hurried pass through the store, grabbing the few things she needed. When she put the basket on the counter Natalia smiled at her, apparently recovered. She gestured toward the parking lot. "That was Mr. Frederick, the landlord. He's not real happy with us right now."

"Legal trouble?" Abby started emptying her basket. "Sorry, it's none of my business."

"No, that's OK." Natalia shot a look toward the door at the rear and lowered her voice. "My daddy did something he shouldn't." She had started to ring Abby's purchases up but now she halted. "I'm afraid he's gonna go to jail."

"Oh, no." Abby stared in dismay. "Oh, Natalia."

Natalia shook her head, tight-lipped, then wiped a tear with a finger. "I'm OK." She went back to ringing up the items. "We just need a good lawyer, Daddy says."

What leapt to Abby's mind was that the local supply of lawyers had been abruptly reduced. "I'm gonna take the SAT again in a couple of months," said Natalia, managing a smile.

Why not, thought Abby, let's do it. "You want some help with the math?"

"Oh, that would be great. Would you really do that?"

"Sure. Let me look at my schedule and figure out a good time, OK?"

Outside in the parking lot voices were raised. Natalia's eyes flicked toward the door in alarm. "Luis," she breathed. She dashed from behind the counter.

Abby followed her to the door. When they went out into the parking lot they saw Jud Frederick and Luis standing face-to-face, in confrontation. Frederick was a head taller but Luis was giving nothing away. Today he was in low-slung jeans and an oversized T-shirt, with a baseball cap on his head, the flat brim cocked slightly to one side.

Frederick jabbed Luis in the chest with a finger. Luis brushed his hand away and lunged forward to knock the taller man back with a two-handed shove. Frederick staggered but kept his feet, and took a swipe at Luis that knocked his cap off. "God damn beaner punk. Keep your hands off me."

"I'll fuckin' take you apart." Luis squared for the fight, fists raised.

Natalia wailed and ran to throw her arms around Luis, pleading in Spanish. Her brother tried to shove her away but she held on. They spun in a clumsy dance and Natalia switched to English to scream at Frederick. "Please, please just go away. Don't hurt him."

Frederick leveled his finger at Luis. "I know what you're up to, you fucking Mex gangster wannabe. It's over, you hear?"

Luis sent Natalia staggering, freeing himself, but he didn't advance on Frederick. "I'll put you in the fuckin' ground."

Frederick didn't seem to want the fight any more than Luis did; he was backing toward his car. "You'll be in jail before you know what hit you, asshole."

Abby watched, stunned, as Natalia herded her brother toward the store and Frederick's car went squealing out onto Jackson Avenue. Luis shook free of Natalia and his eye lit on Abby. He barked, "Are you with him? You here to spy on the Mexicans, are you?"

Abby stiffened. She was speechless for an instant and then she bristled. "I'm not with anybody," she said. "I'm here because your sister was nice to me, and if that bothers you, maybe you're the one with the problem."

Luis glared at her. Abby waited for a reaction, rigid and unblinking, but he swaggered past her into the store. She watched him until he disappeared down an aisle. She exhaled, astonished at her own sudden anger. A little weak in the knees, she shook her head.

Natalia was staring at her. She said, "I'm sorry, Abby."

Abby put a hand on her arm. "Don't be sorry for me," she said. "Just tell me what I can do."

Natalia wiped tears, took a deep breath. "Help me learn math."

"That I can do," Abby said. "That I can do, for sure."

9 |||||||

"Nobody ever showed me this before," said Natalia. She looked up from the paper, wide-eyed. "I wish I'd had you in high school. Mr. Jenkins was hopeless. It was like he was only talking to the kids who already knew it. The rest of us, it was like, good luck."

Abby smiled, gratified. "Here, I'm going to e-mail you the link to this web page. See if you can work through all these problems before the next time we meet, OK?" She turned the laptop toward Natalia.

They were in Abby's study, papers spread across the desktop, the view beyond the window tempting the occasional stray glance. Natalia had been timid and hesitant at first but Abby had been able to tease out the strands of what appeared to be a reasonable grasp of the basics of algebra and geometry.

Natalia nodded and closed her notebook. "Yeah, sure." She looked at Abby, hesitant. "I feel like I should pay you something."

"No, we made a deal. You get above five hundred in math on the SAT and you owe me a good Mexican dinner."

"All right." Natalia sat back on the chair, closed her eyes, and exhaled. "I have to get back to the store." She opened her eyes and stared out at the greenery for a moment. "My father had to go to Indianapolis to see a lawyer."

Abby let a few seconds go by in uncomfortable silence. "What's going on with that?"

Natalia's head drooped. "I don't know."

"I'm sorry. None of my business."

"No, it's OK." She turned big, wide eyes to Abby, brimming with tears. "I think my daddy's in a lot of trouble. A bunch of FBI guys came and took a lot of stuff out of his office. I think it's about the documents."

"What documents?"

"He helps people. He helps them get documents."

"Ah."

"Like . . . fake documents, I think. You know? Drivers' licenses and stuff."

"Uh-huh."

"And he got busted. I don't know what we're gonna do if he goes to jail. We already had enough trouble with my brother."

"Luis?"

"Yeah. He got in trouble in Indianapolis. He was hanging with some gang guys and got arrested last year. For selling drugs. He got probation, so he was lucky. And he came back here. But he still goes to Indianapolis a lot, and I think he's hanging with the same people. I'm afraid he's gonna get hurt, or go to prison." Natalia was staring out the window, tears tracking down her cheeks. "My mama can't run the store herself. Her English isn't good enough. And I don't know if I can, either. Not if I want to go back to school."

Abby sat dismayed and helpless, watching her fight for composure. "Well. I can't tell you what's going to happen. But I think you should plan on going back to school. Prepare for that, and if things work out you'll be ready."

Natalia nodded, wiping her eyes with the back of her hand. "I know. There's nothing else I can do." She flashed Abby a smile. "I didn't make this mess."

"That's the spirit."

Natalia pushed away from the desk but halted. "Oh, I almost forgot. I wanted to invite you to something." She took her purse from the floor and dug in it. "You gotta come to the LUCES benefit."

"The what benefit?"

"LUCES. It's an organization. It stands for, lemme see, 'Latinos United for Cooperation, Enterprise and Success,' I think. See, *luces* means 'lights.' It supports stuff, like job programs and English classes and things like that. And they have this benefit every year. There's music and food, and there's a raffle and a silent auction and stuff. It's a lot of fun, and a lot of white people come, too. I'm supposed to sell tickets, but I'll give you one for free." Natalia pulled a ticket out of her purse and offered it to Abby.

"When is it?"

"I think it's like a week from Saturday."

Abby saw no way to refuse gracefully, so she took the ticket. "Sounds like fun. But I want to pay my way. What is it, twenty dollars?"

"You don't have to. You can be my guest. To pay you for the lessons, OK? Please?"

This girl is going to go far with that smile, thought Abby, giving in. "All right, thanks. For that you get an extra ten minutes of tutoring. Let me see you solve these equations."

"Five thousand? Come on, Ray. I wasn't born yesterday. A 2005 Ford Focus with a hundred and forty thousand miles on it? And that Carfax report? Anything more than four would be taking advantage of this young lady's innocence."

Ray was an affable man with a good head of black hair and a walrus moustache to match his walrus physique. He gave Abby a rueful look. "You said you were from Manhattan? I think it was Lisa Beth here who talked the Indians into giving it away for twenty-four bucks."

"If the Dutch had had me on their team," Lisa Beth said, "I'd have gotten it knocked down to twenty, for lack of infrastructure. Now what do you say?"

Abby smiled sweetly, content to be a bystander. She had been watching Lisa Beth at work on her behalf for an hour and had learned a great deal about the process of purchasing an automobile and about female empowerment.

Ray sighed and looked at Abby. "Can you do forty-five hundred?"

Abby would have given him the five thousand, but she knew better than to open her mouth. She looked at Lisa Beth, who winked at her. "Forty-two, Ray. Or we walk."

"You're killing me, Lisa Beth. Forty-two five."

Now Lisa Beth looked at Abby and raised her eyebrows. "Um, that's fine," said Abby.

Half an hour later she was the somewhat apprehensive owner of a slightly road-weary but fully functional automobile. She sat behind the wheel, the engine ticking over. "You can go to the BMV on Monday," said Lisa Beth, leaning down at the window. "It's cocktail hour. Let's go get a drink to celebrate."

"I don't know," said Abby. "I don't want to get busted for drunk driving on my first day."

"Come on, the Azteca's a hundred yards down the road. One drink and we're done. Meet you there."

Abby managed to cover the hundred yards without incident. The test drives had been a little nerve-racking at first but she had quickly gained confidence. Traffic in Lewisburg was not especially harrowing. She parked and got out as Lisa Beth pulled in beside her.

The place was nearly empty; two old men sat at the end of the bar and a solitary woman was tucking into an early dinner at a table. The hostess who had seated them on their previous visit was behind the bar. Lisa Beth ordered a margarita, frozen with salt on the rim. Abby settled for a grapefruit juice.

"Suit yourself," said Lisa Beth. "One drink won't send you off the road."

"I really appreciate your help, Lisa Beth. I would have been happy to go on walking three blocks for a gallon of milk. But the Poza Rica doesn't have bagels or pasta sauce."

"You go to the Poza Rica?" Lisa Beth's look was suddenly intent. "Oh, of course, it's just up the street from you. You know Miguel Menéndez then, do you?"

"The owner? Seen him, that's all. I'm tutoring his daughter in math."

"What a sweetheart you are. Was she in on the monkey business?"

"The fake documents? I don't think so. She did mention her dad's legal troubles."

"Legal troubles, my God. That man's going to go away for a long time."

"For forging documents?"

"Honey, it was a lot more than that. Cheers." The drinks had arrived and Lisa Beth devoted herself to the first swallow. She set the glass down, leaned forward, elbows on the bar, and lowered her voice, putting her head close to Abby's. "I told you about that, remember? The tax fraud case? That man scammed the government for more than a million bucks."

"You're kidding. What did he do?"

"He filed tax documents with phony names and addresses and got refunds. He stole people's personal data and filed for unemployment and got the state to send him their benefits. The Mexicans all trusted him because he helped them get papers, helped them navigate the bureaucracies. And all the time he was gaming the system for his own benefit."

"Oh, God. Poor Natalia."

"I'm afraid she's going to have to kiss Daddy good-bye for a few years. There's a son, too, apparently. I don't know that he was involved at all."

"I met him. I saw him fighting with what's-his-name, that Frederick guy."

Lisa Beth drew back, a theatrical gesture of surprise. "My goodness, you have a way of being on the scene, don't you? You should be in my business. What were they fighting about?"

"Frederick was accusing the son of being a gangster. They were about to start throwing punches, but the daughter separated them."

"Hmm. I've never heard anything about the son."

"Natalia told me he had gotten in trouble in Indianapolis for running around with a gang."

"Oh, that's always good news for a family. You know, I hope this doesn't get ugly. So far there hasn't been much in the way of anti-Mexican agitation around here. But with this murder, on top of Menéndez and his scams, it makes me nervous."

They brooded together for a moment, staring at a lurid rendition of an Aztec warrior in a beaked eagle headdress hanging on the wall behind the bar, mariachi trumpets bleating merrily above their heads. A door behind the bar opened and two men came out of an office. One was a Hispanic man somewhere in his forties and the other was Jud Frederick. When Frederick saw Abby and Lisa Beth he stopped dead in his tracks. "Oh, for Christ's sake," he said. "What now? You gonna dig up the parking lot looking for bodies?"

Lisa Beth gave him a contemptuous look. "Chill, Jud. We're here to have a drink. Believe it or not, I'm not always on the job."

Frederick's eyes flicked back and forth between Lisa Beth and Abby. "Right. And your girlfriend here just happened to wander into Menéndez's store the other day. Lisa Beth, you'd be funny if you weren't so pathetic. You think you're gonna win a Pulitzer catching me in code violations? Nobody gives a shit. And as for your intern, or whatever she is, her cover's blown. Stick to making copies, OK, sweetheart?"

This last was addressed to Abby, who watched, speechless, as Frederick went out the door. Lisa Beth said, "Well. Somebody's getting a little touchy."

At the end of the bar one of the two old men said, "You gals with the TV?"

Lisa Beth gave him a withering look. "Does this look like a TV face to you?"

Evan's father bowed, obsequious, and swept a hand toward the double doors that led to the dining room. "Right this way," he said, eyes twinkling behind the rimless glasses. "He's waiting for you."

"But I don't want to," said Abby. "I'm not hungry."

"But he's waiting for you," said Evan's father. "He's expecting you."

"No!" Abby tried to turn and run, but her legs wouldn't move. Evan's father grabbed her by the wrist and dragged her toward the double doors, and Abby wanted to scream but she couldn't. Evan's father pulled her with an iron grip, and with his free hand he shoved through the left-hand door, and then they were in the dining room and there sat Evan, waiting for her at a table in the middle of the room, in the heart of a ball of flame. He was blackened and faceless, his skin beginning to split, the fat bubbling up from beneath, and as Abby writhed and strained to cry out, Evan leaned forward, his limbs contracting, and then slowly pushed away from the table and stood up, blackened, peeling, smoking, but intent on her. He took a step toward her, out of the heart of the flames, and reached for her.

Abby thrashed and woke up, a low guttural cry finally making it out of her constricted throat. She lay in the dark gasping, her heart thumping madly in her chest, panicked and lost.

Why was it so dark? Why so silent? Where was she?

The sight of the digital clock on the bedside table brought her fully awake. It was 4:32 in the morning and she was in her bedroom in her new home, lost in the vast dark middle of the continent, and outside there were only the woods and houses where people who did not know her or care about her slept unconcerned. She struggled out of bed, walked into her living room in the dark and sat on the sofa.

Absorbed in her work, Abby had barely noticed as a solitary Sunday had passed. In a few hours she would be on campus again, engaged with people; now there was only this black abyss of loneliness to endure.

The silence, she realized, was not absolute. She could hear the crickets buzzing faintly outside. At long intervals she could hear cars purring by on Jackson Avenue.

She could hear Evan saying, "I'm terrified of losing you."

Well, Evan, you lost me, she thought. And you're going to haunt me for the rest of my life.

Beyond the curtain in front of her, outside, a light went on, the edges of the window glowing. Something had triggered the motion-sensitive light high on the eaves. Abby sat holding her breath. She strained to listen, but there was only the murmur of the night. Eventually she breathed, but she did not move.

Abby listened until she thought she heard a step, a scrape, a soft scuffing on the grass. Then there was nothing again. She sat with her heart pounding until the light went off, leaving her in darkness.

10 | | | | | | |

Abby stood just outside the door to her apartment, watching branches toss gently in the breeze. The morning air was cool; the sun did not reach the shaded backyard. Birds flitted and fluttered in the shadowy woods at the bottom of the slope. Their twittering was the only sound above the sighing of the trees.

A deer, she thought, scanning the ground near the door and the big picture window. A deer bold enough to forage near the house in the sheltering darkness would trigger the light. The ground told her nothing, the long grass and clover taking no tracks. A deer would have been spooked by the light and gone skittering away, Abby thought. You would have heard something more than the soft step you heard.

Or thought you heard. Abby locked her apartment door, shrugged into her backpack, and went up the steps at the side of the house. On the porch she halted, startled by the sight of her landlord bent over on the front lawn, hands on knees, panting and dripping sweat onto the grass. He was shirtless, in running shorts and shoes with low-cut socks, holding a T-shirt in his right hand. A stopwatch hung from a lanyard around his neck. He straightened up and saw her, then smiled. "Morning," he managed to say.

Abby went down the steps. "I didn't know you were a runner."

McLaren laughed, a single puff. "Used to be. More of a jogger now." He wiped his face with the shirt and grinned at her. "Age takes a toll."

More with some than with others, Abby thought, looking at the lean, cut torso slicked with sweat. For a man past the prime of youth he looked pretty fit. "Where do you run?"

He recovered for a few more breaths before answering. "I have a couple of different routes I take. Out south of town, sometimes east. I try to avoid hills."

"I hear you." Abby hesitated, her lips parted. Did she want to get into this? "I like to run myself. I've been looking for a good safe route. I've been running on the track over on campus but it's really boring."

He nodded. "I could never run on a track."

"I hate it. But . . ." Careful, Abby thought. "I ran out along South Street the other day, but I got a little spooked."

McLaren nodded. "I heard." He took in Abby's surprised look and added, "I have a friend in the police department. He told me what happened."

"Would that be Detective Ruffner?"

"It would. He thought I should know because you're my tenant."

"Well, anyway, I want to get back to doing roadwork but I don't know if it's safe."

He wiped his face again. "I'd offer to run with you but you'd probably leave me in the dust."

"I don't know. I'm kind of out of shape."

He smiled. "What's a nice comfortable mile time for you?"

"Now? Maybe six and a half minutes."

He considered for a moment. "You'd be making me work, but I think I could do it, for a while, anyway." He waved a hand, his body language saying he didn't want to presume too much. "Just a thought. If you want a partner some time."

Abby smiled. Did she? "I'll let you know."

"Well, we know a lot more than we did last week," said Detective Ruffner. "We know Lyman was last seen in a bar he owns out on Lafayette Road and was probably carjacked in the parking lot. We know a jerry can full of gasoline was stolen from a maintenance shed at the cemetery down the road from the bar and was probably the one found on the back seat of the car. We know Lyman was stabbed to death inside the vehicle. We just don't know who did it."

Abby stood at the window of her office, phone to her ear, looking out at the campus green, people ambling across the grass or lounging in the shade of the big maples. "I see," she said. "So he could still be around."

"Sure he could. Or he could be a thousand miles away. I can't tell you anything for sure. What I can say is that it doesn't appear he was a local. We've pretty much turned the local criminal class upside down and shaken them at this point, and nothing's fallen out. We've got our snitches and our contacts like any other department, and what we hear is that the local bad guys are as upset about this as we are. A lot of them were clients and friends of Lyman's, and I think if it was somebody local who'd done this, we'd have heard about it by now. So we're looking at outsiders, and the thing that jumps out at us there is the Mexican connection. Last week a Mexican national named Pedro Gutiérrez was arrested by the FBI in Indianapolis for trading guns for drugs to a Mexican cartel down in Texas and bringing the drugs back to sell in Indiana. They'd been tracking him for a while. And this guy had been a client of Lyman's here in Lewisburg."

"Really."

"Yeah. And some of the guns were traced to a store here owned by another client of Lyman's. Except they hadn't been purchased, they'd been stolen. The owner had reported a burglary a couple of months ago."

"So . . . one of his clients stole from another?"

"Looks like it. And Lyman and the store owner put their heads together, maybe. The feds grabbed Gutiérrez at a relative's house over on the east side of Indianapolis, and the word is, it was Lyman who gave them his whereabouts. And that would seriously piss some people off."

Abby stood looking out at the inconsequential movements of people who showed no signs of care, much less trauma. She envied them. "Thank you," she said. "That's helpful."

After the call ended, Abby stood at the window for a moment longer and then sat at her desk. She brought up a browser on her phone and searched until she found the news story about Pedro Gutiérrez on the *Indianapolis Star* website. The idea of Mexican drug gangs having a presence in central Indiana was so outlandish to her that she could hardly credit it. The story gave the bare bones of what Ruffner had told her, without much background.

She started a new search and browsed until she found herself looking at a story headlined: *Feds say Mexican drugs move through heartland.* An FBI spokesman was quoted as saying, *"This operation is run out of Mexico. The cocaine comes from California and the meth from Arizona. The drugs get distributed as far east as New Jersey. Indiana is an important transit point."* A few more taps at her phone brought up an interview with a DEA agent from the Indianapolis office. *"They keep discipline in the networks with violence. Murder, intimidation, torture. These are some of the most ruthless people we have ever faced. And they're here."*

Abby laid her phone on the desktop and put her face in her hands.

The snack bar in the student union had windows that looked out onto the green and offered ample light to work by. Abby was grading problem sets and finishing off a yogurt when Graham came over to her table, briefcase in one hand and a soft drink in the other. "Are you in work mode or can you be distracted?" he said, flashing the high-powered smile. He was in a suit today, the jacket slung casually over the briefcase, a well-groomed, well-dressed, not-hard-to-look-at man.

"If I didn't want to be distracted I'd be in my office with the door barred." Abby smiled and shifted papers to make room on the tabletop.

Graham sat down across from her. "I have found that the solution to the problem of homework is not to assign any. You'd be amazed at the effect that has on your workload."

She cocked an eyebrow at him. "I'll assume you're joking, though the idea is appealing. Do you always dress this way for class? You're making me feel slovenly."

"Nah, not always. I had a meeting out at the steel plant this morning."

"The steel plant?"

"Meteor Steel, out by the highway. It's my moonlighting gig."

"Somebody mentioned something about a steel plant but I don't know anything about it."

"It's a big local employer. They're a minimill company, meaning they melt down scrap steel instead of making it from scratch in big blast furnaces. Their corporate headquarters are in Indy. I'm not sure why they chose to put a plant here, but they kind of saved the town when they did. They brought a lot of jobs."

"And how did you get hooked up with them?"

He leaned forward, elbows on the table. "Well, I'm an economist, and international trade is my area, particularly in heavy industry. And companies always need to know what the long-term economic picture looks like. Does it make sense for them to expand? Can they compete with the Chinese? Is it time to add capacity, or is the whole industry doomed? I got interested in what they were doing and went and talked to them and they wound up offering me a consultant gig. I tell them what they should be doing, what they should be paying their lobbyists to do, and so forth. It's fun, a little bit of money, and not that much work. Of course, I have to do a little homework from time to time so I have something to tell them."

"Sounds interesting. It must be nice to have real-world expertise. The kind of math I do has applications in gambling, but I haven't had any casino executives offer me money for my opinions."

"How about the other side? If you can come up with a way to beat the casinos they'll come flocking to your door."

"If I can come up with a way to beat the casinos, what makes you think I'd share it?"

He laughed, and they were suddenly veering too close to flirting for Abby's comfort. She picked up her pen, the smile lingering on her face.

Graham watched her for a moment. He lowered his voice and said, "So, how's the morale? Holding up OK?"

"Under the strain of having witnessed a murder, you mean? All right, I guess."

"What are the police telling you?"

"They're telling me they have no idea who did it but I'm probably not in any danger. I'm assuming I can live a more or less normal life. Frankly I don't really think I have a choice. What am I supposed to do, go underground?"

Graham sat nodding, his look grave. "Let me know if there's anything I can do. Anything at all. A ride, an escort, somebody to sit up with you at night." He smiled, just a little. "That's not a come-on."

Abby almost believed him, and she returned the smile. "Thanks. I'll let you know."

"Look at this term again," said Abby. "Check your multiplication."

Ben Larch stared at the paper for a few seconds, then made a noise of mild disgust, erased his calculation, and redid it. "I always do that. I forget the xy part of it."

"Free throws. Do these until it's second nature. There's a bunch of these problems on that site I showed you. Do ten or twenty of them.

When the lower-level stuff is solid, the higher concepts will come easier to you. But I think you're starting to get the idea."

Ben nodded. "This really helps, thanks. I can see how you get from here to here now."

"Good. Do those problems and then have another go at the homework from last time. And if you need to come in again before the quiz, you know where to find me."

Ben smiled, shoving things into a backpack. "If I pass this course, they should give you a medal. Nobody's ever explained this stuff to me like this before."

"Glad I can help."

"Really. You're amazing." Suddenly Ben was gazing raptly at her across the desk. "I love your class."

Alarm bells went off, faintly, in Abby's head. She pushed away from the desk on her wheeled chair. "I'm glad. Thanks. See you next time."

"Uh, here." He was digging in a pocket. "I got you something." He pulled out a small cardboard box, a couple of inches square, and slid it across the desk. "This is for you."

Abby froze, her eyes going from the box to the boy and back again a few times. "What's this?"

"It's just something I got for you. To show my appreciation."

Abby frowned. "Um, I'm not sure that's appropriate," she said.

"It's nothing much. Look." Ben opened the box and showed her a small turquoise pendant, lying on a coiled silver chain. "I think it would look really good on you."

Abby pulled herself back to the desk. "Ben."

"It's just to say thank you." His eyes came up and locked onto hers.

"You said thank you. And you're welcome. Gifts really aren't appropriate. It's nice of you, but I couldn't possibly accept it." She shoved the box back toward him with her fingertips. She gave him a perfunctory smile and his gaze dropped to the desktop again. He made no move to pick up the box.

"I just want to show you I'm grateful."

"Ace the next quiz. That's the best way to show your gratitude."

A silence followed, the boy motionless, staring at the box while Abby groped frantically for a strategy. "Please take it," Ben said.

"I can't, Ben. It would be improper. There are rules. It's my job to help you. I get a paycheck. I can't accept gifts." She reached for the box, replaced the lid, and held it out to him. "I appreciate the thought, but it's really not appropriate."

He made her wait through an agonizing few seconds, but finally he took the box and put it back in his pocket. "I thought you'd be happy," he said.

"I'm happy to see you learning the material. That's as far as it goes. As far as it can go. You can see that, right?"

Now he was giving her an earnest, searching look. "Just because of the rules?"

God help me, thought Abby. "Because I am interested in you as a student, and only as a student," she said. "We will maintain a thoroughly professional relationship, in and out of class. OK?"

Another excruciating moment passed, Abby trying to harden her look, and then abruptly the boy stood up, slung his bag over his shoulder, and stalked out of her office. Abby listened as his footsteps died away down the hall. A student with a crush on me, she thought. Just what I need.

Abby had been raised to consider herself fortunate; she had been a happy child, only a moderately unruly teenager, and a driven and focused young woman. She had never been a person things happened to. Things happened to other people, careless people, undisciplined people, people who made bad choices. Things happened to schlimazels and losers.

And me, Abby thought, turning to her laptop with a sigh. All of a sudden, I can't turn around without something happening to me.

Get ready, she thought. What next?

It was not until Abby turned up Hickory Lane that she managed to put a name to what she was feeling, faintly but undeniably: dread. After a solitary supper she had returned to campus for a lecture by a celebrity intellectual, one of the occasional cultural perks the college offered. The lecture had drawn a crowd and been reasonably entertaining, and it was only when Abby emerged from the arts center to see that night had fallen that she realized she would be coming home in the dark.

Abby walked past her neighbors' houses, looking longingly into lighted windows, catching glimpses of placid domestic life, feeling the dread grow. She had begun to think she had left dread behind her in Manhattan. After Evan's death, walking into an empty apartment had become an ordeal; even after moving back in with her mother, opening the door and hearing no answer to her hello had triggered physical symptoms and visual memories that sometimes made her slide down the wall to the floor, face in her hands. But with a radical change in environment, the effect had gone. Ned McLaren's house was so different from her former habitat that walking into it had triggered nothing. The link had been broken.

In its place was something new. She crossed Ned McLaren's porch, triggering the motion-sensitive light, and stood for a moment at the top of the steps. The area illuminated by the light shaded into a penumbra at the edge of the yard and then there was a blackness made all the greater. Down there was her home, and all she had to do was get there. All she had to do was cover fifty feet of lawn, brightly lit, exposed to whatever was out there in the dark woods.

Abby went down the steps, reaching into her purse for her keys. She turned the corner and made for the door, stepping quickly. As she fitted the key into the lock she glanced over her shoulder, quelling the terror of things behind her coming out of the dark. She pushed open the door, slipped inside, slammed the door and threw the deadbolt, and turned to stand with her back to the door, facing the lamp-lit room, letting the beating of her heart subside, convincing herself she was safe.

11 |||||||

Behind its forbidding façade, the Masonic Temple on Main Street was just a big room, like the rental hall in Chelsea where Samantha and Tom had been married. Abby surrendered her ticket at the door to the ballroom and went in to join the throng. At one end of the room was a low stage on which several Mexican men with odd-looking undersized guitars were pumping out twangy up-tempo music. At the other end open doors revealed a kitchen; a buffet had been set up and ranks of tables filled the center of the room.

The company was heavily Mexican, with a scattering of upscale Anglo types. Abby drifted, looking for familiar faces, smiling when smiled at and feeling conspicuous. Still guilty about crashing the benefit with her free ticket, she was desperately searching the silent auction offerings arrayed on tables along one wall for something she could bid on when a voice just behind her said, "If I'd known you were coming we could have carpooled."

Startled, she turned to see Ned McLaren. Tonight he was looking trim and suave in a cream-colored sport jacket over a green T-shirt that set off his eyes. "I walked," said Abby. "I thought about driving my new car over, but it seemed kind of silly. It's not that far."

"Nothing's that far in this town," said McLaren. "What brings you here?"

"You know Natalia, the girl at the Poza Rica?"

"Never been in there."

"She gave me a ticket. What about you? Why are you here?"

He shrugged. "I wasn't doing anything else tonight. And a friend of mine kind of runs the thing. Come on, I'll introduce you." He put his hand on Abby's arm briefly to steer her toward the back of the room, where a knot of people had gathered near a drinks table. They were evidently the VIP posse, all older and fairly prosperous looking, some Latino and some Anglo, the men in suits and the women in outfits they had not acquired at Walmart. A tall, well-fed Anglo who was compensating for his retreating hairline by cultivating a neat line of beard along his jaw turned at McLaren's touch. "Ned, hey."

"Everett, let me introduce you to my tenant."

"Please do." The tall man beamed at her, extending his hand. "Everett Elford."

His handshake was firm; his look was appreciative, and Abby was, as always, gratified. "I'm Abigail Markstein. Pleased to meet you."

"You're living in Ned's basement, huh? I hope he's not charging you too much." Elford's beard was gray and his eyes behind black-rimmed glasses were brown. He looked like a man who enjoyed a good meal and a good laugh.

"It's a pretty nice basement, actually," said Abby. "No complaints."

McLaren said, "It's not like the basement in the old house where we used to shoot BB guns at the mice."

Elford laughed. "I don't think we ever hit any. But that light bulb made a pretty great noise when you shot it out."

McLaren laughed. "Boy, did I catch hell for that."

"You guys must go back a long way," said Abby.

"Third grade," said Elford.

"Second," said McLaren. "Miss Hall's class. You had just moved into the mansion on Maple."

"OK, second. I taught Ned here how to ride a bike."

"The hell you did. I seem to recall my dad pulling your bike out of Mrs. Dick's fishpond."

They laughed, and Elford slapped McLaren on the back. To Abby he said, "Here, let me introduce you to some people," bringing her into the group. "This is Emilio Azuela, president of LUCES." Abby's eyebrows rose as she recognized the man who had come out of the office at the Azteca with Jud Frederick a couple of days before. Azuela nodded and smiled but made no sign he recognized her. His wife was at his side, a dark-eyed former beauty carrying extra weight, though gracefully, in early middle age. "And this is Ron Ingstrom, who's come all the way from Indianapolis for some good Mexican food." Ingstrom was short and burly, his tie constricting a thick neck. He had given into baldness by shaving his head completely. "Ron's the governor's right-hand man," said Elford. "If we show him a good enough time tonight we hope he'll drop a few coins in our hat." This brought a laugh but Elford didn't linger, moving on to a gaunt white-haired man in a black suit and clerical collar whom he introduced as "Father Pete McGrath from Saint Benedict's." Father Pete bowed gravely. "Father Pete's had to learn Spanish so he can talk with his parishioners. He'll be delivering the keynote address tonight, in Spanish." Father Pete shook his head in good-natured denial, while Azuela burst out in wild laughter, leading Abby to suspect he had been exposed to the priest's Spanish.

Abby said, "So tell me what LUCES does."

Elford said, "Lots of things. We've set up ESL courses, job counseling and training. Child care, after-school programs. We've endowed scholarships and we've got volunteers to help kids through the college application process. Education's a big focus. A lot of times Mexican kids who grow up here are the first generation to get more than rudimentary schooling. We've done some good work."

"That's impressive."

"And we just try to bring people together." Elford looked toward the stage, where the musicians were working up a sweat. "It's good to see people mixing, having fun."

"Especially now," said Azuela.

There was an uncomfortable silence. "Yeah," said Elford. "Especially now, with this murder."

Azuela said, "Which they say it was Mexicans that did it, with no evidence."

The man from Indianapolis said, "What do they base that on?"

Elford traded a look with Azuela and said, "I don't know. I don't think they're sure of anything. I talked to the chief the other day. I think he's aware of the danger of getting people stirred up."

Azuela frowned. "Did you see Frederick on TV today?"

Elford shook his head. "I heard about it." To Abby's puzzled look he said, "Jud Frederick was interviewed by a station in Lafayette this morning. He said some things you might consider a little provocative. Like how the Mexicans had brought in drugs and crime and it was time to crack down on illegal immigrants."

"Not very helpful," said the priest.

"Not in the current climate, no."

Azuela's wife shifted things abruptly by commenting on the music and Elford managed to detach Abby and McLaren again. "Let's skedaddle before they bring up Menéndez. I don't feel like having a discussion about undocumented workers tonight."

"Yours are all documented, of course," said McLaren.

Elford bristled, just a little. "We do what we can, Ned. We don't have the resources to run thorough checks on everybody who applies for a job. If a guy shows up with a social security card, we'll hire him. They're good workers and they deserve a decent day's pay and we give it to them."

Abby said, "So how did you get involved in all this?"

Elford shrugged. "Noblesse oblige, my wife calls it."

McLaren rolled his eyes. "He means he employs a lot of Mexicans."

"And good old native-soil Hoosiers, too. I've got plenty of those." He turned to Abby. "I have a farming operation in the north part of the county. So yeah, I've got a number of Mexican employees."

Just then Natalia emerged from the crowd, dressed to the nines in a tight blue dress and looking fabulous. "Abby! You came."

"Of course I came. Wouldn't miss it."

The men were ogling; Abby introduced her to them, and then Natalia pulled her away with an apology. "I want you to meet my mom." Abby spent the next half hour meeting Mom and various female relatives, only a few of whom spoke English. Dad was not in evidence, and Abby wondered if he was in jail or merely in disgrace. Nor was there any sign of the refractory brother. There were other young Mexican guys present, some of them with the same borderline gangster look, though without Luis's sullen demeanor.

The music wound up, there was much applause, and dinner was announced. Going with the flow toward the buffet, Abby ran into Lisa Beth, standing near the entrance. "Good Lord," Lisa Beth said. "What are you doing here?"

"I might ask you the same."

"Me? I'm working. I'm covering this gala event for the *Herald Gazette*. It's not the White House correspondents' dinner but it's what I have. Aha, the lord of the manor is here, I see." She was looking at Everett Elford at the back of the room.

"Oh, I met him. Why the lord of the manor?"

"Well, I would say Everett Elford's probably the richest man in the county. He's a philanthropist and a pillar of the community."

"Where does the money come from?"

"Land. The Elfords have owned land around here for a long time. A lot of land. And the bank there on Main Street. Everett's dad left him with a pretty good empire, and Everett has a law degree and an MBA, so he's taken pretty good care of it. I think the next move for Everett is, he's probably going to run for Congress one of these days. My God, is that Ron Ingstrom next to him?"

"Yeah, I think that was the name I heard."

"Well, that does it. Now I know he's running for Congress. Or something, anyway. Ingstrom's probably the top Republican political fixer in the state. If he's here, it means Everett's made Golden Boy status. Good for him." Lisa Beth smiled. "Excuse me, will you? I have to go do a little discreet ass kissing."

Abby joined the line for the buffet, feeling abandoned; she wasn't sure she wanted to spend the rest of her evening eating with strangers. She was rescued by Ned McLaren, who came by with a full plate and said, "I'll save you a spot over there," pointing to a table.

When they got there, she and Ned were the only English speakers at the table. After some earnest greetings all around, everybody tucked in to dinner, the Mexicans reverting to Spanish, leaving Ned and Abby tête-à- tête.

"So your friend's kind of a big shot around here, huh?"

"Everett? He's a local VIP, yeah. But to me he'll always be the kid who had the first Atari console on the block."

Abby laughed. "It's nice that you kept in touch."

"We didn't, really. I was gone for a long time. We just kind of reconnected since I came back last year."

Abby poked at her shellfish and rice with a fork. "Where were you all that time? If you don't mind my asking."

Ned shrugged. "Africa, mostly." Abby waited while he ate. Just when she had decided that was all she was going to get, he swallowed, looked up and said, "I was a mining engineer. I worked in a few different places. Mostly in central Africa. Extracting coltan, cobalt, copper. I spent about fifteen years out there altogether. Kind of a rough lifestyle, though the furloughs were generous. And the money was good. But I finally got tired of it and quit, came back with some decent savings and a desire to do nothing much for a while." He smiled. "Which ambition I have fulfilled."

Just a touch disingenuously, fishing, Abby said, "You seem to keep busy."

"The house kept me busy for a while. But it's pretty much done. And honestly? I don't know how long the excitement of life in Lewisburg, Indiana, is going to be enough for me. I can feel the wanderlust starting to stir again. But I'm probably good for another year or two here, anyway. Meanwhile I want to see if I can get my 5K time down under twenty minutes. Speaking of projects."

"That would be respectable." Go for it, she thought. "Could I take you up on your offer to run with me some time? I'd really love to get back on the road, but I don't want to do it alone."

"Sure." He gave her a brief, appraising look. "Tomorrow morning?"

"Name a time," she said.

Running for the first time with a new partner had aspects of a first date; this occurred to Abby despite her resistance to any and all thoughts in that direction. Don't go too fast, don't let things drag; try to impress him without strutting your stuff too obviously, find a mutual comfort zone.

Ned led her south along Jackson out of town, past the mall, past the high school, past the windowless Hall of Jehovah's Witnesses sitting like a bunker in the middle of its parking lot. When they were free of the town he turned onto an asphalt road that led west.

They had agreed that he would set the pace, being possibly the lesser runner. Abby was so glad to be released from the prison of the track that she was for once unconcerned about pace or mile times. It was a joy to be moving. After the first couple of miles Abby was aware that had she been on her own, she would probably have been pushing it a little harder, but not by much.

The land sank toward Shawnee Creek and the road dipped into a zone of mixed farm and woodland, patches of pasture with a few cows, half-hidden in the trees, lonely houses secluded at the end of long gravel drives. Ned took her south onto a road that then curved back east away from the creek, and they climbed, laboring a little, back up into the corn and bean fields. They came to an intersection and Ned pointed to the right. They turned and the road stretched out ahead, running straight south for a mile or more, past a couple of farmsteads.

Neither of them had spoken, but now Ned gasped out, "Push it a little? To the silo?"

"OK." Abby located the silo two hundred yards ahead and kicked it up a gear. As she pulled slowly ahead she thought, here we go, this is the test. This will determine if we can train together. She concentrated on her form, working hard now, approaching the pace she would have tried to maintain in a race, feeling how much she had declined from competitive condition. She passed the silo and slowed, hearing Ned's footsteps a few yards behind her. He drew even with her within a hundred feet and settled in at her shoulder again.

After that it was work. He led her on a circuit back to town, turning east on a road that dipped into a glade and tested them a little on the mild hill beyond, then turning north for the gut-check stretch back into town. Abby was working but still had reserves; she could tell that Ned was laboring now, head down, feet starting to slap a little as his stride deteriorated, but refusing to give in. Abby was now setting the pace.

Etiquette, thought Abby. You don't want to show him up.

He asked for it, she thought in the next moment. She held the pace.

They came in from the east, hit Jackson just north of the mall, and then it was blessedly downhill to the entrance to Hickory Lane, with the short sharp uphill stretch through the trees hitting them hard at the end. Abby could not resist pushing it a little, reaching the driveway of 6 Hickory Lane ahead of her landlord. She slowed to a walk and kept

Sam Reaves

moving, hands on hips; he caught up and together they walked, recovering, to the end of the lane, around the turnaround and back.

"You made me work," Ned said hoarsely as they turned up the drive.

In Abby's experience guys could be weird about getting outrun by a woman. Some of them were good sports and some weren't. Abby waited for the excuse: I'm nursing an injury; I've been too busy to run; ten years ago I would have beaten you.

It never came. When he reached the porch Ned turned and smiled at her and said, "I hope I didn't hold you back too much."

Abby shook her head. "It was good. Thanks."

"You want to go again, let me know."

"I will."

"Have a good one." Ned opened his door and went inside with no further ceremony.

OK, thought Abby. What were you expecting, a good-night kiss? She went down the stone steps at the side of the house.

For a first date, she thought, not too bad.

12 |||||||

Frat house row was along South Street just west of the campus, a three-block stretch where a half-dozen grand old houses had had fire escapes and large Greek letters tacked on to them to convert them to communal residences, designed to cultivate character and scholarship in the inmates.

"It's been four years since we had a death from alcohol poisoning at one of these houses," said Graham, slowing and putting on his turn signal. "I'd say we're about due for another one."

Abby gave it a nervous laugh. She had been just a trifle suspicious that Graham was secretly behind the invitation from the start, but she had been unable to think of a plausible reason to decline the ride he had offered.

The Tau Kappa Zeta house was the last one in the row on the south side of the street. It was a three-story brick pile, a mansion by local standards, with a white-columned portico in front that gave it the air of a poor man's plantation house, minus the long avenue of live oaks. Graham pulled into a driveway that led along the side of the house to a gravel parking lot behind it, where a motley collection of a dozen or so cars sat. Behind the lot the ground fell away steeply into thick woods.

"These things can be excruciating if they're trying too hard to impress you," said Graham as they walked back along the side of the house toward the front door. "And I've had a few students try to use the occasion to butter me up for a better grade. But it can also be a lot of fun."

"How's the food?" Abby asked, stifling a sense of dread.

"The food is edible. They have a hired cook who usually produces something you can get down without too much trouble."

"That's certainly what I look for in a meal."

Inside, things were not as bad as she had feared. Abby was relieved to see that there were at least half a dozen women there, girlfriends no doubt, in skirts or dresses. The jocks had all dressed up to varying degrees, the tie being the common element, clashing in some instances with jeans and tennis shoes. The big front room in which they were received with handshakes and iced tea was handsome, with elegant woodwork, the paint a little battered in places but no actual holes in the wall. The furniture bore signs of wear and abuse, but the house had been tidied and a general air of civility prevailed.

Graham was an old hand at this, Abby saw, mixing easily, bantering. Abby survived a few stiff introductions and scanned desperately for familiar faces.

"Dr. Markstein." Cole West loomed, looking very adult in an actual suit, groomed and handsome. "Welcome to Tau Kappa Zeta. Glad you could come."

"Thanks for having me. This is quite a house."

"Oh, thanks. It used to be the mayor's house, or somebody like that. Before the college bought it and gave it to us to tear up."

"Well, you better get with it. I see some unbroken windows."

He laughed. "Give us time. The semester just started." He cocked a thumb at her, looking at his crew. "What'd I tell you? She cracks us up in class."

Abby began to relax a little, and by the time they were ushered in to lunch she was beginning to feel at ease. Luncheon was served in what had once been a formal dining room, now a bit overcrowded with long tables, thirty or forty people squeezed in elbow to elbow. Abby was seated at a table with Cole West at the head, while Graham was across the room at another table. Abby's suspicions of a setup subsided. The meal, as promised, was edible but unremarkable except for a quivering slab of Jell-O, which Abby stared at in fascination before attacking it with her spoon. The conversation was a little constrained at first but waxed as bellies filled.

"So, Dr. Markstein." Cole West wiped his mouth and laid his napkin on the table. "We heard a rumor about you talking to the police, about this murder that happened just down the road here. What's up with that?"

Abby froze for a second, spoon in the air. She set the spoon down. "Nothing much. I just happened to go jogging out there that morning and saw the car burning. I reported it, that's all."

"Wow. Did you see the guy inside the car?"

"No. I didn't get that close."

A boy down at the other end of the table said, "One of our guys snuck around through the bushes past the police line and saw them taking the body out. He said it was like burned to a crisp."

Abby frowned at her Jell-O. West growled, "Hey, we're eating lunch here."

A youth across from Abby, another bruiser, said, "That's a sinister damn place, that overpass. One of the old alums that was here at homecoming said there was a suicide there like twenty years ago. Some girl jumped off the top of the arch."

"I've heard that," said West. "Except I heard it was a guy. He'd been caught getting it on with the preacher's son or something, some kind of weird scandal."

A pimpled specimen to Abby's left said, "You'd be amazed what goes on in a town like this. My uncle's a sheriff's deputy, and he was telling me all the stuff that goes on. There was a guy shotgunned his whole family on a farm just north of town. My uncle was the first guy on the scene. And he said once two guys got in a fight in a bowling alley and one of them beat the other one to death with a bowling ball. I am not making this up."

The bruiser said, "These yokels around here, man. They scare me. It's like *Deliverance* once you get two blocks from campus."

Down the table, another boy scoffed. "Aw, Jesus. Don't give me that. You Indianapolis guys and your attitude."

This diverted things to a spirited bout of intrastate rivalry, to Abby's relief. When that petered out the company repaired to the front room again for coffee. The talk was anodyne, and when the yawns began Abby and Graham made eye contact and shortly afterward took their leave. In the car Graham vented a brief laugh, wheeling out of the drive. "Well, that was fairly painless. Nobody made improper advances, I assume?"

"No, it was fine."

A silence ensued; as Graham turned down Jackson toward Hickory Hill he said, "So forgive me for asking, but I can't help being concerned. Is there any word from the police on this investigation? Have they made any progress?"

"I don't know. I went and looked at some pictures. They're not really keeping me in the loop. The police don't seem to think I'm particularly in danger, so I'm just doing my best to forget about it."

That killed the conversation, as Abby had hoped. When he pulled into the driveway of Ned McLaren's house Graham sat for a moment looking gravely at her. "See you at the office."

"Thanks for the ride."

"No problem. Listen, can I take you to dinner some time? No frat guys involved?"

Abby's heart sank. She met his gaze and said, "Let's just keep it at the office for a while, OK? I have enough on my plate right now."

His look darkened for a moment, but then he smiled. "OK, I understand. Forget I asked."

I will do my best, Abby thought, getting out of the car.

Abby stood at the edge of the woods, enjoying the early evening cool and putting off going inside. Inside there was nothing but work, solitude, yearning and regret. And with darkness, possibly an attack of the terrors. Every day that passed put a little more distance between her and the sight of a blackened corpse contracting in a fireball, but her nerves were still raw. She lingered, hoping to catch another glimpse of the deer, but none appeared and after a while she turned to go back into the house.

"Evening."

Abby was startled by the sight of her landlord standing on the covered porch at the top of the steps. "Oh, hi."

He was in his version of evening dress, white duck trousers and a blue batik shirt, tail out. His left hand was in his pocket and his right hand dangled at his side, holding a bottle of beer by the neck. "Didn't mean to scare you."

"That's OK. Just daydreaming. It's nice out here."

"Yeah." Ned nodded, surveying the woods with a solemn look. He fixed on Abby and said, "Can I offer you a drink?"

This was a lifeline. "Thank you, yes. That would be nice."

They sat in the director's chairs, looking out over the woods as the light faded. Abby had opted for a glass of pinot grigio, crisp and cold. She sipped and said, "That was good this morning. Thank you. I really needed a good hard run. Life's been a little stressful recently."

"I can imagine."

Abby let her head loll back and released a long sigh. "As in, the whole last year of my life." She let that hang in the air, already regretting the slip.

Ned was studying the label of his beer bottle. "I'm all ears."

Abby realized how badly she wanted to talk about it and how pathetic it might sound. "I'm sorry, I won't bore you with it if you don't want me to."

"After an intro like that? Please, bore me."

Abby gave it a token laugh. Here we go, she thought. "I should be in my second year of teaching at Amherst. But just as I was packing to move there, a little over a year ago, the boyfriend I had just broken up with killed himself."

There was no sound but the buzz of the crickets in the failing light. After a long moment Ned said, "Man. I'm sorry."

"It really knocked me off the rails. I was a wreck for a while, just long enough that Amherst had to give the position to someone else. I found a mindless retail job and started learning how to live with guilt."

"That's a tough one."

"Yeah. The one thing I can say for this murder is, it's distracted me from thinking about Evan. I'm not sure that's a good long-term therapeutic approach, though."

They sat in silence for a while. Ned said, "Don't let him do that to you."

"Yeah, that's what everybody says. But he's doing it." Abby emptied her wineglass. "We were together for three years. I thought we would probably get married. We met at MIT. He was a physicist. He was really brilliant. But his depression was always a problem. Maybe that went with the brilliance, I don't know. But he struggled with it. There was medication, there was therapy, there were good times and bad. It got easier for me when I realized I wasn't responsible for making him happy, that in fact I couldn't. That made daily life easier, but it was bad for our long-term prospects. He sensed I was sealing off a part of me from him and he resented it. He got needier. When I'd had enough and started trying to disengage, that's when he really sank his claws into me, with the guilt. And I didn't react very well to that. I finally snapped and told him to stop feeling sorry for himself. In other words, I completely repudiated the idea of his depression as a clinical condition. I essentially told him it was nothing more than a personal failure. And I ended things, just ripped the bandage off. Big scene, it's all over, good-bye. He moved out, a couple of weeks went by, things were calm, the tearful phone calls had stopped, I thought I was out of the woods. Then one night I came home and found him hanging from a light fixture in my apartment."

They listened to the crickets for a while. Ned drained his bottle and stood up. "Want some more wine?"

"If I have any more wine I might start crying."

Ned shrugged. "I can bring you a Kleenex, too."

"I better not."

"OK." He stood looking down at her. "Give him credit. He killed himself instead of you."

Abby blinked at him. "That's pretty hard-hearted."

"You need to stop feeling sorry for him and get mad at him." Abby could just see him smiling. "Take it from me. I'm an expert in guilt. I've been on both sides."

Ned went inside. Abby was gathering herself to get up and take her leave when he came back with a fresh beer in hand. "I'm sorry if that was cold," he said. "I know there's grief involved, too."

Abby said, "Yeah, there's grief. It's terrible sometimes."

Ned settled back into his chair, took a drink, and looked out into the dark woods. "I had a lady friend in Paris. I met her in Africa. She worked for one of the NGOs out there. We hit it off, had a little thing for a while, and then she went back to France. We kept it going long-distance for a couple of years. I would go and stay with her on my furloughs and that would keep me going for another few months. We went on little trips or just hung out in Paris, being in love. There was never any explicit talk about the future, but I thought we had an understanding. Then one day I got the Dear John e-mail. The subject line said, *Je ne t'aime plus*: I don't love you anymore. That was all I needed to see. I didn't even open the e-mail for three days. And it said pretty much what I thought it would."

Abby turned her head to look at him. "I'm sorry," she said.

The ghost of a smile stretched his lips. "That was the only time I ever gave serious thought to killing myself. Just for a day or two, but

I was looking it in the eye. And I remember thinking, man, would she feel bad. I have the power to make her hurt. But I knew she didn't deserve it. She didn't do anything wrong. Things just changed. So that's why I come down hard on your guy. He had that power and he used it, and you didn't deserve it. You didn't do anything wrong."

The night hummed with the electric noise of crickets, the black woods shifting in a gentle breeze. "I'm not sure we can assume he did it to punish me," said Abby. "I don't think I'm capable of knowing what went on in his mind. I'm trying not to blame him for what everyone tells me is a clinical condition. But yeah, the effect on me was . . . brutal. And it helps to hear that it wasn't my fault. So thanks."

"Don't mention it." Ned took a drink of beer. "Just one of the many services we provide."

13 |||||||

Abby locked the door of her apartment, stowed the key in her purse, and wandered across the grass toward the trees, slinging her backpack over one shoulder. Monday morning had dawned a little cooler, promising an easing of the heat as September progressed. She had a class to teach at 11:10; she was well prepared and not pressed for time and looking forward to an unencumbered hour or so in her office. She stood at the top of the slope, looking down into the cool shadowed woods, the stream betrayed by fleeting ripples glinting through the foliage. She turned and looked at the windows of Ned McLaren's living room, above her own. The past twenty-four hours had expanded her comfort zone by just this much: that the man who lived behind those curtains was no longer completely a stranger.

A siren rose, keening on the morning air. Abby listened, trying to discern its direction, as it grew louder. The vehicle tore down Jackson Avenue past the entrance to Hickory Lane, screened from her by the trees, and away up toward the center of town; simultaneously a second siren swelled faintly in the distance.

She had been hearing sirens all her life and ignoring them, but now the sound terrified her. Suddenly all she could see in her mind's eye was a man being roasted, skin blackening and splitting. She sank to her knees on the grass, dropping her backpack, taking deep gulping breaths. Abby knelt there with her heart pounding as the sound of emergency vehicles arose in every direction, a dissonant chorus in the bright morning air.

She listened until the sirens died away and there was nothing but the sound of the birds in the trees. When her heartbeat had calmed, she stood up, shrugged into her backpack and mounted the stone steps at the side of the house.

"All right. Chapter One test on Friday. Be ready. If you need help, you know where my office is. Don't be shy." Abby bestowed what she hoped was a benevolent smile on the dozen or so members of her Calculus I section and snapped the cap onto her dry-erase marker with authority, signaling the end of the session. The assemblage stirred and broke up, chairs scraping, voices rising.

Except you, Abby thought, watching as Ben Larch crammed his things into a shoulder bag. You could afford to be a little shyer. She had come into class with some trepidation, anxious to see how Ben would respond to what she hoped were brighter lines of demarcation. She had made routine eye contact with him a couple of times during the class, meeting a blank stare she imagined was just a shade on the sullen side. Ben had asked no questions, volunteered nothing, made no notes as far as Abby had seen. Now he slung the bag over his shoulder and went out of the room without looking at her.

Eat something, Abby told herself. Get a grip and go have lunch. Her stomach was just beginning to recover from the tension that had gripped her when she heard the sirens and again when she saw Ben walk into class. She dumped her books in her office, locked it, and left the building. In the snack bar she bought a chicken-salad wrap and a yogurt and headed directly for the round table in the corner that by long-settled convention was reserved for faculty at lunchtime. As she approached she saw Jerry Collins holding forth. With him were Adam Linseth, Philip Herzler and a man she didn't know. "Can I join you?"

"Of course." Jerry beamed at her. She took a seat and he introduced the stranger, who turned out to be a historian whose name went right over Abby's head. "Abigail here is the new star of the math department," said Jerry.

"I don't know about that," said Abby. "New kid on the block, anyway."

The usual questions and subtle flaunting of credentials followed. The historian was from Brown and his specialty was the Carolingian Empire. "Star or not, if you can do math, I bow before you," he said.

"If you can read Medieval Latin," said Abby, "I think you just trumped me."

They laughed and then Jerry frowned abruptly and said, "We were just talking about Jud Frederick."

Abby blinked at him. "What about him?"

"You didn't hear, huh? Apparently he was murdered last night."

Abby set down her wrap. "Oh, my God."

"Yeah, it's a shock, isn't it? He was found dead in his home this morning, and it wasn't an accident."

Abby drew a deep breath. "I heard the sirens."

"We all did. Lisa Beth was still at home, but when she heard them she tore off in the car to go chase them. I called her a little while ago and she said she was at the police station waiting for somebody to talk to her. She said it was a home invasion."

"Are you OK, Abby?" Philip Herzler was sending her a concerned look across the table.

"Oh, my God. That's horrible." Abby slumped back on her chair. "What is going on?"

"Well, I can tell you what the police think is going on," said Jerry. "After Frederick's TV interview the other day, they're going to be looking even harder at the Mexicans."

"The Mexicans?" said the historian.

"They think Lyman was killed because he informed on a Mexican client of his," said Jerry. "And Frederick was ranting on TV the other day about Mexican criminals. So I think that's kind of at the forefront of the investigation right now."

"How was he killed?" said the historian.

"Lisa Beth didn't say. All she said was, she heard it was a bad crime scene." Jerry looked at Abby and opened his mouth to say something and then hesitated. No, thought Abby, please don't.

Adam Linseth came to her rescue. "Who was this guy, anyway?"

Jerry leapt for it, enjoying being in the know. "He was a real estate guy. A slumlord, Lisa Beth called him. He owned a lot of properties around town, including the trailer park."

"Where a lot of Mexicans live," said Linseth.

"The plot thickens," said the historian.

"I think we might be jumping to conclusions," said Herzler.

"And that's the job of the police," said the historian. "I'm happy to leave it to them."

Jerry was still looking at Abby, as if he were considering whether to out her. "You know, actually I have a pile of papers to grade," Abby said. "I'm afraid I'm going to have to go have lunch at my desk."

"I seem to have triggered a murder epidemic. I hit town, and people start dying." Abby sat with her phone to her ear and her eyes closed, a hand over her face.

"What on earth is going on out there in the heartland?" her father said. "It used to be, I'd get calls from out-of-town friends asking if I was OK in the hellhole that was New York. Now we're sitting here wondering if you're in mortal peril out there in the cornfields."

"I don't know what's going on. Nothing to do with me, that's all I know. I'm OK, Daddy. Really. I'm handling it."

After a time he said, "All right. You know where I am. Call when you need to."

When they ended the call Abby sat staring at her phone. She would have loved to talk to Samantha, but the last couple of conversations had been unsatisfactory, Samantha too absorbed in her own travails to focus on Abby's distress. Her phone buzzed in her hand. She recognized the number with a sinking sensation of dread. "Yes?"

"Ms. Markstein? Detective Ruffner here. I'm sorry to call you so late."

"That's OK. I'm just sitting here trying not to be scared."

"I can imagine. You heard about this new murder, I assume?"

"I heard."

"Well, I was wondering if I could swing by tomorrow morning and pick you up to come and look at some pictures again."

Abby sighed. "More mug shots?"

"No, actually, we have something better than that today. Jud Frederick had security cameras on his property, and we think we may have the killer on video."

14 |||||||

The office in the rear of the police station was crowded: There were two uniformed officers and three in plain clothes, one of them a woman in her thirties, in jeans and a black blouse, brown hair in a ponytail, badge and holstered automatic on her belt. She was sitting at a desk with a laptop in front of her.

"Have a seat," said Ruffner, waving Abby to a chair at the corner of the desk. "This is Detective Perkins from the ISP."

The woman nodded at Abby. "How you doing?"

"I don't know," said Abby. "Ask me when this is all over."

Perkins gave her a brief, sympathetic tightening of the lips. "It's no fun, I know. We appreciate your help."

"So what am I going to look at? Am I going to have to look at a body?"

"No." Perkins was frowning at the laptop, manipulating a mouse. "We got the feed from Frederick's home security camera. He had a pretty good setup. Cameras front and back. And they caught somebody. Not much good for a positive ID, as you'll see. But we're hoping you can tell us if it's the same guy you saw."

While Perkins peered at the computer, Abby looked at Ruffner. "When did this happen?"

"Some time last night. Or early this morning, probably. Frederick lived in a subdivision west of town called River Woods. The houses back onto Shawnee Creek. We think the killer came up from the creek. He shows up on the camera at the rear. But there was no forced entry, so he might have waited for Frederick to come home and jumped him then, or slipped in when the garage was opened or something. But Frederick was killed inside the house."

Abby closed her eyes for a second or two. She could see Jud Frederick coming down the room at the Azteca with a decorative blonde in tow. "Was anybody else home?"

"No, thank God. Frederick was divorced. He's got a couple of kids at IU. But he lived by himself. The killer stayed in there for a while, it looks like, going through drawers and such. Frederick had a gun in the house, and apparently this guy took it. He left the holster."

"Here we go." Perkins turned the laptop toward Abby. She saw a screen with a blurry black-and-white video still. It showed a stretch of patio at the side of a house, with what looked like a sliding glass door to the right. Perkins hit a key and the counter at the bottom of the screen began to tick off seconds, starting at 1:57:44. "This was about two in the morning," said Perkins. "But the back of the house is pretty well lit at night, so the image is good. And there's our guy."

As Abby watched, a dark figure came from the bottom of the screen, below the camera, and walked along the patio, pausing at the glass door to lean close and shield his face as he looked through the glass.

Abby caught her breath. There were the cargo shorts, the sneakers without socks, the black hair curling on the neck. "I can't see his face," she said.

"Wait," said Perkins. "He'll be back."

The figure disappeared off the top of the screen. The seconds ticked off. Abby realized her heart rate had accelerated. At 1:58:16 the figure reappeared, facing the camera now, and halted just below it. The view was from above, and the face would have been clearly visible, but for the bandanna tied over it, western-outlaw style.

"He got smart," said Perkins. "He knew he was on camera, and instead of trying to disable the system he just put on the mask."

"And I'm supposed to identify him?" said Abby, though the chill of recognition had intensified the second he came into view.

Ruffner said, "Just, if you can, from stature, body language and so forth, tell us if it's the same guy you saw."

The mask obscured the bottom half of the face, but the shape of the head was the same, the dark hair slicked back from the forehead. He was wearing a shirt this time but the tattoos on the arms were visible, blurry indecipherable markings crawling down to the wrists. "I think it's him," said Abby. She pulled away from the desk and closed her eyes. "That's the man I saw."

The police officers traded a look among themselves. "Thank you," said Perkins. "That's helpful."

"Not to me," said Abby.

Ruffner pulled a chair from a neighboring desk and sat down next to Abby. "You're not out jogging by yourself anymore, I'm assuming."

"No, that's over. Am I safe just walking around? Should I leave town? Are we at that point?"

Ruffner sighed and another look went around among the cops, producing nothing more helpful than shrugs. Ruffner said, "We don't have any reason to think this guy is actively looking for you. If you could positively ID him, if you knew who he was, it would be another matter. That's when witnesses are really in danger. But you didn't know this guy. He's probably not going to waste energy trying to find you. Now, he could just see you by chance, there's always that, but would he recognize you? I don't know that he would, in a totally different context. If you're really worried, we can put on extra patrol for your residence. Or we could get you a place in the Family Crisis Shelter. Going some-place else for a while would be another option."

"I have a job here. I can't really run away."

Perkins had been watching, frowning faintly. Now she said, "Cut your hair."

"Excuse me?"

"Cut your hair. Nothing changes your appearance faster. If you're worried about this guy spotting you on the street or something, change your appearance."

Abby nodded. "I can do that."

"Turn off the Facebook location feature on your phone. Probably not a factor, but just in case."

"Did it a long time ago."

Ruffner said, "Drive rather than walk, and keep the doors locked. Hang with people when you can. You're renting from Ned McLaren, right?"

"That's right."

"He can keep an eye out for strangers and so forth."

Perkins said, "I think the risk is manageable. And we are working as hard as we can to reel this guy in, believe me."

Ruffner said, "We've got some federal help, too, in view of the possible, uh . . . foreign angle. There's a lot of resources on this."

Abby could see that was all she was going to get. "This is two. Two men I just happened to see on practically my first night in town who have been murdered now. Why? What's going on?"

"They're related," Ruffner said. "The victims knew each other and were apparently killed by the same guy. As for why you happened to see them, it's a small town. There's a limited number of places people go. You were just there."

"And then the next morning I went for a run."

"Yeah. That's the anomaly. You went for a run."

"Well, that's over, believe me," Abby said, bitterly. "That's all over."

- - - - - - - - - - - - - - - -

Lisa Beth answered her phone on the third ring. "Abby. How are you?"

"I could be better. I could be a lot better."

"You heard about Jud Frederick?"

"I just got back from talking to the police."

"Did you, by God? What did they want with you?"

"They wanted me to look at more pictures."

"Don't tell me anything if you don't want to. I will not abuse your friendship by trying to make a source out of you."

"Thank you. It would help me to talk about it with you, actually. But first I have a practical question."

"What's that?"

"Who does your hair?"

There was a silence and then Lisa Beth's bellowing laugh sounded in Abby's ear. "I swear to you, that is the last thing on earth I would have expected anybody to ask me."

"I need to get my hair cut. Like, today. Can you recommend someone?"

"Well, I can tell you who keeps me shorn. Is that the look you're going for?"

"Maybe not so . . ."

"So extreme? You may be frank, I don't mind."

"Not quite as short as yours. But shorter, yeah. You know somebody who could do me a bob or a pixie or something like that?"

"Honey, my guy Dexter can do anything. Let me call him and see if he can fit you in."

Dexter, it turned out, could fit Abby in at four o'clock. That worked with Abby's schedule, and Lisa Beth offered to swing by and pick her up. "My source at the police station has promised to call me if anything breaks. In the meantime it's a slow news day and I can do what I want."

Dexter was a gay male of a certain age who worked in a salon a block off Main Street, a three-chair operation with crimson walls, towering racks of hair products and ample mirrors. Dexter had made a gallant attempt to offset the ravages of time by dyeing his hair a luminescent blond, with indifferent success. "So we have decided to go with a more gamine type of look, have we?" He stood with hands clasped and head canted to one side, the artist surveying his canvas.

"We have decided to go with significantly less hair," said Abby. "It's hot and I haven't done anything with my hair for five or six years and, basically, what the hell?" Here at the brink Abby suddenly had a bad case of nerves, her natural conservatism shying at the prospect of radical change. But the image of a man peering in through a glass door carried the day. "What are my options?"

"For a ravishing beauty like you, with naturally thick and wavy hair and a heart-shaped face, I think a nice textured pixie with bangs a wee bit on the long side will be *exquisite*."

"Do it." Abby settled into the chair and abandoned herself, stomping on her misgivings. Lisa Beth had installed herself in an armchair opposite with a cup of coffee, and she watched the proceedings with an amused smile while carrying on a back-and-forth with Dexter that testified to long acquaintance and a shared, somewhat jaundiced view of life in Lewisburg, Indiana. Abby mostly sat with her eyes closed, listening to the snick of the scissors and feeling a part of her persona fall away.

It took time. When it was all over, Abby was stunned, looking into the eyes of the stranger in the mirror. "Weeeell," drawled Dexter. "What do we think?"

It's not me, was what Abby thought. But it's not bad. "It's fine," she said. "I like it. It's good, thanks."

"You are superb," said Lisa Beth, who had come to stand at Abby's shoulder. "Oh, my. Dexter, you're a master."

"I am humbled by your praise." Dexter beamed at Abby in the mirror. "Sweetie, you are going to knock them absolutely *dead*."

Actually, somebody else is taking care of that, Abby thought.

"It's cocktail hour," said Lisa Beth, starting her car. "Can I buy you a drink?"

"I think I'd better not. I have work to do this evening. I'd probably better get home."

"What a work ethic you have. You are an inspiration to us all. Talk to me."

"Huh?"

"You said you wanted to talk to me about this investigation." She pulled away from the curb. "Off the record. With you, there is no record. I promise you that."

Abby exhaled. "I identified the guy who they think killed Frederick. On the security camera footage. It was the same guy I saw with Lyman. That's what the haircut is about. The police told me to change my appearance. Because the guy is obviously still around. And I can identify him."

"My God." Lisa Beth drove, scowling out at the world. "No wonder you're scared."

"Mostly I can function OK. Coming home at night is hard."

"Get yourself a dog. They bark and slobber and shed, but they are company."

"Sounds like a lot of work. I just want the cops to catch this guy."

"Well, they're working on it." Lisa Beth turned onto Jackson. "They're beating this supposed Mexican connection to death. This guy you saw, could he have been Mexican?"

"He could have been just about anything. I saw him once in limited light and once on a surveillance cam. I didn't exactly get a chance to study his features."

Lisa Beth nodded. "So it's possible he doesn't give a damn about your having seen him. If he's from down there, he's used to impunity. The line the cops are following goes back to Veracruz, where all our Mexicans come from. You know about Veracruz?"

"I know it's in Mexico."

"It's a battleground. Some of the worst drug cartel violence has gone down there. That's where the Zetas operate."

"OK, I've heard of the Zetas, but that's about it. Educate me."

"They're former Mexican army commandos who hired themselves out to the Gulf Cartel as muscle and then decided to take over. They're the biggest and meanest organized crime group down there. They like to leave bodies in cars and set them on fire, and they like to behead people. So, bingo, especially with the Veracruz connection around here, that just jumps right out at the cops."

"Wait a second. Bingo? Behead people?"

Lisa Beth shot her a look. "They didn't tell you? Frederick was decapitated."

The bottom dropped out of Abby's stomach. "Oh, God."

"Just wait, it gets better."

"Better?"

Lisa Beth smiled grimly at the road ahead. "They brought in Frederick's doctor to identify the body, from scars and so forth. And they took fingerprints. They had to do that because the head is missing."

15 |||||||

Abby looked up from her desk to see Ben Larch in the doorway of her office. They just stared at each other for a moment and then Ben smiled and said, "Hi. Can I get some help with these differentiation problems?"

"That's what I'm here for." Abby returned the smile and shoved her laptop away. Please, she thought. Let it just be normal. Just let him be a normal student again. "Have a seat and let's see what's going on."

He sat at the corner of the desk, next to her, set the textbook on the desk with a thump, and opened his notebook. "In class I thought I was following you OK, but then when I sat down to do these I kind of got confused."

"OK, let me look at what you've done." Abby ran her eye over the scrawl in the notebook and saw that like most struggling math students Ben was handicapped by a disorderly approach. It was hard to make sense of what he had done, as lines straggled off crookedly to the margins and calculations were crossed out with heavy strokes of the pen. "What's this term here? Where does it come from?" She pointed and Ben leaned closer to peer at it.

"I don't know. I did this last night. I was kind of tired."

"OK. Let's start over." Abby turned to a clean page in the notebook. "Problem number one. Look at it and tell me what you see."

They went at it for a few minutes, Abby trying to coax out what Ben knew and pinpoint what he didn't. The art of teaching was to get people to figure it out for themselves. It was a tough slog sometimes.

Ben had a small eureka moment and successfully nailed the first problem. He laid the pen on the notebook, sat back on his chair, and looked at Abby. "Why'd you cut your hair?"

A chill ran through Abby. She met Ben's unwavering gaze and said, "That's really none of your business."

"I liked it long. I mean, it looks OK now, it's kind of cute, but I really liked the way you looked before." He was giving her an earnest look that in other circumstances would have made him appealing; now it made Abby's hair stand on end.

"Ben. I thought we settled this. Personal remarks are not appropriate. We are not friends."

"What do you mean we're not friends?"

"I am your teacher. It's a working relationship and we will maintain a proper distance."

Now his look hardened just a little. "Why are you so cold?"

Abby could only gawk at him, astonished. "Ben, I am cold, as you put it, because we are not here to discuss my appearance or your opinion of it. We are here to help you learn to do calculus. And that is as far as it goes. As far as it can ever go. If you are incapable of avoiding personal remarks and excessive familiarity, then it's going to make my job a lot harder. Impossible, in fact. And yes, I know I sound harsh. But that's the way it has to be. Now, can we return to the matter at hand and do a few more of these problems?"

Ben Larch just looked at her, the appealing look gone, replaced by a remote, affectless gaze. "That's OK," he said. He closed the notebook, slapped the textbook on top of it, and stood up. "I'll try and figure it out on my own."

Abby drew breath to toss him a bone, a parting offer of reconciliation, but something stopped her. He turned in the doorway for one last glance and she met his stony look with what she hoped was an appropriately resolute one. "Thanks a lot," he said, and vanished.

Abby sat with her heart pounding. All I wanted to do was teach, she thought. What did I do to deserve this?

Abby had plenty of milk at home but needed to talk to Natalia about their next tutoring date; she could have texted her but the Poza Rica was on the way home and she badly needed a friendly interaction. Bill Olsen had not been in his office when Abby had gone looking for him; she had drafted and sent a careful e-mail documenting her encounter with Ben and then fled the campus. It felt ridiculous to be driving the few short blocks home, and a man in a pickup truck behind her leaned on the horn when, lost in her thoughts, she was a little slow to notice that a traffic light had changed. By the time she walked into the Poza Rica she was frazzled.

She instantly regretted her impulse when she saw that instead of Natalia it was Luis Menéndez that stood behind the counter. Abby stopped just inside the door and almost turned and bolted, but Luis had seen her, and as dejected as she was, Abby was not prepared to lose that much face. She approached the counter, Luis watching her with a sullen, heavy-lidded look. There were a couple of customers down one aisle but Abby barely noticed them. "Hi, Luis. Is your sister around?"

He shifted just slightly, slouching, his chin rising. "We don't serve snitches in here."

Abby blinked a few times. "Excuse me?"

"You heard me. I don't want your business and I don't want you hanging around my sister. Go back and tell the cops it's over. They gotta find a new snitch."

"I don't know what the hell you're talking about."

"Yeah, right. Frederick gets killed and the cops come for me. Because we had a fight, they said. How'd they know about that? Who was there? I don't think my sister told them about it."

Abby drew a sharp breath, anger flaring. "Well, it wasn't me. That's ridiculous."

"Yeah. Get the fuck out of here." He flapped a hand toward the door. "Go on, go tell your bosses if they want to infiltrate this here big Mexican drug cartel, they gotta do better than a silly-ass white bitch who can't even speak Spanish."

"You are out of your mind."

"Get out of my store."

Abby glared for a couple of seconds longer and got out. She got in her car and drove the three blocks to her house a little recklessly, telling herself: you will not cry. She parked on the lawn under the tree but sat with the engine idling. For a moment she wanted to turn the car around, point it toward the interstate, and floor it until she hit the George Washington Bridge. Better yet, ditch the car at the Indianapolis airport and be home tonight. She turned off the ignition, got out and went down the steps at the side of the house and let herself into her apartment. She slammed the door, went into her bedroom, flopped on the bed and pulled a pillow over her head and cried.

Abby was not especially a fan of the classical lute, but a renowned virtuoso was on campus for the first guest concert of the year, and she quailed at the thought of an evening alone. She devoted an hour to grading problem sets, five minutes to hair and makeup, and thirty seconds to the question of whether to drive. The concert was in the college's spanking-new arts center on the north side of campus, an easy walk and a trivial drive away. Abby considered the prospect of walking home alone after nightfall and grabbed her keys.

The parking lot at the side of the arts center was nearly full when she got there. She sat in her car, watching a steady flow of students coming across the green, making for the broad front steps of the auditorium. Ben will be here, she thought. For a moment she was on the point of restarting the car and fleeing.

The sight of Philip and Ruth Herzler emerging from their car rescued her. Abby took the keys out of the ignition and timed her exit to cross paths with them. She managed to put on a bright face as she greeted them and fell in step. They seemed glad to see her and her spirits rose. "I'm not sure I could even reliably identify a lute," she confessed as they entered the hall.

The classical lute, it turned out, produced music that was melodic, soothing and highly soporific. Abby began to fight heavy eyelids shortly before intermission. When the lights came up she revived enough to follow the Herzlers up the steps into the lobby. Coffee was being dispensed from behind a counter on one side and Abby gave it a long look, but the Herzlers seemed uninterested and she felt inclined to cling to them. She smiled at a couple of students who caught her eye but tried not to let her gaze wander.

"So, things running smoothly, I hope?" said Philip. "I got the impression the other day at lunch that you were feeling a bit harried. I hope you got your papers graded."

"I did. But that wasn't the real problem." She hesitated: Did she want to unburden herself here? The looks of expectant concern on the Herzlers' faces decided her. She made a quick scan of the crowd, lowered her voice, and said, "I've got a student who's veering way over the line with personal remarks." She told them about Ben.

"Not unheard of," said Herzler when she had finished. "But it's always disturbing. Did you talk to Bill Olsen?"

"Just by e-mail. He told me to document everything, and if it happens again refer it to the dean of students. I'm not sure why I have to wait for another creepy remark to do that, but I'm willing to follow the rules."

"You can always go talk to Richard Spassky. There are procedures, and they're excruciatingly slow, but he'll appreciate the heads-up. And he'll be on your side. Talk to him tomorrow."

The crowd around them shifted and Lisa Beth loomed at Abby's elbow, gaunt and gimlet-eyed. "Hello, kids. Everybody enjoying the show?" Just behind her came her husband, beaming at them with his usual bonhomie.

"It's a change of pace from the Rachmaninoff, isn't it?" said Ruth.

"Real toe-tapping stuff," said Jerry.

"Jerry's under orders to pinch me if I start to snore," said Lisa Beth.

Herzler's face took on a frown. "I saw your story about this killing," he said. "That is just unbelievable. Have they really not found the man's head?"

"Not as of this afternoon. Hence the media circus over by the police station. They've had all the Indianapolis TV stations and one from Chicago jostling for space in the parking lot. They've confirmed it's Jud Frederick's body, from the prints, I believe, but his head's still AWOL."

Ruth shuddered. "Horrible. Why would anyone do that?"

Lisa Beth shrugged. "It's not unprecedented. There was a case in Texas, I believe, not too long ago, where the killer made off with the head. The cartels down in Mexico started the fad, apparently. They dump the head with the person they want to send a message to."

They all contemplated that for an uncomfortable moment. "Not that I think that's what's going on here," said Lisa Beth. "I'm a skeptic about this Mexican angle." She turned to Abby. "How are you, sweetheart? Hanging in there?"

Startled, Abby said, "So far, so good."

"Is your landlord here tonight?"

"Um, not that I know of."

"OK, didn't mean to insinuate anything. His folks always came to these things. I guess he's not a lute enthusiast. How is young Ned as a landlord? Satisfactory?"

"As a landlord? Great."

They stared at her, apparently waiting for more. Herzler rescued her by saying, "Young Ned? I think he must be in his midforties by now. He was still in high school, I think, when we first got here."

Ruth laughed. "Goodness, have we been here that long? I remember he was a really friendly kid, but kind of wild, or so they said."

Lisa Beth said, "Yeah, there was some friction in the family, as I recall." She looked at her husband.

Jerry shrugged and said, "I heard Tom McLaren call him a wastrel and a prodigal son and so forth on occasion. It just seemed they were estranged. It was kind of sad. I don't know if they ever reconciled before Tom died."

"Ned had a somewhat mysterious career," said Ruth.

Abby said, "He was a mining engineer. Mostly in Africa. That's what he told me."

"Yes. But there was always something . . . vague about that. We would ask about Ned, and Tom and Nancy would say something like, 'Well, we're not really sure where he is right now.' And then somebody said, on the usual good authority that is never identified, that he was in the CIA."

Lisa Beth made a scoffing noise. "Sounds dubious to me. Sounds like Tom McLaren romanticizing. But who knows?"

Ruth shrugged. "Anyway, he was away for years and then came back. And he's kept pretty much to himself since he did."

A chime sounded and the lobby lights dimmed for a moment, and people began to move toward the doors to the auditorium. Abby started to drift in the wake of the Herzlers but felt Lisa Beth's hand on her arm, gently holding her back. They halted and Lisa Beth murmured in her ear, "So how's the morale? I'm sorry if I shocked you the other day."

"Well, there's been no sign of Mexican hit men in Hickory Lane yet. Or severed heads." Abby flashed a smile. "I'm all right as long as it's light out. At night it gets a little scary."

"I can imagine. Listen, if you need company, don't hesitate to call. I can come over and just be there if you want. Or you could come over to our place, just hang out for an evening, get some work done, have a glass of wine, just not be alone. I don't know if that appeals to you. I'd put Jerry on notice not to pester you with shaggy-dog stories and reminiscences of student days in Bloomington."

"Thank you, Lisa Beth." Abby looked into the older woman's face, seeing past the cultivated severity of her looks to something softer in the dark eyes. "I may take you up on that. I appreciate it."

"Oh, honey, any time. Well, you'd better go catch up with Philip and Ruth if you want a comfortable seat to nap through the rest of this. What's the matter?"

Abby had started to turn but stopped, catching sight of a figure on the other side of the lobby, alone in the thinning crowd.

Ben Larch stood staring at her, hands in his pockets, head jutting forward, the look on his face troubled, as if the sight of her pained him.

"Nothing," said Abby, breaking eye contact and starting to move again. "Nobody worth talking to."

Abby prided herself on her rational faculties, her power to dominate the lizard brain with the primate brain. It comes down to timing, she thought, stepping carefully as she descended the stone steps at the side of the house, keys in hand, the light high on the eaves illuminating grass and trees within a fifty-foot radius behind the house. I can get the door open, slip inside, and throw the bolt in three to five seconds, faster than a man waiting in the darkness at the edge of the woods can cover those fifty feet.

I just have to make it to the door before he steps into the light. She paused at the foot of the steps, searching the penumbra, listening. Two hundred yards away there was the sound of traffic on Jackson Avenue behind its screen of trees. There was the soft rustling of branches, the distant trickle of water in the stream, somewhere out in the dark the high-pitched cry of an animal. Abby waited, feeling her primate brain asserting itself. When she felt sure, she stepped briskly toward her door. As she pulled open the screen door she took a look over her shoulder, saw nothing, and froze.

Sight and hearing were not her only senses. She sniffed, aware of a pungent odor, familiar but surprising, wafting on the gentle breeze. Someone was smoking marijuana, not too far away.

Abby twisted the key in the lock and ducked inside, slamming the door and shooting the deadbolt home. Primate brain, she thought, do your stuff. Who smokes dope around here? Ned? The retired doctor next door? How far can a night breeze carry a scent? All the way from frat house row?

Abby turned and leaned back against the door, replacing her keys in her purse, shoulders sagging. The smell of a burning joint near a college campus was nothing to panic over. There were other matters to attend to. She put down her purse, kicked off her shoes, and then stood for a moment, wavering, looking at the sideboard backed against the wall at the foot of the stairs.

Early on, mildly curious and by way of familiarizing herself with her new home, Abby had poked around briefly in the sideboard, sliding open the drawers, turning the key that sat in the lock to pull open the double doors enclosing the bottom shelves. The drawers were full of junk, dog-eared decks of cards and stray lenses from long-broken pairs of glasses; the shelves underneath held old board games, discarded glassware and a box full of old photographs and envelopes.

Abby had scrupulously replaced the box after identifying it as a trove of family memorabilia; it was none of her business. It still wasn't any of her business, but her curiosity regarding her landlord had been piqued again, and now a mischievous voice was telling her that if there was anything especially private here, it wouldn't have been left for her to find. She opened the sideboard, pulled out the box, and took it to the sofa. She set it on the coffee table and with the slightest twinge of guilt began to paw through the photographs, faded prints from a time before digital cameras.

They appeared to date from the seventies and eighties, judging by clothes and hair. Ned was easy to spot in a Little League uniform or a high school yearbook shot, impossibly young but unmistakable. With him were people Abby identified as the family: Here he was with his parents and sister, all dressed up at her high school graduation. Here was Ned with a prom date, looking self-conscious in a rented tux, the girl smiling dutifully, clutching her corsage. Here was Ned with Everett Elford.

They were standing side by side, T-shirted and squinting on a sunny day, farm buildings visible behind them. Ned was thin and wiry, Everett more solidly built but not yet going soft, a couple of robust kids in their late teens. They were working hard to look tough, scowling at the camera, and not quite pulling it off despite the guns they were brandishing. They both held handguns, fingers on the triggers, muzzles to the sky, affecting a gunslinger pose. They didn't look particularly tough, but all it takes is a gun to make a boy look dangerous.

Abby frowned at the photo for a moment and then shoved it back into the box. She rose and took the box back to the sideboard and shut it away, turning the key in the lock. None of my business, she thought. All he is is my landlord, and anything else is idle curiosity.

16 |||||||

Richard Spassky was a squat bulldog of a man who affected a handlebar moustache, a tweed jacket with leather patches on the elbows and a gruff demeanor that no doubt served him well in his capacity as dean of students at Tippecanoe College. "These things are lamentably common," he said, giving Abby a sour look across the desktop. "Hormones and all that. But you have to stamp on it, of course."

"It's an aggression," said Abby. "Once I've made it clear the attention is unwanted, anything after that is an aggression. I hope I don't sound too stridently feminist."

Spassky raised a placating hand. "Please. I am entirely in sympathy with you. We don't tolerate this kind of thing. We have procedures to deal with cases like this."

"Yes, I looked at them. They seemed a bit . . . cumbersome." Abby had scrolled through them on her laptop, trying to follow the trail from *Initial Assessment* through *Title IX Investigative Report* to *Appeal Process*. "I don't want a Trial of the Century. I want this resolved as quickly and quietly as possible so the class isn't disrupted. For starters I wonder if somebody couldn't just sit this kid down and tell him to behave. And if he doesn't, I want him out of my class. Is that reasonable?"

Spassky nodded once, failing to look Abby in the eye. "Perfectly. Unfortunately, people aren't always reasonable, and that's why we have impersonal, cumbersome procedures." He sighed and met Abby's gaze at last. "I'll start by talking to him. What was the name again?"

Abby could see that Natalia's head was not in the game today. The poor girl was stuck, staring at the figures on the page with the desperate look of a trapped animal scanning the walls of the cage. "Can you factor that out for me?" Abby asked gently.

Natalia gave it five more seconds and then closed her eyes and let her head droop until it rested on the notebook. "I'm sorry."

Beyond the window, branches tossed in the sunlight. Abby put a hand on the girl's back. "What's the matter?"

When Natalia's head came up, her eyes were glistening. "We're going to lose the store."

"What? Why? What happened?"

Natalia wiped tears from the corners of her eyes with a single finger, the nail painted bright red. "My daddy's cooperating with the government. His lawyer is trying to get him a deal. But part of it is that they're taking the store away from us."

"How can they do that?"

"I don't know. It's all something the lawyer did. My daddy might not have to go to jail, but he won't have the store anymore. I think the government's going to sell it. I don't know what we're going to do."

"Oh, Natalia. I'm so sorry."

"I know he did wrong. There's no excuse. He said so. But if they take the store, then we don't have anything. My daddy's just like, going crazy. He looks like he's sick, he's walking around talking to himself. And he gets these phone calls, people yell at him and he goes out into the yard where nobody can hear what he says and he argues with these people, and then afterwards he just stands out there rubbing his face and looking worried. My mama just sits in the kitchen and cries. And Luis is mad at everybody all the time."

Natalia sat with her eyes closed, one hand over her face. Abby waited for a while and said, "Luis thinks I told the police about him fighting with Frederick. Just in case you have any doubts, I didn't."

"I know that. That's stupid. I told Luis so. He's just being a jerk." She turned wide eyes to Abby. "My father's a criminal. My brother is, too. Do you know how hard that is for me? I don't even know how to think about it. I mean, I love them both. But how can they be so bad? Luis, OK, it was these terrible guys he started hanging out with in Indianapolis. But how could my daddy do that? How could he steal all that money? I actually asked him that. I freaked out at him and screamed at him. And he just said he was trying to make money for us, for the family. And I told him I would rather be poor. And now it looks like I'm going to get the chance."

The look she gave Abby was so desolate that Abby had to reach for her, and they just sat in an awkward embrace for a short while. When Natalia drew back she said, "If my daddy goes to jail, or if they go back to Mexico, I don't know what will happen to me. I don't want to go to Mexico. This is my home. What am I going to do?"

Abby had no answer for that. She said, "You're going to find a way. You're going to do what you have to do to have the life you want to have. You're not responsible for your father. You're just responsible for you."

It wasn't much of a lifeline, but Natalia seemed to grab it; she stared out the window a while longer and then heaved a sigh and bent toward the desk again. "I don't get this," she said.

"Forget it, then," said Abby, flipping the notebook shut. "It's not going anywhere. We'll tackle it again tomorrow. Maybe today you start paying me for the lessons. Let's go buy some groceries and you can teach me how to make *pambazos*."

- - - - - - - - - - - - - - - -

"This is as close to an elegant cocktail lounge as it gets in Lewisburg," said Lisa Beth, sliding onto a barstool. "Sad to say, we have no Musso and Frank or Toots Shor's."

What they had was the bar at the Holiday Inn, which was full of flat-screen TVs and middle-aged men in polo shirts. Lisa Beth had waved or nodded at some of them as she and Abby proceeded to an uninhabited stretch at the end of the bar and installed themselves where they could survey the room. "They have a house specialty cocktail, but I don't recommend it," said Lisa Beth. "Stick to the classics that only the clumsiest bartender can screw up, and you'll be OK."

"Um, you're going to have to help me out," said Abby. "I'm not much of a drinker, really."

"And I am." Lisa Beth smiled at the slightly pudgy young man who was ambling down the bar toward them. "Hello, Ricky. My usual, please. My friend here will try a Manhattan, in honor of her hometown."

Abby had had a Manhattan once, and she didn't recall especially liking it, but she was in a mood to be led. She nodded at Ricky and he went away to make the drinks.

Lisa Beth said, "I am an alcoholic, as I'm sure you have noted. All I have to say in my defense is that I'm a very high-functioning one. I managed to quit smoking five years ago, so I figure I'm entitled to this vice. At this point in my life, I don't have anything to prove, it doesn't impair me notably, and it gives me something to look forward to every afternoon. If my liver gives out one of these days, that's better than wasting away with dementia, in my book. There. That's my apologia, in case you felt one was needed."

Abby managed to say, "Not really. I did notice, but it's none of my business."

"If you prefer to have a soft drink, it's probably not too late to cancel the Manhattan," said Lisa Beth with a look that might have been slightly abashed. "We drunks just enjoy the company, that's all."

"No, the Manhattan will be fine. But I'll probably just have one. What's Jerry up to this evening?"

"Cooking, I hope. I'll be hungry when we're done here." Lisa Beth smiled. "Yes, we have in many ways completely reversed the traditional gender roles in our marriage. Jerry is the domestic one. He likes to cook, and he's pretty good at it. He keeps the house tidy, balances the bank statement every month and loves those tony British dramas on TV. Me, I'm the one who likes hanging out in bars and talking to dubious people. Present company excluded of course. It's kind of a strange formula for a marriage, but it's worked for almost forty years. No kids, and you'd think that would have been it for the marriage, but it wasn't. I guess we're just too lazy to get a divorce. Ah, here we go."

They took delivery of the drinks; Lisa Beth's usual appeared to be a martini with three olives on a tiny plastic sword. They clinked glasses and Lisa Beth said, "Cheers. Now, what's on your mind?"

Abby was a little startled; she had not mentioned anything beyond a desire to get out of the house on a Saturday night when she had called Lisa Beth, but in fact she did have an agenda. She frowned and said, "I was wondering what you'd heard about Miguel Menéndez and his legal case. His daughter's worried sick. She says his lawyer's trying to cut a deal, but it will involve their losing the store. And she says he's getting angry phone calls. I'm wondering if he's in danger."

Lisa Beth raised an eyebrow. "I don't know who from. Unless it would be the Hoosier taxpayers. There's been some muttering about Mexican criminals, from the usual hotheads. You heard about the bust?"

"No. What bust?"

Lisa Beth swallowed and set down her glass. "The state police and the local flatfeet raided the trailer park on the east side of town today. They arrested three Mexican nationals and found weapons and drugs. They didn't find any missing heads, but I don't think they expected to."

"Oh, my God. Do they think they got this killer?"

"I don't know what they think, because they're still not saying much. But I can tell you what I think. I think this Mexican angle is a load of hooey."

Abby waited while Lisa Beth drank deep. "OK, why?"

"Precisely because Miguel Menéndez is still alive."

Abby worked on it for a second or two and said, "I'm not following you."

Lisa Beth leaned closer. "Listen. How do criminal gangs operate? What's the modus operandi? If the Zetas really are active in this part of the world, do you think there would be any independent Mexican criminals?"

Abby frowned. "I give up."

"The answer is no. When a big-time gang like the Zetas moves in some place, they get control of everything. They identify the rackets, the ones they think they're entitled to, and they take them over. Anything significant, anyway. And Menéndez was making big money. I guarantee you, if the Zetas were concerned with what goes on around here, they would be taking a big cut of what Menéndez made from his scam in exchange for protection, and the second there was a hint he was trying to cut a deal with the feds, he would be the one going up like a Roman candle in his car. I'm sorry, that was callous. But last I heard, Menéndez was still peddling peppers there on the corner near you. He's not scared enough. So I don't believe the big bad Zeta bogeyman theory. I just don't. If there's any serious organized crime around here, it's much more likely to be run by biker gangs. The Outlaws, for example, have been into drugs and extortion and loan sharking for years. As for these characters they scooped up today, I think they're just garden-variety punks. Probably with ties to some minor-league street gang in Naptown. But I don't believe they're the ones who killed Lyman and Frederick. I just don't see it." She leaned back and reached for her glass.

Abby sat and watched Lisa Beth drink. "So who did kill them?" she said finally.

Lisa Beth fished an olive off the tiny plastic sword with her teeth, consumed it and said, "I don't know. Not yet. But I'm going to find out. I've been thinking I need a new hobby, and this could be it."

As Abby pulled into Ned McLaren's driveway, her headlights washed over the covered porch, illuminating three men sitting there. Coming up the steps, she identified Ned, Everett Elford and Ron Ingstrom. They were dimly lit by the glow coming through the open door to the house. Inside, men were laughing. The three men on the porch had drinks in their hands; from the looks on their faces she had the impression she had interrupted something more than casual chat. Elford said, "Do you know what time it is, young lady?"

"It's not quite nine," said Abby. "Ned lets me stay out till ten on weekends."

They all grinned, and Ned said, "You're just in time to get into the poker game. Twenty-dollar buy-in."

"Not my game," said Abby. "The mathematics are only moderately interesting and I'm too honest to bluff."

"Pull up a chair. Everett's just been telling us about the big bust."

"I heard." Abby took a chair from its place against the wall and unfolded it. "Lisa Beth Quinton was telling me about it."

"You're as thick as thieves with Lisa Beth these days," said Ned.

Abby shrugged. "She's been very helpful to me."

"She's a good one to know if you want to keep your finger on the pulse of the community," said Elford. "She's been minding other people's business for a long time around here."

Ned laughed. "Touched a nerve, has she?"

Elford smiled. "She's a good reporter. Let's just say her approach is a little adversarial sometimes. She's got a bit of an attitude about wealth."

"And privilege," said Ned. "Don't forget the privilege."

"Oh, yes. The feudal sway I supposedly hold over this county."

"Well, these guys they just arrested work for you, don't they?"

Elford shot him a sour look. "Two of them do. The other one is unemployed, I believe. And let me be the first to say, they *used to* work for me." He turned to Abby and said, "These guys they arrested are small-time dope dealers. Apparently they have some links to one of the Indianapolis street gangs. Whether they're the ones who did these murders, I have no idea. The police are looking hard at the forensics, and we'll see what turns up."

Abby said, "Lisa Beth has a theory. She says that if there really was a Mexican organized-crime presence here, Miguel Menéndez would not still be alive. She thinks he would be dead already, because he's talking to the government. So she doesn't buy the Mexican crime theory."

The men digested this. Elford said, "Lisa Beth's always got a theory. Who knows? But it's also possible that Menéndez is still alive because he *is* the big enchilada. Maybe he's the boss. Maybe he's the guy who had Lyman and Frederick whacked, because they had snitched on him."

They fell silent for a while. "Deep waters," said Ned. "If it was Menéndez, then it's over, right? Is there anybody else around who pissed him off?"

Nobody said anything to that, though Abby sat thinking about how she had pissed off his son. After a moment Ingstrom spoke for the first time. "You'll want to make a statement," he said to Elford. "Condemning these guys. Illegal behavior won't be tolerated at Elford Enterprises, et cetera. It wouldn't hurt to fire a few illegals if you can spare them. You can't afford to have people identifying you with Mexican criminals."

Elford nodded and gave Abby a rueful look. "Ron's trying to get me elected to Congress."

"Keep it under your hat if you don't mind," Ingstrom said. "The official announcement isn't until next week."

"I won't tell a soul," said Abby. "But I think the rumor's already out there. Lisa Beth Quinton guessed when she saw you two at the LUCES benefit."

"It's not really a secret," said Ingstrom. "But we like to try to maximize the surprise."

Elford said, "Right now we're going over all the skeletons in my closet, trying to assess whether any of them will shoot down my candidacy. I think we've decided that the drunk and disorderly arrest when I was at IU might just pass unnoticed."

"It won't," said Ingstrom. "But you should survive. Youthful indiscretion."

Elford shook his head, trading a look with Ned. "Everyone's got a skeleton or two in the closet, right?"

"I have an entire ossuary," said Ned.

"A what?" Elford laughed, his ample belly shaking. "Isn't that a kind of bird?"

"Bones," said Ned. "A whole lot of bones. That's what I've got."

Elford casually tapped Ingstrom's knee with the back of his hand. "This guy's got more than both of us put together, between being a crack defense attorney and a top political operator. Right, Ron?"

Ingstrom smiled. "That's why you're running instead of me," he said. His eyes met Abby's and she did not see a lot of humor there.

17 |||||||

The *Herald Gazette* website was not exactly a go-to source for world news. The top story this morning, judging from its placement just beneath the ads for car dealers and furniture stores that dominated the home page, was an antique car rally in the mall parking lot south of town. Abby had to scroll down to *News* to find Lisa Beth's report on the trailer park arrests, nestled between *Meteor Steel seeks land to expand* and *Garage damaged.*

Lisa Beth had gotten somebody at the police station to talk to her, it appeared; her account contained the names of the arrestees and a list of the weapons confiscated: two handguns and a semiautomatic assault rifle. That was in addition to approximately twenty-five grams of heroin, with an estimated street value of $5,000. Two of the arrestees were employees of Tippecanoe Agricultural Enterprises. Their immigration status was under investigation.

To Abby that didn't sound like a drug operation on a scale that would rate imported hit men and envoys from Mexico putting the arm on local rackets, but it was hardly her area of expertise. Abby spent a little time on the site, looking for other articles by Lisa Beth. Only the features bore a byline, and most of those were Lisa Beth's. Most of the items were short, uncredited and, as far as Abby was concerned, utterly inconsequential. There was no mention of Miguel Menéndez and his troubles except in a pair of archived articles several weeks old. The few items on world or national news were from the AP.

Abby left the site and mused for a moment, trying to picture a young Lisa Beth Quinton. She would have gotten her journalism degree more or less in the Watergate era and been fired up to take on the world, speak truth to power, and bring down the high and mighty. A job in Cincinnati might have given her a start, but she had chosen to come here, yoked in a marriage that she herself didn't seem to value much.

You are not going to wind up like that, Abby told herself. You will do what you have to do to get to a place where you really want to be. This is an exile; at the end of it you will go out and take on the world.

At least, Abby thought, you will not be yoked in a marriage. There is nothing left of that but a chair toppled on its side.

Abby pulled into a parking spot in the faculty lot behind the library and shut off the ignition. The drive from home had taken her all of three minutes. The fear that came with darkness had receded in the light of day, and she had stood under the tree on Ned McLaren's lawn, debating with herself, preferring to walk to campus on a fine late-summer morning but finally opting for the greater security of her car.

She grabbed her bag off the seat and got out. She stepped onto the sidewalk and was startled to see Ben Larch sitting on the steps to the library entrance. He looked up from his phone and seemed equally startled; Abby halted and they stared at one another for a couple of seconds.

You are the boss, Abby thought. Act like it. She took a couple of slow steps toward him. "Hello, Ben. Are you coming back to class?"

Ben Larch just stared at her, his look hardening. "I thought you wanted me out of there."

Abby knew she had made a tactical mistake by asking the question. "What I want is for you to get from the class what you need to get.

And that means observing certain conventions of behavior. If you can do that, I'm happy to have you in the class."

"So why did you set the dogs on me?" Now he was giving her the remote, affectless gaze he had given her when he had stormed out of her office.

Walk, Abby thought. Walk away from this. Instead she said, "I informed the dean what was going on. That was the proper procedure. I'm not going to debate it."

"No, you're always right, aren't you?"

Abby stiffened. "OK. Don't come back. Not if you're not prepared to be cooperative and compliant." Abby walked on past him.

She had almost rounded the corner of the library when Ben called after her, "I'll be back, don't worry."

Ben was not in class, much to Abby's relief. Even so, it was not her best performance. She was distracted and unfocused, and a couple of times caught students looking at her with expressions of mild puzzlement and concern. She rallied and managed to wrap up the session with a reasonable summation and a pep talk for the next quiz. But she fled down the hall to her office without lingering for her usual relaxed wind-down after class.

There was an e-mail waiting for her on her laptop from Richard Spassky.

> I spoke with Ben Larch this morning about your concerns. He was somewhat uncommunicative but he seemed to understand what was at issue and he agreed that there would be no further untoward advances. If there are, please don't hesitate to notify me and we will begin formal proceedings. But I think it's always better if these things can be dealt with informally without setting the machinery in motion. Sometimes students just need to be made aware.

Sam Reaves

And sometimes, thought Abby, they need to be slapped down. She replied, noting that she had spoken with Ben but he had not been in class, and turned to the pile of homework she had to grade, grateful that she had work to distract her from the minefield that her life seemed to be turning into.

She had barely begun when she looked up at a knock on the door frame to see Graham standing there. "Got a second?"

"Sure. What's up?"

Graham came in and sat down across from her, a slight frown settling in. "I got a heads-up from Spassky about one of my advisees. Ben Larch?"

Abby sat back, sighing. "Ah. He's one of yours, is he?"

"Well, I am his academic advisor, yes. What's the story?"

Abby leaned forward, elbows on the desk. "The story is, he has no idea of boundaries. Or the proper relationship between student and teacher. He tried to give me a present, he makes remarks about my appearance, he got a little surly when I told him we weren't friends. He's creepy and he's over the line."

Graham nodded, frowning. "He's a little problematic, yeah."

"You've had problems with him before?"

"Not me personally. He had a nervous breakdown his sophomore year, I think. Year before last. If I recall correctly, there was a suicide attempt, kind of halfhearted, with pills. He had to drop out for a semester. But he got help, apparently, and he was readmitted. He's one of these high-strung kids. I think there's medication involved. But he seemed to be back on an even keel, in my dealings with him, anyway. I'm sorry he's made trouble for you."

Abby slumped on her chair, exhaling. "The last thing in the world I want to be is a coldhearted bitch, believe me. I'm sorry if he's got problems, I really am. People very dear to me have had problems." She had to catch her breath for a moment before raising her eyes to Graham again. "But I'm not responsible for whatever's bothering him.

136

I'm responsible for seeing that the people in my classes learn something. So I feel like I have to be a bit of a hard-ass about this."

"I get that." Graham looked genuinely afflicted. "I thought he was recovered and back on track. I should have paid closer attention."

"I don't hold you responsible. I just need to know what to do. I don't need any more drama in my life."

"No, I guess not. Well, you did the right thing talking to Spassky, for starters."

Abby reached for her laptop and showed him the e-mail Spassky had sent her. "Think that'll do it? How fast can I get him out of my class if a lecture from the dean doesn't work?"

Graham stood. "I don't know the procedures that well because I've never had to use them. But I can promise you I'll do what I can to expedite matters. You shouldn't have to be afraid of this kid."

Abby watched him go and then turned to her work with a sigh. The message light on her phone was blinking and when she brought up the voice mail it was Ruffner's number; she just stared at it for a few seconds. Good or bad? She swiped and put the phone to her ear.

"Ms. Markstein, Detective Ruffner again. Please contact me as soon as possible. We'd like you to come in and try to make an identification in the Lyman murder."

Abby was starting to feel at home in the detectives' office; she went directly to her usual chair and found a cup of vending-machine coffee waiting for her on the corner of the desk. "Thank you," she said. "But it wouldn't do good things to my stomach right now."

"That's OK. Somebody will drink it." Ruffner handed it to a patrolman who gave him a wry look and carried it out of the room. Ruffner sat at the desk, emitting a soft grunt as he settled. He passed a hand over his face, eyes squeezed shut, and Abby realized that the detective was a very tired man. "We have detained a suspect in these killings," he said.

"That's good news. Did you find the missing head?"

"No sign of it yet. We are hoping to get him to tell us what happened to it." He sketched a sour little smile. "Though at this point, there can't be a lot left to find, unless he's had it on ice or something. Anyway, our investigations led us in the direction of a particular guy, and we went and found him. We can hold him for seventy-two hours before we have to charge him or let him go. So our task now is to make sure we have the right guy and have all the evidence we need to take to the prosecutor's office. And part of that is for you to take a look at him and tell us if he's the man you saw at the scene of the Lyman murder."

Abby nodded. "OK."

"Now, in view of the time that has passed since you saw him, and the need to have an airtight identification that will stand up in court, we have to do a lineup. You've probably seen this in the movies. Six guys up against a wall, and the witness points to a guy and says, 'That's him.'"

"Yeah."

"Well, we do it with photos here. And there are a few wrinkles designed to make it as objective as possible, to avoid false IDs. To begin with, I'm not going to be the one showing you the pictures, because I know which one the suspect is, and I might influence you by body language or whatever. So I'm going to have an officer who was not involved in the arrest come in and show you the pictures. That's called a 'double-blind' setup."

"All right, I understand."

"You will see them sequentially, one after another, and I'm going to ask you to think carefully, comparing each one to your memory of the man you saw."

Got it, thought Abby, I'm not stupid. Aloud she said, "I understand."

Ruffner nodded. "Now, I also have to remind you that the guy you saw at the scene might not be here at all. If none of the people you see here looks like the guy you saw, don't hesitate to say so."

"OK, I understand."

Ruffner pushed away from the desk and stood up. "OK. I'm going to bring in Officer Keller and he'll administer the lineup. Just relax and try not to have any particular expectations. Just look at these guys and tell him if you've seen any of them before."

Officer Keller was the one who had taken the coffee away; he was big, heavy and baby-faced, with a shaved head and a neck that bulged against the collar of his black uniform shirt. He had evidently been instructed to be as robotic as possible; he nodded perfunctorily at Abby but said nothing as he took Ruffner's seat behind the desk and opened the file folder. "Suspect number one," he said, and slid an eight-by-eleven sheet of paper with a computer-printed mug shot centered on it across the desk.

How much of my life am I going to spend looking at these guys? Abby thought. Here was another one, a dead-ender staring into the camera with a glum, defeated look. He had dark hair and eyes and a ragged moustache on a face that showed a lot of wear and tear. Abby gave him five seconds or so and then closed her eyes and summoned the image of the man by the side of the road, smiling at her in the glare from the fire where Rex Lyman was being consumed. "No," she said. "I don't think so."

"OK." Keller turned the photo facedown on the desk and pulled the next one out of the folder.

Abby had seen this one before; it took her a second, but the penny dropped. This was one of the mug shots the state police detective had showed her in her second session. "Um, no. I saw him before. This photo, I mean. He's not the guy."

The third was also one she had seen before: same general type, Hispanic-looking tough guy with dark eyes and moustache, unhappy to be sitting for a police portrait. "No."

Number four took her a moment: the face provoked a little twinge of familiarity, but she was fairly sure she had not seen this photo before. She closed her eyes again. The man by the side of the road had longer hair than this, and the moustache crawled down to his chin on either side. But there was a certain similarity in the shape of the head, the general aspect of hard-bitten contrariness. Abby opened her mouth and hesitated and then remembered. "I saw, I think, a different picture of this guy, the last time." She frowned. "And I said he was a maybe. Just a maybe."

Keller reflected her frown and scrawled something at the bottom of the sheet before turning it over on the pile and going to the next one.

There were six in all. Abby had seen three of the photos before; two were entirely new to her and one was the new photo of the man she had picked out at the last session. Keller thanked her, swept the photos into the folder, and left the room.

Abby sat pondering until Ruffner came back into the room. "Thank you," he said, sitting down. "That was helpful."

"I still haven't seen anybody that jumps out at me."

Ruffner nodded. "Understood."

"The one guy, the guy I picked before. Why is the photo different this time?"

"Because we took a fresh one when we brought him in yesterday."

"So he's your suspect."

"He is."

Abby thought for a second. "What about the tattoos? Does he have tattoos?"

Ruffner smiled and reached for a file folder on the desk. He took a sheet out of the file and pushed it toward Abby. This was a photograph of the same man from the waist up, shirtless, glaring into the lens. His bare torso was covered with tattoos, intricate and detailed, most of them illegible. Over one nipple Abby could make out the words "*Vato Loco.*" She closed her eyes again, trying to picture the man she had seen. He had also had a scattering of crude blue tattoos across his upper body. Was this the pattern she had seen?

She opened her eyes. "Have you gone back and looked at the security camera images?"

"We have. They're inconclusive, as you saw. The image is too blurry. You saw him close up. You're the best judge of whether this is the same guy."

Abby stared at the picture. "He's the same type. If you wrote down a description of the two guys, they would read the same. But I'm not looking at him and going, yeah, that's him. When I picture the other guy, I see the tattoos, for example, but I can't swear it's *these* tattoos." She looked at the detective. "But that might just be my fallible memory."

He nodded, looking grave. "Let me ask you this. When you look at this guy, do you see anything that rules him out? Do you instantly go, 'No, it's not the same guy'?"

Abby was already questioning her image of the man at the end of the bridge: How much had she seen and how much was after-the-fact construction? "No," she said. "He could be the guy. But I'm not getting a thrill of recognition here. I'm sorry."

"OK," he said. "That tells us something. Thank you."

"So why this guy? I told you I wasn't sure about him."

"I know. But he turned out to be very interesting. This is Mr. Gómez, Alejandro Gómez. We looked at his record, talked to people who knew him, finally tracked him down in Indianapolis. It turns out he was evicted from a property by Jud Frederick last year, and they had a violent confrontation."

"Really."

"And then we talked to some more people and found out he was a close associate of Pedro Gutiérrez."

"I'm sorry, who?"

"The man who was arrested down in Texas for trading guns to the cartels. Possibly after Rex Lyman informed on him to the FBI. He and Gómez were arrested together on drug charges a few years back. We thought it was enough to go get him and have a serious talk."

Abby stared at him, stunned at the thought she might have actually fingered the right man. She drew a deep breath. "I see," she said. "Well, I hope that's it, then."

"So do I," said Ruffner. "Believe me."

18 |||||||

The first thing Abby did when she walked into class was to scan to see if Ben was there. The knot in her stomach eased a little as she saw he wasn't. The faces turned to her struck her as a little apprehensive today, maybe because of her shaky performance last time out. She had taken an extra minute in her office to put her thoughts in order, get psyched, put on her game face. Now she gave the students a smile and said, "All right. Get ready to rumble. I've got some inverse trig functions here that will knock your pretty pink socks off."

She was greeted with a groan that told her she had the class back, and she proceeded to nail the presentation. Sitting in the back of the class watching two students work through a problem on the board, she let her mind drift for a moment to thoughts of the man in the mug shot she had seen the night before. He was beginning to resemble more and more the man smiling at her in uncertain light by the side of the road. Shear off the hair and trim the moustache and that nightmare figure would be reduced to Alejandro Gómez, petty criminal and murder suspect with ties to both of the victims. The cops know what they're doing, Abby told herself. They wouldn't have arrested him if they didn't have a good case. "Check that last line," she said. "Is the exponent right?"

After class, morale seemed high, hers and the students'. "Thanks, Dr. Markstein," said Giselle McCullers, ponytailed and beaming. "That all makes sense now. Last night I was like, 'Just shoot me now.' I was so confused."

"Euthanasia's a little extreme for homework trouble. See me first."

Cole West had hung back, hulking and unshaven in a New Orleans Saints T-shirt stretched tight over his massive shoulders, wearing a faint smirk. Abby had assumed he was waiting for Giselle, but she flounced out without him and he approached the desk as Abby packed up her things. "Hi, Cole. What's up?"

"Uh, I just wanted to let you know." The smirk was gone, and his eyes flitted from the desk to the board and back, avoiding hers.

"Yeah?"

Now he looked at her, frowning faintly. "The guy, Ben. The kid that's been bothering you. He won't anymore. He got told."

Abby stared at him in astonishment for several seconds. "Told? What do you mean? Who told him what?"

Cole shrugged. "A couple of us. We just told him . . ." He made a brushing-away gesture with his hand. "Don't bother Dr. Markstein again." The look he gave Abby was suddenly cold. "I think he got the message."

Abby opened her mouth, hesitated, groped wildly for words, and finally nodded. "I see. Um, thank you. I guess. I mean, thank you for being concerned. It's being handled, actually. The dean knows, he talked with Ben. I don't anticipate any more problems."

"If there are, let me know. OK?" He was serious, apparently.

She drew a deep breath. "There are procedures. And I think it's important to follow them, for everybody's protection. OK? But thank you."

Cole West shrugged, and now the little smile was back. "Don't mention it," he said. "I really like your class. I'm learning a lot."

Me, too, thought Abby, watching his broad back as he left the room.

Abby was struggling to concentrate on a quiz she was supposed to be composing when her phone started buzzing on the desktop. The number was Lisa Beth's.

"You must have been pretty convincing," said Lisa Beth when Abby put the phone to her ear. "They've decided to charge him."

It took Abby a moment to catch up. "Who? The Mexican guy?"

"Your pal, Mr. Gómez. They just released a statement. He has his initial hearing tomorrow."

It took Abby a few seconds to find her voice. "So they're sure it was him."

"Evidently. They mentioned an eyewitness identification."

"God, I hope they're not basing this on my identification."

"They must have something else. I know they were waiting to hear from the state crime lab in Indianapolis. It must have come just in time. They were coming up to the end of the seventy-two hours and they had to charge him or cut him loose."

Abby sat back on her chair. "Oh, God, please, let it be over."

"Honey, I think it's over. I'm not a big Lewisburg PD booster, as you've probably noticed, but they got a lot of help from the state police on this. And our local prosecutor's office is reasonably sound. I don't think they'd be charging him if they didn't have a case. I'm jumping the gun a little here. I got a tip at the courthouse. I thought you'd want to know. Now I gotta go write a story. I'll call you later."

She rang off and Abby sat with the phone in her hand, staring at the desktop. Please, she thought. Let it be over.

The call from Ruffner came a few minutes later. "We've decided to charge Alejandro Gómez."

"That's good to hear. You must have found some evidence."

"Enough to charge him, we think. We're still working on it. But we got some testimony and found some things that indicate he's our guy. We talked to his girlfriend. Former girlfriend at this point, probably.

She says he was out all night when both murders occurred and came home with blood on him the night Frederick was killed."

"Wow. That sounds pretty conclusive."

"Well, we'd prefer to be able to put him at the scene with physical evidence. The state crime lab is still processing material from Frederick's scene. One of the things we found at Gómez's house was a knife that had been recently given a good, thorough cleaning. We're hoping he missed a spot. You don't need much for a DNA sample."

Abby hesitated, then said, "Will I have to testify in court?"

"If you are confident in your identification, that would help us make the case, yes."

Abby let a few seconds go by. "I'm not sure how confident I am. I'm sorry, I tried to make that clear. It could be him. But it's a maybe. I have to be honest."

"OK. As I said, we've got other evidence. The case isn't going to rest entirely on your identification. We think this is the guy."

Abby closed her eyes. "Thank you," said Abby. "Thank you so much."

Abby wanted to tell somebody the good news. She went by Graham's office but he wasn't in. She made a pass through the student union but saw nobody she knew. She was done for the day and she decided to go home. Ned would be there and she could tell him.

Driving down Jackson, Abby's heart sank as she passed the Poza Rica. She had been unable to read the hand-lettered sign in Spanish posted on the door, but the message was clear: the store had been closed for three days. Abby had texted Natalia twice but gotten no answer.

A knock at Ned's door brought no response, and a peek through a window in the garage door showed her his car was gone. Abby went down the steps at the side of the house with a new sense of freedom. Her phone went off as she was changing into shorts and a tank top: the number on the screen was Natalia's. "I'm sorry I didn't get back to you," the girl said.

"That's OK. I saw the store was closed. How are you doing?"

"I'm all right. But I had to get out of my house today. Everybody is like going crazy there. With us losing the store and everything, lawyers and cops coming around, it's nuts. So I left. We could do a lesson today if you want. I brought my books and stuff."

"Sure. Let me get a bite to eat first. Say seven?"

"Yeah, fine. I'm at my friend Leticia's house. And I don't have a car. I'm kind of stuck here. Can you come to the trailer park?"

"The trailer park. Um, sure. Can you give me directions?"

For Abby the phrase "trailer park" conjured up images of stray dogs, shoeless children and tornado damage, but when she turned up the main street of the park she saw tidy, pastel-painted trailers on permanent foundations, set in neat rows, each with a house number and a mailbox out front. The grass was mowed and the trash bins neatly aligned; it was just a neighborhood where all the houses were long and narrow.

Abby had to make a turn or two to find the address Natalia had given her. She went slowly, wary of the children playing on the grass between the trailers and sprinting heedless across the street. A lot of them looked Mexican but a lot didn't, and Abby wondered about the ethnic mix.

She passed a playground, but there were no children here. The young guys perched idly on the swings and lounging on the merry-go-round with cigarettes in the corners of their mouths were a decade or so too old for it. They were Hoosiers, townies, and not the local bourgeoisie. There were sideburns and mullets and NASCAR caps, sleeveless Lynyrd Skynyrd T-shirts. Abby met pale eyes tracking her as she rolled by and she remembered Ruth Herzler's fear: Look, there goes a Jew.

Fifty yards farther on was the address she was looking for, a pink trailer with a satellite dish on top, a gas grill by the steps and a pickup truck parked on a little patch of asphalt. Abby swore under her breath: Here was another reception committee. She counted six young Mexican guys by the open tailgate of the truck while she pulled over onto the grass and shut off the car. There was a cooler in the bed of the truck and the guys all had beers in hand. They had been looking down the way at the posse on the playground, but now they were staring at her, and she almost lost her nerve and cut and ran. But the number was right, and she got out of the car. "Hi. I'm looking for Leticia's house."

"Leticia. Lemme see. Never heard of her." This one had been at work all day; his clothes and boots were dirty, his hair tousled and sweaty. "But you can hang with us. Want a beer?" One of his friends said something under his breath in Spanish and a couple more laughed. All of them were giving her the once-over, head to toe.

Abby was wishing her outfit didn't display quite so much skin. She gave the offer the token smile it deserved. "No, thanks. You think somebody inside might know Leticia?"

He grinned and cocked a thumb toward the trailer. "I'm just messin' with you. You got the right place."

As Abby made for the steps, the door to the trailer opened and Natalia appeared. "Abby, hi, you made it. Come on in." Natalia's look went beyond Abby to the young men gathered behind the truck. "What are you guys looking at?"

There was a murmur of Spanish and an explosion of laughter. Abby ducked inside the trailer with relief. Here there was cool air and a smell of something spicy simmering. Abby was presented to Leticia, cast in the same mold as Natalia, pretty and dark-eyed, and to her mother, gray haired and plump. The mother was bustling about the tiny kitchen and apparently spoke no English. Leticia said something to Natalia in Spanish and went outside. Her mother cleared a space on a small table so that Abby and Natalia could work there.

"I'm sorry," said Natalia. "I know this isn't the best place to work. My daddy wouldn't let me take the car. Next time I'll try and come to your place." She exhaled and Abby could see the strain in her face. "I didn't study or anything since the last time, I'm sorry."

"You've had other things on your mind. Don't worry about it."

"But I really want to do this. I'm gonna have the time to study, now, without the store. I'm gonna do an hour a day. Whatever happens. Leticia says I can stay here if I have to."

Abby frowned. "What's going on with your family?"

"My mama's going back to Mexico. She said I have to come with her, but I told her I won't. We had a big fight about it. So then my daddy says I can only stay here if I can get a job. Leticia says I can live with her, here. That would be really tight. But if I can get a job I can maybe get my own place after a while. And a car. I'm gonna need a car."

"Why is your mother going by herself? What's your father doing?"

The look in the big bright eyes was desolate. "He's probably going to jail."

"Oh, Natalia."

"The lawyer says the best he can do is cut a deal where my daddy will only have to do four or five years. And he'll have to pay restitution. We're gonna be so broke. But the lawyer says we should be grateful. The government wanted to give him twenty years."

"What about Luis, what's he doing?"

"I don't know. I think he's back in Indianapolis with those gang guys again."

Abby reached out and took her hand. "I'm sorry."

Natalia sniffed and gave her a smile. "I'm OK. Let's do this."

Abby drew a deep breath. "All right, let's try to get some momentum back," she said, opening her notebook. "Do we need to review the trigonometric functions?"

"I think we need to review just about everything," said Natalia. "Two plus two is four, right?"

They had been working for maybe twenty minutes when the door burst open and Leticia leaned in, looking frantic. "They're fighting!"

Natalia looked up. "Who's fighting?"

"The guys, my brother and his friends. With those rednecks." A torrent of Spanish directed at her mother followed. Natalia jumped up and followed Leticia out the door. Abby exchanged a look with Leticia's mother and stood up slowly. Leticia's mother said something in Spanish, looking frightened, and went to a window. There was also one near Abby but all she could see was the neighboring trailer.

"I'll go see," she said pointlessly, out of her depth, and headed for the door.

By the time she got to the end of the drive, by the now-deserted pickup, it was over. Down by the playground, the rednecks were dispersing, yelling the last insults and thrusting middle fingers into the air. One of them took his hand from his face and shook blood onto the ground. Natalia, Leticia and two of the Mexican guys were coming back toward the trailer. One of the guys was bleeding from the mouth, spitting red onto the grass. Leticia was crying. Neighbors had come out of their trailers and the street was full of people, mostly Mexican.

Abby spent the next ten minutes standing ineffectually in a corner of the trailer while the women fussed over the injury and the men recapped the fight, in a mixture of Spanish and English. The split lip belonged to Leticia's brother, and he wasn't saying much, but his friend looked at Abby and said, "Those fuckin' guys, they been looking for trouble since all this bullshit about Mexican killers started."

Natalia came over to Abby and said, "We've never had this before. People always got along. This is real bad."

Abby reached for her and they hugged for a few seconds. "Call me when you're ready. I'll come pick you up if I have to." She gathered her things and left.

An LPD squad car had appeared by the playground and two officers were talking to a knot of Mexican residents. Abby got in her car. Braking at the stop sign at the exit from the trailer park, Abby eased to a halt directly in front of a Lynyrd Skynyrd T-shirt, leaning on the gatepost, smoking. The man gave her a look full of contempt and said, "You like to fuck Mexicans, huh? We got a name for bitches like you."

19 |||||||

As her topology class broke up into pockets of small talk and banter, Abby turned her phone on and saw a light flashing, signaling a text message from Richard Spassky: *Please come see me in my office ASAP.*

When Abby rapped on the door frame, Spassky was shoving something into a drawer in a filing cabinet. He looked at Abby over the top of his reading glasses and said, "Ah, Abigail." He pushed the drawer shut and pointed to the chair in front of his desk. "Have a seat." He whipped off his glasses, walked past her to the door, and closed it gently. "Thank you for coming."

"He hasn't been in class since we last spoke." Abby was prepared for the worst; there were lots of academic horror stories about nightmare students protected by rules, impossible to expel.

Spassky laid his glasses on the desktop and settled onto the chair behind it with a sigh. "And he won't be," he said. "Not anymore." He frowned at a paper on the desk and shifted it an inch or two to his left.

"I see," Abby said. "Thank you."

"Don't thank me." Spassky was looking at her now. "I have to tell you that I received a call just now from Mercy Hospital. Ben is there, getting emergency care, unconscious after apparently taking an overdose of some kind of medication."

Abby gaped at him for a moment and then closed her eyes. She sighed and sagged on the chair. "Is he going to make it?"

"I couldn't say. He was found in bed this morning by his roommate. Ben lives off campus, as you may or may not know, in one of those houses over on Sycamore Street. The roommate went to wake Ben for a class and found him in bed, unresponsive. He called the ambulance, and there we are."

"Oh, my God. That's horrible." Abby stared out the window, thinking: You need to be very cold about this or it will eat you alive. She took a deep breath before turning to the dean. "I assure you, I did nothing to lead this kid on. Nothing. You can ask anybody in the class."

Spassky nodded. "I don't doubt that for an instant. This young man has a history of instability. Nobody's blaming you. Not at all. I'm sorry you had to go through this."

Abby opened her mouth but found that the questions she wanted to ask were too jumbled in her head to come out. "God. I have to go in and face that class tomorrow."

Spassky exhaled, heavily. "I'll be sending out a campus e-mail about it some time this afternoon." He reached for his reading glasses. "At least you didn't have to call his parents," he said, and for a moment Abby felt sorry for him.

Graham waylaid Abby as she crossed the green. "I got a text from Spassky," he said, brow contracted in concern. "Did you hear about Ben?"

"I've just come from Spassky's office. You could say my feelings are kind of mixed right now."

They stood frowning at each other in the middle of the walk, the flow of passing students parting around them. "Well, this ought to get him out of your class," Graham said finally.

"I'm not going to lie to you, that's a relief. But I didn't want this. I didn't want anything like this. I wanted him to get help and get straightened out."

Much to her surprise she was suddenly close to losing it. Abby had to look away from Graham. She clamped down hard on herself, staring out across the green.

She felt Graham's hand on her arm. "You've had a rough time. I'm sorry."

Cold, she thought, ice cold. "I didn't do anything to provoke any of this."

"I know." He squeezed gently and his hand fell away. "Hey, you want to go get a cup of coffee or something? Just sit and vent for a while? We could go somewhere off campus if you want."

Abby glared at the distant chapel until she was sure her voice was reliable. She looked at Graham and gave him a brief smile. "No, thanks. I'm OK. I need to go get some work done. But I appreciate it."

There was genuine sympathy in Graham's eyes; the swagger was gone and he looked completely guileless for the first time in Abby's experience. "All right. Please let me know if there's anything I can do to help."

"I will, thanks."

Walking toward her office, heart rate slowing and self-possession returning, Abby remembered Graham's touch on her arm. She found she did not resent it, and she wondered briefly if perhaps she had misjudged him.

"I seem to have developed an amazing talent for antagonizing people. I don't know how I got to be so God damn irritating. I've always tried to get along with people." Abby took a generous sip of her second Manhattan.

Across the table from her Lisa Beth was perusing her with a mild frown. "Easy on that drink," she said. "That's all liquor." Around them swelled the hubbub of a moderately full bar with two baseball games and a football game in progress on multiple TV screens. Abby had made it halfway through a solitary evening in her apartment, frenetically working, texting and instant messaging, before admitting to herself that Graham had been right: she needed to vent, and she needed a live companion to sit there and take it. Finally she had called Lisa Beth.

"I'm sorry to dump all this on you," Abby said. "I know I'm just feeling sorry for myself."

Lisa Beth shrugged. "Sometimes you're entitled."

"I thought coming here would be some kind of retreat. I thought it would be like going into a nunnery or something. Just feed me gruel and let me do my penance."

"Well, the gruel we can do. As for the penance, I don't see where you've done anything wrong. Your guy in New York was obviously a bad bet from the get-go, if you'll allow me to be blunt. As for this little creep in your class, my only regret would be that he's an incompetent suicide."

"Oh, God. I swear to you I wish this kid no harm. I'm sorry for him, I really am. I just want him to be someone else's problem and not mine."

"I believe you. Did I tell you I actually know him?"

"Ben? God, no."

"Jerry had him in one of his classes, and he's been to our house. I thought he was a little strange. And Jerry said there were some drug issues, some heavy recreational use on top of his medications."

Abby gaped at her. "Oh, shit."

"What?"

"I smelled dope coming home one night. Behind my house."

Lisa Beth waved the notion away. "Could have been anybody."

"Ned doesn't smoke, as far as I know, and the neighbors are elderly. Oh, God, he knew where I lived." Abby shuddered.

Lisa Beth looked dubious but said, "Well, all the more reason to be glad he's gone. You are the victim in this case, with absolutely nothing to apologize for. As for Luis Menéndez, he's a criminal like his father."

"Don't forget the trailer park rednecks. I managed to piss them off just by speaking civilly to some Mexicans, apparently."

"Mmm, yes. Did you ever hear of the cluster effect? Any random pattern, like pepper spilled on a tablecloth, will show clusters. Events are like that, too. Every once in a while there's a cluster of anomalous events. This is one."

"That's a good try. I'll work on that."

"Take it from me. You just had the bad luck to cross paths with this little cluster of sewer rats, and as a native Hoosier I apologize for the poor impression we must be making." Lisa Beth took a sip of her martini. "There was a bad fight at a bar out on Indianapolis Road last night. Mexicans versus Hoosiers, three people to the hospital. That's the worst part of this nonsense about Mexican killers. We're starting to see the kind of animosity we've avoided so far."

"Nonsense?" Abby frowned at her. "Excuse me, but what are you saying? You don't think this Gómez is the killer?"

"Oh, he may have done the killings. But it had nothing to do with the drug cartels."

Abby nodded. "I think the police know that. Ruffner told me Gómez had quarreled with Frederick and was a pal of the guy Lyman snitched on."

"That may be. Or it could be something else. Rex Lyman and Jud Frederick were into so much hanky-panky there's a smorgasbord of options." Lisa Beth leaned closer across the table. "My guy Dexter is a great source for dirt, all the gossip he hears. And you know what Dexter told me? Just before he got toasted, Rex Lyman had a serious tiff with your landlord's old pal Everett Elford."

"Really."

"Gospel. Dexter got it from Elford's office manager."

"So what does that mean?"

"God knows. Maybe nothing. But if there's anything there I hope to find it."

"You're always looking for dirt, are you?"

"You don't have to look too hard. In a place like this they all know each other. The rich folks, the lawyers, the bankers. They all grow up together, go off to school together, come back and do business together. It's cozy. It's small-town life. It's intimate. It's all stitched up."

"I think it's the same everywhere. I think there's a lot of insider stitching up that goes on in New York."

"No doubt, no doubt. Boys will be boys. Did you know Elford is looking for a new secretary?"

Abby peered at Lisa Beth. "Why would I know that? Why would I care?"

"No reason. You know who the old one was?"

"I give up."

"The blonde we saw with Jud Frederick at the Azteca that night."

"You're kidding."

"Nope. Somebody told me Frederick had been dating Elford's secretary and the penny dropped. And now Dexter tells me she has decamped, if that's the word I want. I think it would be very interesting to talk to her. But nobody can tell me where she's gone. I just find it intriguing that Jud Frederick was intimate with Everett Elford's secretary. Elford's got a clean reputation. I wonder if he knew that his secretary was putting out for one of the top sleazeballs in the county."

"Why don't you ask him?"

"Oh, I will. But I'm not quite ready to talk to young Everett. I don't have all my ducks in a row yet."

Abby gaped at her. "Do you mean you're really digging up something new on these murders? And you think Elford's involved?"

Lisa Beth leaned closer. "Elford's involved in everything in this county. I don't mean he's a crook. I'm not accusing him of anything.

But when you have a lot of money and influence and interests in a place, things that happen affect you. And I'd like to know how these murders affect Everett Elford, I really would." Lisa Beth leaned back, waving it all away. "Forget I said anything. For you the only thing that matters is that the guy that did it is under lock and key. I think the local flatfeet may have gotten it right."

Abby raised her glass. Her head was spinning a little. "Here's to them."

I will pay for this tomorrow, thought Abby as Lisa Beth pulled into the driveway of 6 Hickory Lane. On the ride home the world had seemed a little less threatening but also a little less stable, the second Manhattan permeating comfortably through her brain. "Thank you," she said. "I needed this. Your patience was much appreciated."

Lisa Beth reached out to give her hand a squeeze. "Honey, any time." She paused, on the verge of saying more, then smiled and released Abby's hand. "Be careful going up those steps, will you? I should have cut you off after one."

"I'll be OK. I have my sensible shoes on."

"Looks like someone's waiting up for you." Lisa Beth nodded at the figure dimly visible on the porch. "Don't let him ply you with drink."

"I'm sure he will see me safely home." Abby got out of the car.

"Watch the cord," said Ned as she came carefully up the steps. He was sitting on the edge of his chair, his face illuminated by a laptop on a footstool in front of him plugged into an outlet in the side of the garage.

Abby managed not to trip over the cord. "Nice night to be outside," she said.

Ned looked up at her. "Yeah. Want to sit for a while? I just have to wrap up this e-mail."

"Thanks." Abby lowered herself onto a chair. The steps would be negotiable even with a mild buzz, but at the bottom there was nothing but an empty apartment. The crickets were in full voice and the night was sultry. She watched Ned pecking at the laptop, his face lit from below, concentrating with a mild frown. After a while his expression eased and he sat back. "Sorry. Dealing with a minor crisis in Angola. Want something to drink?"

"No, I'm good, thanks." Abby blinked at him. "I thought you were retired."

"More like between jobs, but yeah. This is sort of a hobby."

"What kind of hobby involves a crisis in Angola?"

Ned let a few seconds pass before answering. "I do some volunteer work for an agency that runs demining operations in various places."

"Demining? What, like filling in mines?" Abby knew the drink was making her stupid.

In the light from the laptop she could just make out his smile. "No. Clearing land mines. Angola has millions of land mines left over from their civil war. People out in the bush step on them all the time. It's going to take decades to get rid of them all. Probably never get them all, in fact. But you have to try."

People surprise you, Abby thought. "How did you get involved in that?"

"Just contacts, networking. I wanted to do something." He looked at her and smiled again. "Call it atonement."

Abby sat nodding stupidly. "You told me you were an expert in guilt because you'd been on both sides. But you only told me about somebody else hurting you. You didn't tell me about the other side." Ned just sat peering at her, and instantly Abby was appalled. "I'm sorry. I've been out drinking with Lisa Beth and I'm drunk. Forget I said that."

He laughed gently. "That's OK. I brought it up. I guess I owe you the rest of it."

"Not if you'd rather not. Just forget it."

A few seconds went by and Abby had decided he was going to forget it when he said, "I did a little work for a government agency out there. One of the ones that are kind of publicity shy. And that's about all I can tell you, because they made me promise not to talk about it. But it wasn't always pretty."

"I see." Abby nodded. "Ruth Herzler told me there was a rumor you were in the CIA."

After a moment Ned said, "That's not true. I can tell you that. And I can tell you that when I was in the Congo there was a terrible war going on that nobody outside Africa ever heard much about. Suffering on a massive scale. But we needed their coltan for our laptops and our cell phones, so the mining companies cut deals with some pretty nasty people to keep the mines going. And that's what I did. And that put me in position to be what those government agencies call an asset. At first it was an adventure and then it was just a job. I did it as long as I could stand it and then I finally quit. And that really is all I can tell you about it."

Abby sat contemplating the spinning of her head. "But you're atoning."

"Giving it a shot." Abby could just make out his mild frown in the light from the computer. His eyes went out into the night and he said, "Too many times in my life I've been in situations where I could have made a stand and maybe stopped something bad. But I settled for just stepping out, not participating. That was better than going along, I guess. But it's not much to be proud of."

Abby leaned forward, hands on the arms of the chair. "I should go to bed. I've had a busy day. I drove another would-be suitor to suicide today. This one botched the attempt, thank God."

"Say what?" Ned slowly reached out and closed the laptop, leaving his face in darkness.

"A kid in my class. He was infatuated, borderline stalking me. I sicced the dean on him and he tried to kill himself."

They exchanged a long look in the scant light from distant lamps. "Not your fault," said Ned. "Really, really not your fault. This is one you just wipe off your shoe. I mean it, Abby. These tormented waifs have no claim on you. None at all."

She nodded a few times. "Thank you. It helps to hear it. Still. It's not a nice thing to go through." Abby sat listening to the crickets buzzing away in the dark. She stood up, a little uncertainly. "All right, bedtime."

"You OK to go down those steps?"

"I think so. I think between jail and the hospital all the potential stalkers are accounted for tonight. Maybe just listen for screams till I'm inside."

The light on the eaves went on as Abby stepped off the porch. She went down the steps very carefully, concentrating on the placement of her feet. At the bottom she stepped onto the grass, reaching into her purse for her keys. Movement in the brightly lit yard drew her eye and she stopped in her tracks.

A raccoon, unmistakable with its black mask and striped tail, was pawing at something in the middle of the lawn. It was a plastic shopping bag, knotted at the top. The raccoon had torn the plastic and was reaching in to scoop out little bits of something red, taking them to its mouth. Whatever was inside the bag appeared to be about the size and shape of a soccer ball.

Abby staggered a little. "Ned?" She retreated to the foot of the steps, calling out again. "Ned?"

She looked up to see him standing there. "What's up?"

"I'm sorry. Maybe I'm being stupid. Could you come look at this? There's a raccoon."

"He won't hurt you."

"It's not that."

He caught her tone of voice, and he came trotting down the steps. He stopped at the corner of the yard and looked. The raccoon paused and looked up. Ned picked up a stick and hurled it. The animal scuttled off into the brush at the top of the slope.

"What's in the bag?" Abby could barely find her voice.

Ned walked slowly across the lawn in the glare from the light on the eaves. He bent down, pulled at the shredded plastic, was motionless for a moment, then, somewhat gingerly, picked it up with both hands, holding it away from his body as it dripped a little onto the grass.

"Oh, God, what is it?"

Ned smiled at her. "About half a watermelon. The Schwartzes were having a picnic in their yard this afternoon. They must have overlooked this when they cleaned up." He turned toward the woods, wound up, and slung the bag out into the darkness. They listened as it whiffed through foliage and thumped into the brush down by the stream. "Nice snack for a raccoon." He came back toward the steps.

There was a moment of suspension and then Abby laughed. She laughed so hard she reeled, nearly losing her balance. "Easy there," said Ned reaching for her. She caught his hand and pulled and suddenly she was in his arms, and for a moment she wanted to stay there; there was nothing she wanted more in the world than to stay there being held by someone who cared about her, because the last person who had held her because he cared about her had been dead for more than a year.

"I'm sorry," she said, pulling away, not sure how long they had been embracing. A couple of seconds, she thought. Only a second or two, she fervently hoped in her drunkenness.

"You OK?" He let her go, a hand trailing on her arm.

"I'm all right," she said, steadying and making for her door. "My imagination got the best of me there for a second. Good night."

She looked back as she got her door open to see Ned standing there, watching her with a grave look.

20 |||||||

The deck behind Tina and Steven Stanley's house had a view of a patch of ill-tended lawn, a stretch of privet hedge lined by flower beds and a garage with peeling white paint, all benignly shaded by a giant elm. To Abby it looked like heaven.

"You can get so much more house for the money in a town like this," said Tina, baby on her hip and wineglass in hand. "We could never have afforded something this big in LA or Madison."

"The only problem is that you have to live in Lewisburg," said her husband, bringing a tray of hamburger patties up from the grill. That brought a knowing laugh from the crowd on the deck, seated at the table or leaning against the rail, a miscellaneous assemblage of men and women some years shy of middle age, all junior members of the Tippecanoe College faculty.

"It's not that bad," said Tina. "I'd rather raise a child here than some place where I'm afraid to let them walk down the street by themselves, like Chicago or New York."

Abby said, "I grew up in lower Manhattan, and I did OK. You learn certain rules when you're small, you learn how to watch your step, but I never felt like I was in danger. I feel like I had a pretty normal childhood. Frankly, this town scares me a lot more than New York ever did."

Looking abashed, Tina said, "Well, that's understandable, seeing what you went through."

Suddenly everyone was looking at Abby. She managed a shrug. "No big deal. They've arrested the guy who did it, apparently."

"Did they ever find the guy's head?" said a man she had just met, a disheveled chemist.

Abby blinked at him and said, "Um, no, I think the head's still missing. But that was the second murder. It was the first one I reported. Anyway, like I said, they've made an arrest."

After a brief silence Steven said, "And let's hope that's it for excitement in Lewisburg for a while."

"I'm good with boring," said Tina, and the conversation moved on. Abby ate a hamburger and fell into conversation with the chemist's wife, who was from New Jersey; the party moved indoors and Abby took a turn sparring with the overstimulated one-year-old, cross-legged on the floor. She had a third beer and drifted from conversation to conversation and at a certain point was startled to discover that she was having a good time.

Tina disappeared to put the baby to bed and the crowd thinned a little. It was not going to be a late night, Abby saw. She was struck with a sudden yearning for loud music, crowded dance floors, jostling at the bar. She wanted to paint the town red. I'm not good with boring, Abby thought, not really. Coming home on the subway with Samantha in the wee hours from some hip club in Brooklyn, tipsy and giggling, barhopping in Boston, plying Evan with drink until she could drag him onto the dance floor. What happened to all that? Samantha had a baby and I had a personal tragedy. And here I am.

She wandered out onto the deck, which was now deserted, and more out of boredom than anything else pulled another beer from the cooler. She moved to the edge of the deck, out of the direct light from the house, and leaned back against the rail, tipsy and bemused. The door opened and Graham came out onto the deck. He fished a beer out of the cooler, straightened, and saw her.

"Hey. Hiding, huh?"

"Drinking alone in the dark. This job is undermining my moral fiber."

Graham twisted the cap off his beer and came to join her in the shadows. "How did your calculus section go yesterday?"

Abby grimaced. "Nobody seemed to want to talk about it. I stammered out something along the lines of 'You probably heard about Ben, let's hope he's all right,' and I was met by deafening silence. Maybe they detected the note of ambivalence in my voice. I don't know how many people knew about the, um, stalking."

Abby watched Graham's eyes flee hers. "Hmm. These things do get around."

"Cole West knew about it. He actually came and told me that Ben had been warned. He said, 'He got told,' whatever that means. How Cole found out about it, I don't know."

Graham was looking distinctly uncomfortable, scowling at the label on his bottle. "I discussed it with Cole," he said after a moment. "I just asked him if he knew what was going on, because I knew he was in the class. Good God, if he went and threatened Ben or something, that's bad."

That hung in the air for a moment. Abby wasn't sure she liked the image that conjured up, and she wondered just how frank Graham was being. "I think that's exactly what happened. Is that what you wanted to happen?"

"My God, no." Graham stiffened and shot her a look. "I just wanted to find out what was going on. I wanted information."

Which you could have gotten, amply, from me, Abby thought. "I'd thank you for looking out for me, but I'm not sure that was the best way to do it."

He broke off eye contact and frowned down at his beer bottle. "If I played it wrong I'm sorry. I was concerned."

Abby shrugged. "I appreciate that."

"Ben's apparently out of the woods medically, for what that's worth. His parents are withdrawing him from school and getting him help, again."

"Let's hope it works this time."

"Hear, hear." He held his bottle toward her and they clinked and drank. Graham said, "There's some talk inside about the possibility of a little jaunt to Naptown. Dave and Lorraine know a music venue there that brings in some pretty good bands. We get going now, we can be there by ten thirty, just in time for the show. You interested?"

It sounded like exactly what Abby had been wishing for. It also sounded a lot like being Graham's date, and she wasn't sure how she felt about Graham right at that moment. "I don't know," she said. "I don't think I'm up for a real late night."

He was smiling at her faintly, just visible in the dim light. Softly he said, "We could go someplace closer, just you and me. A nightcap and some conversation."

It had been a long time since Abby had been courted, and she had missed it. He was devilish handsome, and the easiest thing in the world would be to say yes. Abby wasn't sure what was stopping her, except a hard-won mistrust of the easiest thing in the world. That, and the image of him breathing a word in Cole West's ear. She was staring at Graham, paralyzed with indecision, when he reached out, put a hand to the back of her neck, and pulled her toward him. Caught by surprise, Abby failed to resist. The kiss had its pleasant aspects, but she pulled away before it went on too long.

Graham murmured, "You're amazing."

Abby sank back against the rail. She took a deep breath. "I won't say I didn't enjoy that, but don't get any big ideas. There's alcohol at work."

"I'm sorry." He managed not to sound sorry.

"My life is complicated enough without a professional relationship turning into something else. OK?" Especially with somebody I don't know if I can trust, she thought but did not voice.

She wasn't sure for a moment how it was going to go; Graham stared solemnly, blinking a couple of times. "OK," he said finally. "Sure."

Score one for the primate brain, Abby thought, stomping on a pang of regret.

An up-tempo version of "Für Elise" jerked Abby out of sleep at two thirty in the morning. It took her several measures to recover enough consciousness to recognize the ringtone of her phone, grab the thing, and silence it. She put it to her ear just beginning to wonder who was calling her and what disaster had occurred. "Hello?"

"Abby? I'm so sorry to wake you up."

It took a second for Abby to identify the girl's voice, tenuous and wavering. "Natalia?"

"I'm so sorry. I didn't know who else to call."

"Where are you? What's wrong?" By this point Abby had taken in the time on the clock and swung her feet to the floor.

"I'm kind of like stranded." Abby could hear tears just below the surface. "I'm out in the country, near Lewisburg. My daddy's in Indianapolis and my mama doesn't drive, and Leticia's brother isn't answering his phone, so I didn't know who to call. I'm so sorry to wake you up."

"Natalia, it's all right. What do you want me to do?"

"I need somebody to come pick me up. I went to a party with this girl, but I wanted to leave and she didn't, and she went off with some guy, and then this other guy started getting weird, and I just left. I started walking. But it's a long way, and I'm scared and I don't know if they're gonna come after me, and . . ."

"Natalia. I'll come get you. But I need to know where you are."

"I'm walking up toward Indianapolis Road, on 600 East. My phone says I'm like half a mile south of it. That's about three miles east of town. You know where Indianapolis Road is?"

"That's what Main Street turns into, right?"

"Yeah. If you just go east out of town you'll come to 600 East. I'm walking north toward Indianapolis Road."

"OK, I'm coming to get you. Just keep walking. Or do you want to stay on the phone?"

"No, that's OK. I'm all right. Abby, I'm sorry."

"Natalia, don't worry about it. I'll be right there. Just keep walking."

Abby was dressed in two minutes. She grabbed her keys and phone and made for the door. She went out into the yard, triggering the light, locked the deadbolt behind her, and ran up the steps.

Abby had gone just under three miles along a deserted Indianapolis Road, creeping at thirty miles an hour, one eye on her phone, peering into the darkness at the limit of her headlights, when she spotted the sign for 600 East. She turned south and had gone just a couple of hundred yards when she spotted Natalia, striding fast toward her on the shoulder of the road. Abby flashed her high beams and pulled over.

The girl trotted to the car, tore open the door, and flopped onto the seat. Before the door slammed Abby could see tear tracks on Natalia's face in the feeble glow from the dome light. "Oh, my God, Abby, thank you. I was so scared. I'm so sorry to bother you. I didn't know what to do."

Abby grabbed her hand and squeezed. "It's OK. I'm happy to do it. What the hell happened?"

Natalia put her face in her hands. "Oh, *shit*. I just did something stupid. I went to a party with this girl I kind of know but not real well, and we came with these guys, and we drove all the way out here and then when we got there it was weird. They were drinking Everclear shots and doing drugs and stuff, and I didn't know anyone and then the girl went off upstairs with a guy and this other guy started coming on to me, and I like just freaked and left. I just ran."

Abby put the car in gear and wheeled around to head back into town. "OK, you're safe now. Listen, did the guy hurt you? Did he, I mean, should we talk to the police? Did he assault you?"

"No, no, no, no, no. Oh, God, no. He was just trying to kiss me and stuff. But I'm OK. I'm OK."

She didn't sound convinced. Abby said, "You're going to have to give me directions to your house."

"I'm not going home. I can't go home. I told my mama I was staying at Leticia's. Can you take me there?"

"Um, sure. Why wasn't Leticia with you?"

"She didn't want to go. I got mad at her, and I went by myself. But she was right. Oh, God, I'm so stupid."

Abby drove in silence for a while. "Natalia, instead of beating yourself up about it, get mad at the guy. When they don't take no for an answer, that's their problem, not yours."

The girl sniffed a couple of times. "I was stupid to go with this girl. I don't even really know her."

"They were drinking Everclear? So, not exactly a wine-and-cheese kind of event."

"I know, right? I mean, what a bunch of lowlifes. Oh, my *God*."

She laughed then, and the tension in Abby's stomach began to ease. In a few minutes they had rolled back into Lewisburg and Natalia was directing her to the trailer park. "Leticia's gonna be so pissed. Her mom's gonna be pissed. And then she'll tell my mom and I'll be in *soooo* much trouble."

Underneath the makeup and the nail polish and the tight jeans this was still a little girl, Abby thought. Biology and culture conspired to make girls irresistible to men before they had sense enough to evaluate risk, and trusting men to restrain themselves was always a bad bet. Suddenly Abby was immensely weary. "Here we go," she said, turning in through the gate of the trailer park. Natalia was on her phone, talking softly to Leticia in Spanish.

"Abby, thank you so much. I'm so sorry to do this to you."

Abby pulled up at Leticia's trailer and put the car in park. "Please, don't worry about it. Just be careful next time. Call me, OK?"

"OK." Natalia was tearing up again, sniffing, and suddenly she reached for Abby and nearly gave her a neck sprain with a vigorous hug. "Thank you. You're so awesome." She got out of the car and ran up the steps, where Leticia, softly lit from inside, was holding the door open for her. Natalia waved once and disappeared inside.

Abby sat with the car idling for a moment, depressed by the prospects for a girl like Natalia, all her support kicked away at a crucial time. She sighed and put the car in gear. She backed out onto the street and headed for home.

She turned onto the road that led to the exit, her lights sweeping over a row of trailers. She was focused on the road but her eye was drawn by movement near the edge of the illuminated arc, and suddenly she leapt with fright because there, ducking back behind a porch but not quite fast enough, unmistakable with his dark feral look, the hair and moustache and intense eyes beneath black brows, was the man she had last seen smiling at her in the light from Rex Lyman's pyre.

21 |||||||

"I'm positive," said Abby. "I have no doubt whatsoever. I felt that certainty that was missing when I looked at the pictures of Gómez. It was the same guy." She was shivering in the cool predawn air coming in through the car window. Behind the steering wheel, Ruffner looked as if he would rather be in bed, which was where he had been when a call from the station had roused him. Abby had raced there through deserted streets and told her story to a desk sergeant, who had showed what Abby considered to be a stubborn lack of urgency before calling Ruffner.

"All right," Ruffner said softly, looking out across the park to where flashlights probed the dark near an idling patrol car. Only a few isolated lights burned behind windows in the trailers. "Looks like we missed him. He was probably long gone before we got here. Either that, or he's inside one of these trailers. I guess we'll have to canvass in the morning. I'm going to take you back to the station and get your statement. Anything else you can think of as far as a description would be helpful."

Abby tensed, arms crossed, trying to quell the shivering. "I didn't get a really long look at him. Just, like I said on the phone, the same cargo shorts, same shoes, like Chuck Taylors, and a shirt this time. A dark T-shirt. Hair, moustache, face, the same. Absolutely the same guy."

"I believe you. And it was this trailer here where you saw him?" He pointed.

"Between that one and the next one. Right by the porch steps."

"Did you get the impression he had just come out of the trailer?"

Abby thought. "No, the impression I got was that he was sneaking around. He didn't want to be seen. He jumped back when my lights hit him. I don't think he had come down those steps. But I could be wrong."

"Was he carrying anything?"

"I think, yeah, he had like a plastic bag. Like a shopping bag. With . . . I don't know. There was something in it."

"Was he near a vehicle? Did he look like he was heading toward a car maybe?"

"Not that I saw. I got the impression he was walking toward those trees there but turned around when my lights hit him."

Ruffner nodded. "So he was heading toward the creek?"

Abby just blinked at him. "That's the creek?"

"That's South Branch, that runs into Shawnee Creek."

"I see." Abby shivered again. "The one that runs behind my house."

Ruffner thought for a second. "Yeah, I guess it is."

Abby pulled herself together. "I'm sorry. I tried to make it clear when I looked at the pictures that I wasn't sure. Now I'm sure. I don't know how I can prove it, but I'm sure. This was the guy I saw, not Gómez."

"You don't need to convince me." He put the car in gear and pulled slowly onto the main street of the park. "To be frank, I thought our case against Gómez was weak. And his lawyer pulled an alibi out of a hat a couple of days ago, which last I heard the state police hadn't been able to crack. What I need from you right now, though, is enough certainty in this identification to take to the prosecutor this morning and convince him we've got the wrong guy locked up. Can you give me that certainty?"

Abby closed her eyes briefly, seeing the man again, ducking away from her headlights, moving just as he had moved when he stepped away from the burning car. She opened her eyes. "Yes. I'm certain."

- - - - - - - - - - - - - - - -

"Where does that stream go?" Abby sat on the edge of an armchair in Ned's living room. Ned stood by the fireplace with his hands on his hips, frowning.

"Well, as I recall, it runs all the way across the southern part of Lewisburg and empties into Shawnee Creek west of town. It runs behind the frat houses a few hundred yards west of here and then through the railroad arch and on for another mile or so till it hits the creek."

"Through the railroad arch."

"Yeah."

They stared at each other for a moment. Abby said, "I've been standing out there in plain sight, looking for deer, talking on the phone, daydreaming, advertising where I live."

"I don't know how likely it is he'd have seen you, even if he's been wandering around down there."

"I don't either, but I'm starting to feel really fucking exposed. Excuse my language. Am I panicking? Am I paranoid?"

Ned stood looking down at her, pensive. "I don't think so," he said. "I'd be scared, too."

"So what do I do?"

He wandered toward the window, crossed his arms, stood looking out. "Go somewhere else for a while. Find a place to lay low until they get this guy. I'm not going to let a lease stand in the way of your being safe."

Abby vented an exasperated breath. "Terrific. Maybe I can go back to the Tarkington. I could probably get my old room back." She stood up. "I have work to do. I can't think about this right now." She was light-headed and queasy.

"Go work. I'll make some phone calls, find you a place to stay."

Abby was looking out the window into the trees. "Right now I'm too freaked out to walk down those steps and show myself back there, even in broad daylight."

"OK, let's do this. You can come and go through the house, by these stairs here. That would be less exposed. I'll give you a key to my door."

"Thanks. That would help. But that door's bolted on the other side."

"OK, I'll go down and unbolt it. You want to give me your key?"

"Sit still. Jerry will do the dishes." Lisa Beth put out a hand to halt Abby, who had started to rise.

"I'm happy to help," said Abby. "I feel like I should pull my weight if I'm going to stay here."

"Ah, don't worry," said Jerry, gathering plates. "You'll get your chance. For tonight you're a guest." He smiled, plump and benign in an apron that had MY KITCHEN MY RULES written on it in large red letters. The fringe of gray hair around his shiny bald dome was tousled and he was slightly flushed, whether with the effort of producing the meal or with excitement, Abby was not sure.

"Well, thank you. That was really delicious."

"I don't get a chance to make *sole meunière* very much because Lisa Beth doesn't like it. But she lets me make it when we have company."

"Not a fish fan," said Lisa Beth. She drained her wineglass. "Would you like some dessert? There may be some ice cream in the freezer if you're interested. We generally skip dessert. Our deal is that Jerry gets to nag me about my drinking if I can nag him about his weight."

"I'm fine, thanks."

"Well, let's repair to the library, shall we? Tradition calls for brandy and cigars, but I've given up smoking. Brandy I can do."

The library was a high-ceilinged room with floor-to-ceiling shelves jammed with books, deep armchairs, and a fireplace under a broad mantel. Through a tall window Abby could see a quiet tree-lined street, four blocks from the college. Lisa Beth strode straight to a sideboard with an array of bottles on it and uncorked one with dark amber contents. "Don't mind if I do," she said. "What can I offer you?"

Abby had brought her glass of water from the table. "I think I'm going to stick with this. What a lovely room."

"It is, isn't it? Most of the books are Jerry's, but it's become more or less my domain. He's got his office upstairs where he works, and I've set up my little nerve center here." She pointed with her chin at a desk in a corner near the fireplace where an open laptop sat in a welter of papers, folders, periodicals and books. "There are at least three unfinished books on that computer. Maybe four. Blistering exposés, every one. Reputation makers. Someday I hope to finish at least one of them. Sit, please. Take a load off. They released this Gómez today, did you hear?"

"I knew they were going to."

"They cut him loose after lunch. Apparently there was a long and contentious meeting in the prosecutor's office this morning. They cited an alibi, which has apparently stood up to investigation, and an unnamed witness who claimed to have seen the suspect at large. There wasn't much in the way of an official statement. This is major egg on the face for the prosecutor's office, of course. They weren't very forthcoming, and they sure as hell weren't happy about it. And you are the unnamed witness who upset the apple cart, aren't you?"

"I'm afraid so. Unnamed but possibly known to the killer."

"I don't know how you're holding up under the strain. You amaze me."

"I guess I just don't have any choice. Actually, I'm OK, except in the dark. I've gone back to being afraid of the dark, like a little kid. And the sound of sirens sets off a panic attack now, like it never did. You hear sirens all the time in Manhattan, you get used to them. Now, they terrify me."

"My God, you've probably got post-traumatic stress syndrome. You should talk to Jerry about it."

"I don't know about that. Lots of people have gone through worse."

Quietly, Lisa Beth said, "Honey, I can't believe what you've had to put up with. But we'll take care of you."

Suddenly, catastrophically, Abby was on the verge of tears. She scowled out the window into the dusk, breathing deeply. "Thank you," she managed to say finally. She raised her glass but it was empty. To cover her distress she stood and made for the sideboard. "Maybe I will have a small drink."

"Help yourself, please." Lisa Beth's old jocular tone was back. "So. Now that they've given up on this Gómez, maybe they'll blunder onto the real story."

Abby opened the cognac, poured half an inch into her glass, and went back to her chair. The cognac was as strong as Abby had expected and she coughed a little. "So what's the real story?"

Lisa Beth's eyes narrowed, looking out the window. "I don't know that I'm prepared to say, not yet. But I've been having all kinds of fun digging around in Mr. Lyman and Mr. Frederick's dirt." She smiled, not pleasantly. "I've got a nice little file on them on my computer. It's not the kind of dirt you'd find in a place like Chicago, for example, because we're not Chicago. They were small-timers, and this is the kind of small-time dirt, petty corruption and monkeyshines that you get in a small-time place like Lewisburg. I don't know that anybody would be prepared to kill over it. But then somebody thought those two were important enough to kill."

"So you think this guy I saw was a hired killer. I mean, isn't it possible he's just a psychopath or something?"

"That's possible, certainly. That may be the way the police are going to lean now. These weren't nice clean hits in the great mafia tradition. It seems to me there are several possibilities. The one the cops have been going on up till now is that they were exemplary executions, designed to scare people into toeing the line. That's the way a really nasty criminal organization like the Mexican cartels operates. Now, if that's not what happened, the second possibility would be that the guy is really,

really pissed off. Some kind of personal vendetta. Like these incidents that supposedly motivated Gómez. But now that seems to have been a dead end. So that leaves, as you said, the possibility that he's just really, really sick."

"And you don't buy that?"

"Well, he can hardly be normal. This business of making off with Jud Frederick's head is not exactly standard operating procedure for junkie burglars, to begin with. Have you asked yourself why he did that, by the way?"

"Um, I haven't given it a lot of thought, no."

"Well, I have. I think there are two obvious cases. One, as per the Mexican scenario, it's a warning. You dump it in front of somebody whose attention you want to get, someone you want to intimidate. Here's your business partner's head, now let's have no more misbehavior. Two, it's a trophy, or proof of fulfillment. You take it to prove to somebody that you've completed the job. Now, it hasn't shown up on anybody's front porch that I'm aware of. And if it was taken as a trophy, God knows where it wound up. But I can see a third way to use it, which would mean it might turn up yet."

"Good God, use it for what?"

"You could use it to incriminate someone. If I wanted to pin a killing on someone else, arranging to have the victim's head found, say, in his car trunk or in the freezer on his back porch would make for some awkward explanations."

Abby frowned. "That seems a little far-fetched to me."

"Perhaps. There's always the possibility he's just sick. But that brings me back to the point I was going to make. People who are really, really sick can be used. They can be employed by people who have more delicate sensibilities."

Abby drank, grimaced and swallowed. "That's horrible."

"Yes." Lisa Beth tossed off the last of her drink. "Much of life is. Did Jerry make up the bed in the den?"

22 |||||||

"The alibi in Indianapolis turned out to be solid. The state police confirmed it. So we were looking at having to let Gómez go anyway. Your sighting was just confirmation." Detective Ruffner's voice was a shade above a growl.

Abby sat at her desk with her phone to her ear. "I'm sorry."

"Please. We should be thanking you. It was a bad arrest, and I'm just glad it fell apart before it got to trial. The good news is, we think we might have a better lead."

"Really."

"We hope so. We put a couple of things together and a name popped up. We're trying to track him down now. This is someone who got out of prison recently. He has local connections and some history with both Lyman and Frederick. His mother actually lives there, at the trailer park. She swears she hasn't seen him since he got out of jail, but mothers lie a lot when cops come asking about their sons. We canvassed the trailer park and turned up nothing. Nobody else saw this guy. But he's on our radar. We're working on getting a current photo and when we do I'd like you to come take a look at it."

"OK, just let me know." Abby hesitated; the last thing a hardworking detective needed was advice from her, but then with a flutter of anger she thought that she did have a fairly high stake in this game. "Can I ask you a question?"

"Of course."

"Do you have any ideas, any leads, I don't know what to call them, about what's behind all this? I mean, if these killings were to cover something up? Or . . . something, I don't know."

There was a brief silence and Abby fancied she could hear Ruffner rolling his eyes. "We've looked pretty extensively into the background, yes. For both victims. I'm not sure what you're asking, specifically."

"Well, for example, I'm wondering if you know that Jud Frederick's girlfriend seems to have disappeared. I mean, that's what I was told. And I was wondering if that might be significant."

"You mean Ms. Atkins?"

"I don't know her name. I'm told she was Everett Elford's secretary."

"We've spoken with her. She's in Chicago, with a sister. She was quite upset by the killing and she went to stay with family."

"I see." So much for that mystery, Abby thought. "I'm sorry, I'm sure you have things well in hand."

"We're working overtime. This guy's around somewhere. He's living somewhere, he's eating and sleeping, leaving traces. We'll find him. I just can't say when."

"Thank you," Abby said. "I'll keep my fingers crossed."

At the student union Abby headed for the faculty table with her yogurt and wrap. She hesitated for an instant when she saw Graham sitting there, but decided she was not going to let him dictate her movements. With him were Adam Linseth and Steven Stanley, along with the chemist she had met at the Stanleys' party, his hair still in disarray. The chemist was saying, "Tammy wants a house. I got tenure and she's tired of renting. We just haven't found anything we really think is worth it. The best bargains seem to be on the east side of town, but that's kind of shaky. We looked at one right across from the trailer park the other day. The house was decent, but who wants to live over there?"

"A buying opportunity," said Graham. "Ripe for development."

"Aha," said Steven. "Is this some kind of *Chinatown* scenario? Is the steel plant planning to buy up all the land around there and send the property values through the roof, making you a wealthy man?"

Graham laughed. "Wrong side of town. And the only people the plant expansion is going to enrich are a couple of farmers. Actually, I advised the board against the expansion. I think there's going to be a worldwide steel glut for a while, and they'll regret this. But it looks like they're not going to listen to me. As for the east side, you never know how things are going to go. Somebody decides to build a shopping center across the stream there, all of a sudden it really is a happening place, and if you have property there, you're sitting pretty."

"Is that a tip?" said the chemist.

"No. Just speculating. But trailer parks have a way of vanishing when something more lucrative gets approved."

"Tough on the people that live there," said Abby.

Graham shrugged. "They get bought out and relocate. People move all the time."

"It could only improve the place, right?" said the chemist.

"I don't know," said Abby. "I actually know people who live there. They seem OK to me."

There was an awkward silence. Looking sheepish, the chemist said, "Sorry, nothing against your friends. Just retailing stereotypes, I guess."

Abby waved it off and the conversation moved on. Her mind wandered as she ate; she looked up and caught Graham watching her, a pensive look on his face. The party broke up as people wandered off to class or office hours. Graham lingered long enough to wind up alone with Abby. "You moved."

"Moved?"

"I ran into Jerry Collins. He said you moved in with them." Graham's look was quizzical. "Because the police advised you to or something?"

"Ah. Yeah. Well, not exactly." Abby frowned. "I had another sighting of the guy I saw at the scene of Lyman's murder."

"You're kidding."

"No. I happened to be out late at night, just giving someone a ride, and I saw him." She waved, vaguely. "Over on the east side of town."

"Whoa, hang on. I thought they had arrested the guy."

"Turns out it was the wrong guy. He had an alibi. They released him yesterday."

"Jesus." Graham looked genuinely shocked.

"And, well, somebody had been sneaking around my house at night. So it was decided I should take no chances and relocate, until the police find this guy. The detective I talk to tells me they've got an idea who it is. But they can't find him."

Graham just stared for a moment. "Oh, my God, Abby."

"He said he's probably got no reason to look for me. Just be careful and I should be OK. They're working overtime and blah, blah, blah. We'll see."

Graham shook his head, slowly. After a moment's hesitation he said, "Can I ask you something?"

"Sure."

"What's your relationship with Lisa Beth?"

Abby gaped, closed her eyes, shook her head. "Excuse me? My relationship? She's been a good friend to me. Why do you ask?"

He shrugged. "Just curious. I couldn't help but notice that you're pretty tight, that's all."

"And that is your business why, exactly?"

Now his look was a little harder. He leaned closer, lowered his voice. "I'm just trying for some clarity. I thought for a moment the other night that there was some chemistry here, you and me. But it kind of comes and goes. And the last thing I want to do is step on somebody else's toes, or get involved in some kind of rivalry. So I just thought I'd ask."

Astonished, Abby just stared. "What on earth are you insinuating?"

Now he was giving her a cold, flat look. "Abby, you can't possibly be unaware that Lisa Beth is gay. Or did the marriage fool you?"

When Abby found her voice she said, calmly, "If you're trying to insinuate that she has designs on me, that I'm in danger of being seduced or something, you're way off base. She has been a good friend to me, and nothing more."

He nodded, looking very slightly abashed. "All right, I'm glad to hear it. I just wanted to make sure you were aware." He sat back, hesitated, and said, "She's kind of notorious, actually, for her little affairs. There was a secretary in the admissions office a couple of years ago. That ended badly, with tears at the president's homecoming reception. And she was seen around town for a while, in some of the rougher bars, with some biker chick. It was a minor scandal. God knows what Jerry thinks of all this. They stay married. I just thought you should know. There's been a little speculation already about you two."

Abby sat oscillating between indignation and dismay. "Idle gossip," she said finally, her voice as cold as she could make it. "I assure you. Thanks for the heads-up."

He raised both hands, a gesture of concession. "I didn't know if I should say anything. I just wanted to be clear."

"Be clear. There's nothing there. As for the chemistry between you and me, just to be clear, I've enjoyed your company and hope to continue to do so. But whatever happened last weekend had a lot to do with alcohol, and that's not the right kind of chemistry. I'm not in the market for romance right now, I'm just not. I hope we can be good friends and colleagues, OK?"

He sat nodding slowly, a look of genuine regret stealing over his face. After a time he smiled, not the full wattage, and said, "Yeah, that's clear. Thank you."

- - - - - - - - - - - - - - - -

Abby considered herself a mathematician first and foremost; the quest for an elegant solution was a passion, and teaching was just a way to support the habit. But her research required large tracts of time and a certain amount of mental tranquility, both of which had been lacking for weeks, and she had been shamefully neglecting her work. Late in the afternoon, caught up on her grading and prepared for the next day's classes, Abby resolved to stay at her desk in Harrison Hall and devote a couple of hours to getting her research project back on track. She pulled her notes out of a drawer and set to.

The building emptied as she sat trying to find her way back into the work. She had previously realized that it would be enough to find a polynomial upper bound on the size of sum-free subsets. Would this follow from Bourgain-Katz-Tao? The last afternoon classes ended and students trooped by, making noise; Abby considered getting up to close her office door but they passed quickly and it was quiet again. Colleagues went ambling by, in conversation; Bill Olsen stuck his head in briefly and she assured him that her calculus class was back on track. A door slammed somewhere and it was quiet.

Absorbed at last, Abby became gradually aware of the dimming light. Outside, the sun was going down. The building had been quiet for some time. Footsteps sounded, somewhere close at hand.

Abby looked up from her notes. She identified the slightly labored sound of feet on stairs, ascending. The noise stopped. A few seconds passed and then somebody began walking up the hall, slowly, the creaking of the floor progressing toward her open door.

Abby waited, frozen, telling herself there was no reason to be afraid of a person walking slowly up the hall in a deserted college building, a building locked to outsiders. She was safe here; the campus was a protected enclave.

The footsteps halted. She could hear a distant clock ticking. She drew breath to call out, to ask who was there, but a reluctance to give away her position stopped her.

And suddenly she realized there was no reason on earth to assume that she was any safer on campus than anywhere else; that was a delusion. She remembered a notice sent around to faculty a couple of weeks before, campus security chiding people for leaving the little-used basement door on the west side unlocked as a shortcut to and from the student union.

Abby sat listening to the pounding of her heart. Jump up and close the door, she thought. Slam it shut and lock it, while there is still time.

The footsteps began again, and now they were close. Abby leapt up, dashed around the end of her desk, and swung the door shut with a bang. She flicked the turn lock and leaned on the door, listening, hearing nothing. Slowly she backed away and stood by the desk, waiting.

I have just embarrassed myself, Abby thought. Some startled colleague is wondering what on earth is wrong with me.

The footsteps resumed. They drew up at her door and Abby held her breath for a long moment. A knock sounded on the door, three times. A man's voice said, "Hello?"

"Who is it?"

"Security. Just checking. I saw your door open."

Abby sagged against the desk, light-headed. "Sorry. Sorry, just a minute." She recovered, stepped to the door, reached for the lock and stopped.

Anybody could say they were security, Abby thought. She drew breath and said, "I'm just working late. Everything's fine. Thanks for checking."

Seconds passed. Abby thought: What do I do if he won't go away?

"All right then, just making sure everything's OK." The man sounded very slightly peeved.

"Fine, everything's fine," Abby said, eyes closed, forehead pressed to the door, listening as the footsteps went away down the hall. "Thank you."

- - - - - - - - - - - - - - - -

When Abby let herself into Lisa Beth's house with the key she had been given, Lisa Beth's voice came from the study. "Walk softly. Ace reporter at work."

Abby stood in the doorway to the study. "Hi. Don't let me interrupt."

Lisa Beth shoved away from the desk. "Pour yourself a drink. How was your day?"

"Fine. A little nerve-racking. Actually, I think I'll skip the drink."

"Suit yourself." Lisa Beth rose and went to the sideboard. "Young Mr. Gill coming on strong, is he?" Lisa Beth smiled over her shoulder at Abby's startled look. "I have spies everywhere." She reached for a bottle of vodka. "Jerry saw you with him in the student union. He said it looked like an earnest conversation."

Abby thought carefully before she spoke. "Graham's doing what guys do. It's flattering."

Lisa Beth turned away from the sideboard, drink in hand. "I'm sorry. I don't mean to pry. The company you keep is none of my business."

Abby shrugged. "We're colleagues. That's all. That's all we're going to be. I've made that clear to him."

Lisa Beth sat at her desk and crossed her legs. She hoisted her drink and leveled a sharp look at Abby. "I have to say, I'm glad. I think he's bad news."

"How so?"

Lisa Beth drank and said, "He's a cad and a bounder. He hits on students."

Abby raised an eyebrow. "Oh, does he?"

"Two or three years ago it emerged he was bonking one of his advisees. Discreetly, but somehow it came out. There was a reprimand, I believe. She was a senior and no dewy-eyed innocent, probably, but it's still frowned upon. And it should be."

Abby nodded. "I see. I can't say I'm surprised."

"I commend your judgment. Sure you won't have a drink?"

"No, thanks, really." Abby hesitated. "He warned me about you, too."

Lisa Beth stared at her over the rim of her glass. Abby was already regretting giving in to the impulse. Lisa Beth said, "Did he? I suppose he told you I have designs on you."

"He said I should be aware of your history. I told him you had been a good friend to me and I was perfectly able to take care of myself." Abby hesitated. "Just for the record and in case there is any doubt, I am completely tolerant but completely heterosexual."

Lisa Beth took a sip of her drink with great deliberation and then sat looking into the glass. Her eyes rose to Abby's. "That was what I assumed from the start, and if I have given you any reason to think that I will not respect your boundaries, I deserve to be tarred, feathered and run out of town on a rail."

"None whatsoever." Abby grimaced. "I'm sorry. I shouldn't have said anything."

"Nonsense. It's always good to clear the air." They sat in silence for a moment, not looking at each other. Lisa Beth drank and said, "I've had a very interesting day. I spent a couple of hours in the basement of the courthouse, looking at records of land sales. You wouldn't believe how much land changes hands in a year around here. Or the hands it goes to. All very interesting."

"And this is in connection with . . . what?"

Lisa Beth rested her chin on her clasped hands, frowning at the computer screen. "Maybe with why Lyman and Frederick got killed. Just maybe."

"Oh, my God."

Lisa Beth relaxed, exhaling, closing her eyes. She swiveled on the chair and smiled at Abby. "But then maybe I'm just a fantasist."

23 |||||||

Abby stood at Lisa Beth's front window, looking out at a peaceful, sunlit small-town street. She needed clean clothes and a couple of hours in her own space. It was broad daylight and her rational mind was in control. She called Ned on her cell phone. "I'll be around," he said. "Come on by."

When Abby pulled into the driveway of 6 Hickory Lane, Ned was sitting on the steps, reading a magazine. He stood up as she approached. "All clear," he said, smiling. "Patrols report no suspicious activity."

"I know," Abby said. "I'm paranoid."

"Not at all." He waved her into the house and closed the door behind them. "I don't mean to make light of it. I talked with Mitch Ruffner again, and he said he doesn't think it's real likely that the guy's looking for you, but it makes sense to be careful."

Abby paused in the living room, wanting to linger. "I just wish I knew how long this was going to go on. I'm OK for now at Lisa Beth's but it's not a permanent solution."

"I can't tell you that." Ned stood with hands on hips. "What I can tell you is, I spent a couple of hours walking the streambed yesterday." He moved toward the window. "From the trailer park almost all the way to Shawnee Creek. The water's low at this time of year and it's easy to navigate. I got mud on my shoes and saw lots of trash and poison ivy, but I didn't see any signs of homicidal maniacs." He shot her a wry look over his shoulder. "For what that's worth."

Abby checked an impulse to go and join him at the window. "Have the police done that? Seems like that would be a good thing to do."

"Mitch told me the state guys went a couple of hundred yards or so each way from the railroad viaduct. I don't think they did much more than that. He said they got some footprints but weren't sure they meant anything. There are plenty of prints here and there, but a lot of them are just made by kids, fooling around. I used to do it. And deer tracks, yeah. Lots of deer."

He turned from the window. "There's a narrow stretch along the bank where you can see the back of the house through the trees. It's muddy, and it didn't look particularly trampled, the way it would if somebody had stood there watching. A few partial footprints, but then there are footprints all along. Probably associated with the beer cans you see everywhere. On the slope up to the yard here, there's some broken brush and matted grass, like from somebody climbing. But then the Schwartzes' grandkids were playing down there the other day. Bottom line, I don't know that there's any indication anybody's been watching you, but I can't rule it out."

Abby nodded. "OK. I'll take that into consideration." She stared out into the woods, wishing somebody could tell her what she should do. "Thank you."

Ned shrugged. "If you want to move back from Lisa Beth's, I don't think it would be wildly risky. You've got the key, and you can come and go through the house. You're not visible on the porch from down there. I don't know that it's any more dangerous here than anywhere else. But if you want to talk to Mitch about it, if you feel better somewhere else, I understand."

Abby took a deep breath. "That's all fine in the daytime. Let me see how I feel tonight, OK?"

Heading back toward campus, Abby did a double take as she approached the Poza Rica: Natalia was coming out the open door, carrying a cardboard box. Abby braked and swerved into the lot. Natalia's face brightened as she saw Abby get out of the car; she set the box on the floor of a van that stood with rear doors open and turned to greet her. They embraced and Natalia said, "The FBI let us back into the store, just to clean our stuff out. But it's all over. My daddy has a hearing in Indianapolis tomorrow about his plea deal and he'll find out how long he has to go to jail. My mama's going back to Mexico next week."

"Oh, Natalia, I'm so sorry."

Natalia shrugged with an expression that told Abby this was a girl who had suddenly left girlhood behind; she looked ten years older. "It is what it is. I'll be OK. I'm gonna live with Leticia and I'm looking for a job."

"Don't give up on going back to school."

"I'm not. I want to keep doing math, OK? Can we keep on meeting?"

"Of course. I'm kind of unsettled right now. I'm not actually staying at my place. But I hope to be back there soon."

"Is everything OK?"

"Oh, God, I wish I could tell you. It's all about . . ." Abby waved it all away. "I'm waiting for them to arrest this killer."

"Well, at least they're not saying it was us Mexicans anymore. Oh, God." Natalia stiffened, looking over Abby's shoulder.

"What?"

"Here's my brother. He was supposed to bring some guys to help out."

A dark-gray car pulled in off the street and skidded to a halt near the entrance to the store. The doors opened and three young Mexican men got out, one of them Luis. The two Abby had never seen nodded at the women and went into the store. Luis started to follow but halted and turned to come toward them, eyeing Abby with a sullen expression.

"You happy now?" he said. "No more Mexicans on the block."

"That's not what I wanted," said Abby.

Natalia exploded in a torrent of Spanish, leaning toward her brother. His expression darkened and he said something back that failed to stop the tirade. He made another couple of attempts to interrupt but finally gave up and listened, scowling, as Natalia shouted at him. Abby tensed as Natalia reached out and gave him a hard shove, but he merely staggered back a step and growled something. Finally Natalia fell silent and folded her arms, tears at the corners of her eyes.

Abby drew breath to beat a retreat but Luis froze her in place by muttering, "I'm sorry if I got the wrong idea. Thank you for helping my sister." He made brief eye contact with Abby and then turned and stalked toward the store.

Abby did not especially regret anything regarding Luis or his father, but she felt a response would be politic. To his back she said, "I'm sorry you lost the store."

Luis stopped and turned slowly to face her. "Yeah, well. Don't worry about it. I know who snitched on us, and I'll take care of it."

Abby and Natalia watched him go inside. "That's just talk," said Natalia, wiping her eyes with a finger. "That's just my brother talking big."

"I hope so," said Abby.

Abby's calculus section went well, considering the distracted state she had been in when she arrived on campus. She felt she was reaching the people she needed to reach. Any class contained some people who would learn no matter what she did and some who would never get it. A teacher earned her salary with the ones in between, who were capable but needed guidance. She had built a good esprit de corps, which had tottered a bit but recovered now that Ben was no longer in the class. Cole was back to being the class clown instead of an arm breaker, and

Giselle had nailed the last quiz and started to look like a serious math student.

I might be able to do this, Abby thought, watching Giselle guide a classmate through a problem on the board. This could be my life, for two years at least. "Well done," she said. "Who can differentiate that hairy-looking function in number six?"

After class she worked in her office for an hour, the door open, students and colleagues passing in the hall, making the old wooden floor creak. It seemed the least sinister place on earth. She finished her grading, dealt with e-mail, made a to-do list, pulled her research notes out of the drawer, and went to the student union for lunch.

She saw Graham holding forth at the faculty table and chose to sit by herself, looking at her notes. She had finished eating and was starting to gather her things when she looked up to see Graham approaching.

She tried to maintain a completely blank expression as he pulled up at her table. "I owe you an apology," he said.

Abby just blinked at him, thoughts racing. "For what?"

"For presuming to butt in to your personal life. For letting petty jealousy make me into an old gossip. For failing to keep things professional between us."

He looked completely sincere, attitude and self-regard under wraps. Abby exhaled. "Thank you. I appreciate that."

"I hope we can be good friends and colleagues."

After a moment she granted him a restrained smile. "Me, too."

He escorted her to her car parked behind the library. "I've got a meeting out at the steel plant this afternoon. They won't listen to anything I have to say, but they'll have gone through the motions of getting expert advice, and I'll get paid, so it's a win-win deal."

"Well, it sounds more interesting than writing a test for my analysis class."

He hesitated for a moment before saying, "Are you still at Lisa Beth's?"

"For the moment. Hoping for some good news from the police soon."

Graham nodded, frowning. His expression eased and he said, "OK. Give my regards to Lisa Beth."

When Abby let herself in she was surprised to hear the clicking of fingers on a keyboard coming from the study. She looked in and saw Lisa Beth at the desk, typing furiously at her laptop. "Working from home today," Lisa Beth said. "Jerry has the car up in Lafayette, seeing doctors."

"Is he OK?"

"Other than the high blood pressure, the cholesterol and the angina he's in the pink of health. Just routine stuff. Me, I'm on a roll here. I've got almost all of it in place."

"All of what?"

"The story. About why Rex Lyman and Jud Frederick got killed."

Abby watched her stab at the keyboard. "Are you serious?"

"Deadly. I can't tell you who that thug was who you saw that morning, but I think I have a pretty good idea who hired him."

Astonishment froze Abby in place for a few seconds. "Have you talked to the police?"

Lisa Beth looked up at her, intent. "Oh, I will. But I don't have anything that meets a legal standard as evidence. I just have a credible outline of the big picture. Everybody involved will have great deniability. And there are a couple of pieces I don't have yet. But I'm going to put it all together. Soon."

"So . . ."

"So whodunnit?" Lisa Beth leaned back on her chair, a deep frown on her face. "Rather than start throwing names around, let me finish this write-up. Then you can read it. OK?" Her look softened. "I want you to follow my reasoning. And it's not quite all there."

Stunned, Abby nodded. "OK. I'll be in the den."

Abby tried to work but couldn't concentrate. If she listened hard she could hear the faint noise of Lisa Beth's fingers on the keys, up front in the study. There were long periods of silence, once a murmur, Lisa Beth's half of a phone conversation. Abby sat with her face in her hands for a while. Up front, Lisa Beth spoke again, inaudibly. Then after a pause her footsteps sounded in the hall, coming back toward Abby's den.

She rapped on the door frame and leaned in. "Abby, sweetheart, I am so sorry to bother you. I'm in a bit of a fix."

"What's up?"

"I just got a call from a source that wants to meet me, like right now, at the Azteca. Would it be too much to ask for you to run me out there, ten minutes of your time? Just to drop me. You wouldn't have to hang around. I have no idea how long this will take."

"Um, sure." Abby shoved away from the desk. "Why don't you just take my car? I won't need it."

"Are you sure? That is so good of you. I will owe you forever."

Abby reached for her purse. "It's parked right out front."

Lisa Beth took the keys. "Thank you so much. You are a sweetheart. I'll bring it back as soon as I can."

"Do what you need to do. I'm not going anywhere."

Turning away, Lisa Beth halted for a moment. She said, "I think this is going to be the final piece," and then strode off up the hall.

Abby gave up on the test and made herself a cup of tea in Jerry's immaculate kitchen. She poked tentatively into the rooms on the ground floor, looking at books, pictures, knickknacks. On a shelf she found an astonishing wedding portrait of Jerry and Lisa Beth, both of them with fewer years and much more hair, Lisa Beth with a dark, severe beauty, clutching a bouquet.

Abby went back into the den and was finally able to settle to work. Time passed. Outside, the shadows began to lengthen. In the distance, a siren sounded, faintly.

Abby looked up from the computer screen. She stared out the back window at tree branches shifting lazily in a light breeze. Abby thought she heard a second siren join the first. It swelled and she was sure; for a moment they made a weird, disquieting harmony before they died away. She pushed away from the desk and sat rigid on the edge of the chair, her heart rate accelerating, drawing deep breaths. "Go away," she said out loud to the vivid image of Rex Lyman in the flames, pushing at the edge of her awareness. The sirens died away again. She listened for a long minute but there were no more. Her heartbeat subsided. She closed her eyes for a long moment and returned to work, fiercely mustering her concentration. Outside, the leaves reflected the golden light of early evening.

Steps sounded on the back porch, the kitchen door opened and Jerry called out, "Attention, ladies. Man on deck."

Abby went into the kitchen and greeted him. "Lisa Beth went off to meet a source. She didn't know when she'd be back."

Jerry smiled, looking skeptical. "Depends on how many drinks she has, probably. You like seafood? I've got some shrimp thawing."

"Seafood's good. Can I give you a hand?"

"Oh, no, thanks. Everything's under control. Just relax. Lisa Beth will come wandering in eventually." He reached for his apron on its hook, and Abby, finding nothing to say, went back into the den. She finished writing her test and picked up her phone. She commented on pictures Samantha had posted of the baby, listening to clatter and Jerry's soft humming in the kitchen. The doorbell rang.

Abby heard Jerry marching up the hall. She heard him open the door, heard soft voices, heard Jerry's voice raised in sudden distress. She put down her phone and stood up, her heart pounding. She went to the door of the den and looked up the hall to the front door. Jerry stood there in his apron; beyond him she could see a Lewisburg police officer in his black uniform standing on the porch.

Jerry turned at the sound of Abby walking up the hall. He looked as if he had taken an unprovoked punch to the face. He met Abby with wide eyes and said in a tone of baffled wonder, "Lisa Beth's been shot."

24 |||||||

Abby knew; she had known from the moment she had seen the policeman at Jerry's front door. She had known as she held Jerry's hand in
the back seat of the patrol car racing up Lafayette Road toward Mercy
Hospital. Rising from a chair in an office just off the emergency room
as a doctor in scrubs came in, she realized she had known the instant
she heard the sirens swelling in the distance in the late afternoon. She
began reaching for Jerry even before the doctor opened his mouth and
hesitated for an instant, looking from her to Jerry, before saying, "I'm
sorry."

Jerry must have known, too; as Abby's arms went around him he
said, "She's dead, isn't she?"

"I'm afraid so," said the doctor. "She probably died instantly. Her
injuries . . ."

"Don't tell me," said Jerry, pulling away from Abby and collapsing
onto a chair, knocking it back against the wall. "I don't want to hear
it." He sat with a dazed, despairing look, focused on nothing. "I don't
believe it. I won't believe it."

Abby sat beside him and slipped her arm through his. The policeman had come quietly into the room behind the doctor and now he
said, "Detective Ruffner's on his way. We're going to need you to
identify the body."

Abby looked at him, feeling a deep, incandescent rage beginning to build. "I have things to tell Detective Ruffner," she said.

"It's all on her computer. She was working on the story when she got the call to go meet her source. She had it all figured out. Look on her laptop."

Ruffner put a hand on her arm to steer her back into the office where she and Jerry had waited. The detective looked harried and distracted, having just entrusted a dazed and shambling Jerry Collins to two patrolmen who were to take him home. He closed the door and turned to Abby. "Did she mention any names?"

"No. She said she didn't want to throw names around until she had all the pieces in place. But she said she had figured out who was behind it. Who paid the killer. And then she . . ." Abby had to stop. Her throat had seized up and she could barely breathe. She closed her eyes, managed to take a breath. "And then she got the call." Abby could feel the first waves of grief pounding against the barrier of her shock like a storm surge against a seawall.

She opened her eyes to see Ruffner giving her an anxious look. "Why don't we sit down," he said gently. "You don't have to do this now."

"I'm all right." Abby drew a deep breath. "Tell me what happened to her."

Ruffner gave her a long look before he answered. "She was shot in her car, in the parking lot. She was shot at close range. Once in the head and once in the neck."

"So it was quick."

"Instantaneous, I'd say. Now tell me something."

"What?"

"What was she doing in your car?"

"I let her borrow it. Jerry had their car up in Lafayette."

"I guess I don't have to spell out the implications of her getting shot sitting in your car."

Abby shook her head. "I wasn't the target."

"Why not?"

"Because of that phone call. She was set up."

"Did she tell you who was on the phone?"

"No. She just said it was a source. She said she thought it was going to be the final piece of the story."

Ruffner thought for a second and said, "If the killer was looking for a woman with short brown hair in a Ford Focus, Lisa Beth fit the bill. But that could be your description, too."

"If I was the target it would have happened somewhere else. There were plenty of chances. If they were looking for my car, they would have picked it up at my house, or at the college. I'd have been shot behind the library, probably. Lisa Beth was shot at the Azteca because somebody told her to go there. I think this was all about her. I don't think I was ever in danger. If that man didn't care that I saw him that morning, he doesn't care now. He's never cared."

Ruffner held her eyes for a long moment. "Did she say anything about a Mexican angle? Because of where it happened, we're back to thinking about that."

"No. She thought the whole Mexican thing was nonsense. But if somebody wanted to get the police thinking about a Mexican angle, setting her up there would be a good way to do it."

"Maybe. It was a good way to produce a bunch of witnesses who suddenly forgot how to speak English, that's for sure."

"Somebody must have seen something."

"Yeah. We found a customer who was in the restaurant, by a window. She noticed Lisa Beth because she pulled up and parked, but she never got out. Then after a while another car pulled in next to hers, but headed the opposite way, window to window. Like the driver wanted to talk to her, the witness said. The next time she looked, the other car was gone and she couldn't see Lisa Beth anymore. She thought she'd just gotten out of the car. Then somebody else pulled in and saw the body, slumped over. That's when we got called."

"So she saw the killer?"

"Not much of a look. She thinks it was a man. Driving a dark-colored car, maybe a Honda. No plate number, but that would be asking a lot."

Abby felt the rage pushing against the lid. "If you take me back to her house I can show you the computer."

Ruffner frowned at her. "What I'd like you to do is come to the station with me and give me a statement. Then we'll see about the computer. I'll need her husband's permission or a warrant for that. OK?"

"Let's go," said Abby.

Abby thanked the policeman who dropped her in front of 6 Hickory Lane and got out of the patrol car. Night had fallen, the electric sound of the crickets pervading the cooling air. An unfamiliar car was parked in Ned's driveway. Abby had intended to go into her apartment directly through the back door, but when she went up onto the porch she pulled Ned's key out of her purse. She hesitated and then rang his bell.

He opened the door and stiffened, surprised. "Hey."

"I'm sorry. I didn't want to just barge in."

Ned stood back, pulling the door open. "Please." He watched her closely as she came in. "Are you all right?"

"No, I'm not all right. You heard about Lisa Beth?"

"We heard. I'm sorry, it's horrible."

"Who's here?"

"Everett. We were just talking about it. Come on in." He led Abby into the kitchen.

Everett Elford sat at the table, one plump forearm resting on it. A bottle of bourbon and two glasses sat in front of him. "Hi," he said. He wore a deep frown.

Ned pulled out a chair. "You want to join us?"

Abby was paralyzed for a moment. Did she? She decided it was better than being alone. "Thank you," she said, and sat.

"Want anything to drink?"

"Water." She hung her purse on the back of the chair. "Please."

Ned opened the refrigerator. Elford said, "Lisa Beth was a pain in the ass sometimes, but she did her best to make that crummy little paper a real news outlet. Even a place like Lewisburg needs somebody to keep the politicians honest and get out the vote. I thought she took herself a little too seriously sometimes, but I give her credit. She made that paper better, and that made this town better."

Ned set a glass of water in front of Abby and sat. He took a drink of bourbon. "Pretty good epitaph."

Abby settled for saying, "She was a good friend to me. My first friend here." Her voice had gone husky.

They sat in silence for a time. Elford emptied his glass, uncorked the bottle, and poured himself two more fingers. Ned waved off the bottle and said, "Have you talked to the police?"

"I just got done with them. They have a witness." Abby halted, poised to tell them about the computer, about Lisa Beth's story. She said, "Somebody saw it happen, from the restaurant. That's all I know."

Ned said, "What was she working on? Do they know?"

Elford said, "I'm sure they'll find out soon enough. The question is: What goes on around here that's worth killing a reporter?"

Ned frowned. "I would have asked the same question about a lawyer and a real estate guy."

Ned and Elford exchanged a long look. "If this is connected to the others," said Elford, "that's really, really interesting."

Abby sat with her mouth firmly shut, remembering Lisa Beth talking about land sales, remembering Ned telling her that Everett Elford was the biggest landowner in the county, remembering Elford and Ingstrom, and Ned talking about skeletons in closets.

"If this is connected to the others," said Ned, "that's really, really frightening. If you ask me." He turned to Abby. "Where are you staying tonight?"

Abby was still thinking about Everett Elford, and it took her a second to refocus. "Probably Jerry's tonight. I just came to pick up a few things." She blinked at Ned. "Can you maybe give me a ride over there? I lent my car to Lisa Beth."

Ned stared, and she could see when the penny dropped. He put his hand over hers. "Ah, shit," he said.

Abby used the key Jerry had given her to let herself into Lisa Beth's house. The first person she saw, coming up the hall, was Ruth Herzler. "Oh, Abby." Ruth reached for her, looking stricken. "So awful." They embraced, and Ruth held her for a few seconds.

Abby disengaged. "How's Jerry?"

Ruth shrugged, on the edge of tears. "As you'd expect. His sister and her husband are driving up from Terre Haute. They should be here soon. We're all in the kitchen. I'm working on getting some kind of dinner together."

In the kitchen Philip Herzler and Jerry were sitting at the table. A teapot and two cups on saucers sat in front of them. Jerry looked old, tired, deflated. Ruth went to the stove, where something was simmering. Abby nodded at Philip and sat down across from Jerry. "I've been talking to the police. They're going to come and look at Lisa Beth's computer."

Jerry's expression was bleak, remote. "They already did. That Ruffner came and took the computer away, along with a lot of papers and things."

Herzler said, "Lisa Beth had everything password protected. He managed to get logged on, but she'd put a password on most of her documents, too. And that's a lot harder to crack. So Ruffner just took everything he could find, notebooks and so on, where she might have written down her passwords. And he said there are ways to get by the passwords if they can't find them. Do you know why they want the computer?"

"Lisa Beth had been working on something that had to do with these other murders. She told me she thought she knew who was behind them. She'd written it all down."

Ruth turned from the stove. "Oh, dear God. Poor Lisa Beth."

Jerry said, "They killed her because she was writing a story about it?"

"She went to meet a source. That's what she told me. So it looks like it was about the story, yeah."

Voice breaking, Ruth said, "Oh, God, it's a *nightmare*." She reached out and Philip took her hand.

"She did it," said Jerry. "She finally did it. She broke a really important story."

25 |||||||

Jerry's sister was a female version of him; her hair had curled and whitened instead of falling out, but she had given in to the same tendency to embonpoint. She limped a little, wincing occasionally as she moved about the kitchen. Her husband sat at the table, gray and hatchet-faced, black brows clamped down in generalized disapproval.

"Are you one of Lisa Beth's friends?" the sister said, moving to the table and sitting with a grimace.

Abby took a second or two trying to decode that and said, "Jerry and Lisa Beth were just about the first friends I made here. They have both been very good to me."

That seemed to satisfy the sister, who put her chin on her hand and assumed a thousand-yard stare.

The husband said, "Probably one of her dyke friends that killed her."

Abby turned on her heel and went up the hall into the library. Lisa Beth's desk looked bare without the computer. Abby stood for a moment thinking of Lisa Beth bent over the keyboard, tapping out the exposés that were going to make her reputation. A weight settled on her heart.

The floor creaked behind her and she turned to see Jerry in the doorway. "I can't believe she's not coming back," he said.

"Oh, Jerry. I'm so sorry." Abby didn't know what there was to say besides platitudes when a man's wife was murdered.

Jerry came into the room, his eyes falling on the sideboard. "Who's going to drink all that booze now?" He picked up a couple of bottles, examining the labels. "The drinking would have killed her eventually. Her liver was going." He turned and gave Abby a rueful look. "But it would have been nice to be able to take care of her when she got sick."

Abby wept silently. Jerry stared for a few seconds and said, "I knew she was gay when I married her. I think I knew it before she did. And she figured out that I was terrified of sex, probably because of my brutally religious upbringing. I guess we were a good match. Her little affairs never bothered me. I was actually happy for her. It was a marriage of convenience. But you know what? I really did love her."

He stood gazing at the floor, one hand on the sideboard. Grumbling voices drifted up the hall from the kitchen; a car sighed by on the street outside. Struggling to find her voice, Abby said, "She was a good friend to me."

After a moment Jerry roused himself and said, "I'm forgetting what I came down here for. I'm so sorry to do this to you. You see, Lisa Beth's nephew Tom is driving over from Indianapolis, it turns out, and he's expecting to stay here. And that's going to make for a very full house. I was wondering . . ." Jerry faltered.

"Jerry, of course." Abby was immensely relieved. "I'll go back to my place."

"I do so appreciate everything you've done. You're such a sweetheart. There's a reason Lisa Beth loved you." He stood in front of her, looking dazed and drained and desolate.

Abby drew a deep breath, knowing she had to cut this off or everyone was going to lose it. "Let me go grab my things."

"Oh. Another thing." Jerry reached into the pocket of his robe. "I found this in the bedroom." He pulled a small spiral-bound notebook from the pocket and held it out to Abby. "Maybe the police should see it, I don't know. Lisa Beth kept notes in it. I don't know if it means anything."

Abby opened the notebook. The pages showed scraps of writing, a haphazard scrawl in black ballpoint, barely legible. Abby made out:

Elford pd $850K for 200 acres ($4,250 / acre) 6/16/15

She turned over a page.

> *easement: 140 acres*
> *IDT to pay $2.41 mil ($17,214 / acre)*
> *profit: $1.56 mil on $850K investment*

Abby's heart had quickened. There were other notations below:

> *appraisers: easement worth $658,800*
> *IDT ignored valuations—Ingstrom?*

Abby flipped pages and saw another name she knew:

Frederick bought 100 acres 7/24/15.

She looked up at Jerry. "Yeah, I think this might be important. I will see that the police get this."

"Thank you so much. I'll have Lou run you home."

"Um, that would be great."

The brother-in-law looked affronted but agreed to give Abby a ride. In the car Abby made no attempt at conversation beyond giving terse directions, thinking about Lisa Beth's notebook in her purse. When they pulled into Ned's driveway, lights were on behind curtains but Elford's car was gone. Abby stood on the porch and watched as the brother-in-law backed out and pulled away. She could feel the rage building. She looked at Ned's door for a moment, thinking about him and Everett Elford sitting together drinking, and dug in her purse for her keys. She hoisted her bags, crossed the porch, and went down the stone steps, triggering the light on the eaves. I am not afraid, she thought. That's over. The halo of light just reached the edge of the woods at the top of the slope.

Abby let herself into her apartment. It was dark inside. She stepped to the nearest lamp and switched it on. She strode across the room, dropping her purse on the coffee table, opened the door to her bedroom, switched on the light and tossed her pack onto her bed. She went into the study and took her laptop out of its bag, set it up on the desk and booted it up. She stood for a moment listening: above her, in Ned's house, she could hear music playing, faintly, a languorous jazz tune. Abby went into the kitchen and turned on the light, poured herself a glass of apple juice. She went back into the study and pulled Lisa Beth's notebook out of her purse.

Abby sat at her desk and read through the notes again. Some were cryptic: *I-69.* Some were clear: *landowners sold easements.* She brought up her web browser on the computer. A search for *I-69 easement IDT* and a little exploration brought up an article that clarified some things: *State acquires land for interstate extension.* Abby read about how the Indiana Department of Transportation was intending to purchase land to complete an interstate that came up from Texas, heading for Canada by way of Indianapolis. *Secrecy in land sales criticized,* read a subheadline.

Upstairs, just audible, cutting through the soft music, the doorbell rang. Above Abby's head the ceiling creaked. Footsteps sounded and then died away. Abby read on: *Elford sold to Frederick: why?* Below that, underlined three times, was the word *blackmail.*

She skimmed through pages of notes, one line catching her eye: *Outlaws Ingstrom clients.* Here was another name at the bottom of a page: *Duggan acquitted 9/19/04.* Abby searched online and found the case without too much trouble, reported in the *Star: Biker walks on murder charge.*

Abby skimmed the article and read how Bart Duggan's attorney, Ron Ingstrom, had persuaded a jury that Duggan could not have beaten a man to death outside a bar on the east side of Indianapolis because the witness's identification of him could not be relied on.

In the accompanying picture Bart Duggan looked nothing like the man Abby had seen; he was too heavy and had a full beard. But here was another note in Lisa Beth's writing: *Outlaws paid Ingstrom retainer.* Abby searched online and found several articles about the Outlaws motorcycle gang and their involvement in racketeering, extortion, drugs and gambling in central Indiana, and their go-to lawyer, Ron Ingstrom. All the articles dated from the first decade of the century, before Ron Ingstrom had gone into politics and become the go-to guy if you wanted to get elected to Congress.

The ceiling creaked above Abby's head. She could just make out the murmur of voices. She opened another online article: *Outlaws gang uses violence to maintain hold on rackets.* A mug shot accompanied the article; a biker convicted of severing a man's finger with pruning shears was glaring into the camera lens. Again the face was not familiar, but a type was emerging.

How could I ever have thought he looked Mexican? Abby asked herself.

A line on the fifth page of Lisa Beth's notes read: *Ingstrom covering up?*

Abby ran her eye over the notes one more time, wanting to be sure she had her thoughts in order before she called Ruffner. She laid the notebook on the desk next to her computer and stood up. Her phone was in her purse, which she had dumped on the coffee table out in the living room.

She heard a door open.

Abby froze. It had sounded as if the door was in her apartment. Her heart began to pound.

When the footsteps began to come slowly down the stairs, Abby almost collapsed with relief. The door she had heard opening was the one at the top of the stairs. Ned had heard her moving around and was coming to offer her a glass of wine. She went out into the living room. "Hello? Ned?"

The man who reached the bottom of the stairs in the far corner of the room and stepped around the newel post into view was not Ned. He wore cargo pants and Chuck Taylors and a black T-shirt that exposed his tattooed arms, and he had long dark hair swept back and hooked over his ears and a moustache that curled around the corners of his mouth down onto his chin and piercing black eyes. He halted as he caught sight of Abby.

He smiled at her, again.

26 |||||||

Shock kept Abby in place for what seemed like a long time; she simply could not process what she was seeing. It was impossible, but here he was. Then her autonomic nervous system went to work, every alarm bell in her psyche going off as the hormones flooded into her blood. Her heart kicked in her chest and she gasped as she sucked in the breath she would need to fight or flee.

"Well, I'll be damned," said the man, still smiling. "Who we got here?" The voice made him real, jolting Abby out of shock mode. It was a Hoosier voice like all the others, and as he came away from the stairs, walking slowly into the middle of the room, amusement in the glittering black eyes, the dread that had haunted Abby for weeks crystallized in her tunnel vision into a very concrete threat.

Her knees had gone weak but she steadied herself with her hands on the door frame. Her mind began to work again. The bathroom was just to her left, and there was a lock on the door. There were also no windows, no way out. The bathroom was a cul-de-sac. Her phone was in the bag on the coffee table, fifteen feet from her and three feet from the man.

"Thanks, don't mind if I do," the man said, advancing past the coffee table. He was ambling, in no hurry, looking around, comfortable.

There were knives in the kitchen. She could dash across the alcove, tear her eight-inch vegetable knife out of the drawer, retreat into the laundry room, and be ready to slash him when he opened the door. Abby started to lean.

"What's the matter, cat got your tongue?" He was ten feet from her now, and Abby had to choose: the long dash to the drawer in the kitchen, a fumble among the utensils, maybe a struggle; or the two steps to the bathroom. Her capacity to plan collapsed and she darted to her left, ducked into the bathroom, slammed the door and pushed the button on the knob to lock it. She leaned on the door, her ear to it. She heard the man take a couple of steps. The doorknob rattled a little and was still. She heard him say, "Well, shit."

Abby backed away from the door. He could not get to her now, but she was trapped. Nobody would hear her, no matter how loudly she screamed. She stood with her heart pounding, listening. She heard soft steps, rubber squeaking faintly on linoleum, then she heard nothing.

The nothing went on for seconds, a minute, then more. Abby sat on the closed toilet, her legs giving way. If he could not get at her, he would go away. He would steal some things and go away.

A truer and more crucial insight followed: he did not come here to steal.

Where is Ned? Abby's thought processes were stabilizing. Her first, horrifying thought was that Ned was hurt, lying bleeding on the floor somewhere above her head.

Her second thought was worse: Ned let him in. She remembered the doorbell. There had been a murmur of voices, and then the man had come down the stairs, through the door that Abby had not bolted.

Ned let him in.

Ned whom she had last seen drinking with Everett Elford. Ned who had an ossuary in his closet. Ned whom she had thought she knew.

Steps approached the door. There was a scratching noise and the button on the knob popped out. The door swung open and there was the man, smiling at her again, close now, close enough that she could see the scars on his brow, the gray in the tails of his Fu Manchu, the gleam in his eye. He held up a thin piece of wire, a straightened paper clip. "These here locks are easy," he said. "They make 'em easy so your kids can't lock themselves in the shitter." He tossed the paper clip onto the vanity, next to the sink.

Abby had backed into the tub, as far as she could get from the door. She was heaving great breaths, hyperventilating. The flight option had never really been there. There was nothing left but the fight. Abby remembered her father talking to her after an escape from a drunken groper on a subway platform: "If it ever really gets serious, fight dirty. Go for the eyes, go for the nuts. Hurt the son of a bitch."

The man leaned casually on the doorjamb, the smile fading. "What the fuck you so agitated about?"

A few more breaths allowed Abby to settle enough to squeeze out in a quavering voice, "What do you want?"

"Well, since you're askin', you got a car?"

This astonished her so much that it took her a few seconds to answer. "No. Not anymore."

"Well, you're no fuckin' help then, are you?" He glared at her for a few seconds. "You a friend of Ned's?"

He does not know who I am, Abby thought, with sudden illumination. And that is why I am still alive. "He's my landlord," she managed.

"You fuckin' him?"

"What? No."

"Well, shit. Don't act so high and mighty. You too good for that, are you?"

Abby could only shake her head. I am about to be raped, she thought. Can I take that? Can I survive that?

He was leering at her, his eyes going up and down the length of her body. "A college girl, huh? God damn, I wish I'da gone to college."

Abby closed her eyes. "Don't hurt me," she said, thinking: here it comes.

Somewhere out in the apartment a voice called out. "Kyle?"

The man looked over his shoulder. "Yo! Down here." He pushed away from the door and ambled back toward the living room.

Stunned, Abby gaped at the empty doorway. That had been Ned's voice. She listened as he came down the stairs. She heard him say, "What the hell, man? This is my tenant's place."

"Yeah, me and your tenant was just gettin' acquainted."

"*What?*"

"Don't get excited, I didn't do nothin' to her. Come on out here, sugar." Abby ran wildly through her options, then stepped out of the tub and walked slowly out into the living room. The tattooed man was standing by the bookshelves, slouching and nonchalant. And there at the foot of the stairs was Ned, staring at her with an appalled look. "What the hell are you doing here?" he said. "I thought you were gone."

It took Abby a couple of seconds to find her voice, and when it came it wavered a little. "Ned, what's going on? Who is this and what is he doing here?"

Ned sagged a little, his eyes going from Abby to the man and back. "This is my friend Kyle. I'm sorry, he shouldn't be down here."

"Shit, man. You run off and left me and I just thought I'd poke around a little, see what your crib's like. And here she was."

Ned's look hardened. "Yeah, this is her place. Look, Kyle. I got the beer, now let's go back upstairs and leave Abby alone."

Kyle looked at Ned for a moment, and then he turned and looked at Abby. He shook his head. "Well, now, I'm not sure I can do that."

"Why not?"

"Because Abby here knows who I am. Even if she ain't lettin' on. The second we leave, she's gonna go right out that door and run to the cops." He turned to Abby. "I like the haircut, by the way. Makes you look kinda cute."

Abby's legs gave way and she slumped back against the wall and then slid slowly down to the floor. Kyle was watching her and there was no smile now; his eyes were absolutely dead. Abby looked at Ned and said, "Help me."

Ned said, "Kyle. It's not going to do you any good to hurt anybody else. What you need now is to get the hell out of the county. Take my car." Ned dug in a pocket and pulled out a ring of keys and tossed them to Kyle. "Take the damn car and split. You're out of time."

Kyle looked at the keys in his hand. He looked at Ned and he looked at Abby sitting with her back to the wall. He looked back at Ned and said, "Fuck, no. I ain't going by myself. You're coming with me."

"And Abby stays."

Kyle reached behind his back, under the tail of the T-shirt, and tugged. When the hand reappeared it was holding a big black automatic. "You're both coming with me. I don't want her talking to police ten seconds after we go out the door. You and her both come with me. I get a good piece down the road, I'll drop you somewhere."

Ned and Kyle had a long staredown then. Abby was still trying to get her head around the fact that her landlord was on first-name terms with the devil; by the time she had worked out that what Kyle was suggesting was a good scenario for a nice isolated shooting, the staredown was over and Ned was saying, "OK, let's go."

Kyle threw the keys back to Ned. "You're driving." He strode to where Abby was sitting and grabbed her arm, pulling her up. "Come on, sweetheart. We're going for a ride."

"I can walk." Abby jerked her arm free of his grip. Her voice was clear and strong; she was discovering the power of rage. Her eyes met Ned's as she crossed the room toward the stairs and what she saw in them looked like shame.

"You go first," Kyle said to Ned.

Ned nodded and turned to the stairs. He looked at Abby and said, "I won't let him hurt you."

Mounting the steps, Abby said, "That would be nice," putting as much acid into it as she could. She was floating now, electric, suffused with adrenaline and a blistering anger.

Over his shoulder Ned said, "Put the gun away, Kyle. We all want the same thing. Everybody here wants you to get free and clear."

"Suits me," said Kyle. "I like it when everyone gets along. Once I'm sure we're all friends, you won't see it no more."

They followed Ned up the stairs and through the kitchen. He opened the back door and led them across the porch, unlocking the garage door with his key. "You're driving, me and Abby'll be in the back," said Kyle.

Abby's mind was racing. She thought for a second about a wild leap off the porch and a sprint for the woods, but the touch of Kyle's hand on her arm kept her going into the garage. Ned pressed a button to raise the garage door and they all got in the car as Kyle had instructed, Abby directly behind Ned and Kyle on her right. He held the gun in his lap, casually, a man without a concern in the world. He didn't bother with his seat belt. Ned started the car and backed out of the garage. He wheeled around to point the car down the road toward Jackson Avenue and said, "I'm assuming you want the interstate."

"Not yet," said Kyle. "I'm not quite done with this town. I got one more thing to do."

Ned said, "I'm not driving the getaway car for any shootings, Kyle. I'm telling you."

Abby drew a sharp breath. Kyle said, "Relax, will ya? I just got a message to deliver."

"So where we going?" Ned was looking at Kyle in the rearview mirror.

"Take us to the Tarkington," said Kyle.

27 |||||||

Nothing seemed to have changed at the Tarkington since Abby had spent her first night in Lewisburg; these could have been the same pick-ups parked in the same spots. "Just pull up by the stairs there and park," said Kyle in a low voice. "Shut her off and gimme the keys."

Ned parked and handed the keys back over the seat. Kyle took them and then they all sat in silence for a moment. Tonight there didn't seem to be a party going; very faintly Abby could hear a murmur of television behind a door somewhere. "What are we doing here?" Ned said finally.

"We're here to get ahead," Kyle said.

"What the hell are you talking about?"

Kyle laughed softly. "You'll see. Here's what's gonna happen. Me and Abby are gonna go up those steps there to the top deck. You're gonna sit here and hold the fort."

"Kyle, I'm telling you. You do anything to her, it's over. All bets are off. You understand me?"

"I ain't gonna hurt her. Just chill." Kyle turned to Abby. "I'm gonna come around and let you out, and we're gonna go up those steps. Holding hands, just like sweethearts. OK?"

Abby drew a deep breath. "OK."

Kyle leaned forward and stuffed the gun down the waistband of his shorts in back. Then he got out and came around to Abby's side and opened the door to let her out. This is where the rape is going to happen, she thought, of course. By the time she had gotten out of the car he was blocking her way, cutting off any chance for a sudden break. He took her hand.

"This is where dudes come to cheat on their wives," he said. "My cousin Susie caught her husband coming out of a room here with some other guy's wife, and she took a baseball bat to him." He and Abby mounted the steps. "Broke his arm with it." He was scanning as they climbed, looking out over the parking lot, searching the deserted walkways on the other wing of the motel.

They reached the second level, nightmarishly familiar. Abby's heart had accelerated again, and she was weighing the idea of starting to scream, struggle, trying to break free. Would he really shoot her?

"Here we are." He had halted at the ice machine, a big white-painted metal cabinet on four legs, ICE stenciled vertically on its side panel. "Too bad we don't have a cooler, but we ain't goin' that far." Still grasping Abby's hand, he raised the lid, revealing a chamber full of glistening cubes. He plunged his hand deep into the ice, frowning with the effort, and began to root around. Abby watched, bewildered, until he gave a soft grunt, stiffened his arm and pulled.

Ice spilled out of the machine onto the concrete with a clatter as he hauled out a plastic bag that had been buried at the bottom of the ice chamber. The bag was knotted at the top and appeared to be holding something about the size of a soccer ball, or maybe half a watermelon. Abby took a step back, pulling against the man's grip.

"Where the fuck you goin'?" He firmed his grip and pulled her back. "Shut that lid, will you?"

Abby steadied and obeyed, and then he was pulling her toward the stairs again. "OK, we got what we came for." Abby was light-headed with relief at not being dragged into a room. They went down the steps, hand in hand. His grip was strong, his hand rough and a little greasy. As they reached the bottom a man was coming along the walk from the direction of the office. With a flare of dismay Abby recognized the pale, thin clerk who had checked her in on her first night.

He was heading directly for them, purposefully. "That ice machine is for the use of our guests only," he said.

"Shit, we're guests." Kyle halted, squaring up for a confrontation.

"No, you're not. I just watched you drive up." The clerk slowed as he neared them; Abby could see him having second thoughts as he got a closer look at the man he was dealing with.

"And you can't spare a little ice for our six-pack here?"

"You can't just come in and grab some ice any time you feel like it. That's for people staying at the motel." The clerk's eyes came to rest on the bag and she could see him wondering what kind of six-pack made a plastic bag bulge like that.

Jutting his chin toward him, Kyle said, "Well, partner, what are you gonna do about it? You gonna make us put it back?"

The clerk backed away a step or two, his expression hardening. "I could call the police. That's theft."

Kyle released Abby's hand and shifted the bag to his left. As he started to reach under his shirttail, Abby said, "I'm sorry. It's my fault. It was my idea."

That halted everything as the two men stared at her. The clerk's eyes widened a little and Abby could see recognition dawning. "I remembered the ice machine from when I stayed here last month. I apologize. Can we just pay you for the ice?" She looked the clerk in the eye, watching as an expression of incredulous disgust grew. Yes, she wanted to tell him, it's me. Things haven't gone so well for me here.

The clerk's face went carefully blank again. "That's OK," he said. "I wouldn't know what to charge you for it. Just, please. Have a little respect. Don't do it again." He turned away, his eyes showing he knew how close he'd come to serious unpleasantness as they met the other man's, fleetingly.

They watched him walk back toward the office and then got back in the car. Kyle handed Ned the keys over the seat. "You done good," he said to Abby. "I didn't have to shoot him."

"If you'd shot him we'd have all kinds of problems," Ned said.

"You owe me one," said Abby.

Kyle laughed softly. "OK, I owe you. Now we got an errand to run. Start 'er up and let's get goin'."

Ned started the car. "Where to?"

"Out South Street. We're going to the big arch."

28 |||||||

"Kyle, what are you doing?" said Ned. "All you should be thinking about is getting the hell out of town." He was steering with one hand on the wheel, keeping it under thirty miles an hour, heading out South Street past the Tippecanoe College campus. On the back seat, Abby sat leaning against the door, as far as she could get from Kyle and the plastic bag that sat between them.

Kyle said, "Well, I gotta do something with my trophy here. And you said Everett don't deserve it, so I guess the best thing to do is just leave it where I left that other motherfucker. Sittin' in the middle of the road. Although I still kinda like the idea of handing it to Everett. Just to see his face."

"I told you, Everett had nothing to do with it."

"And I believe you. I guess I don't really have no problem with Everett except he's richer 'n shit. Always had everything handed to him. Never had to fight for nothin'."

"Some people are just lucky," Ned said.

"And some of us are fucked from the git-go, I know." A minute passed in silence as they cruised along frat house row. Kyle said, "Everett and his daddy used to come by our house every year, delivering Christmas baskets from the Elks Club, for the poor folks. Which was us, we didn't have shit. And my ma would make me say thank you to

Everett, who sat next to me in school and used to laugh at me and my sister, along with all the others."

"Yeah, kids can be assholes," said Ned. "I'm sorry if I ever laughed at you."

"Naw, you were cool. Anyway, I got over it. I guess all I wanted was for Mr. Everett Elford to have his nose rubbed in it a little bit."

"Let it go, Kyle."

"Well, I gotta do something with this thing. When the cops started talking about Mexicans, that gave me the idea. I was gonna plant it somewhere, make this look like a Mexican deal, but they didn't seem to need any more hints. So now we'll just drop off Mr. Jud Frederick and be on our way."

Ned was slowing for the curve down into the black hollow. Abby had started to hyperventilate, eyes closed. Don't lose it now, she told herself. Hang on to your rage and it will guide you. The road dipped and Abby was in full flashback, seeing Rex Lyman's skin blister in the heart of the flames, the horror flooding back. "Are you all right, Abby?" said Ned.

She drew a heaving breath and managed to say, "Yeah. I'm fine. Don't mind me, I'm just the witness. Don't let me stand in your way."

"Slow down," said Kyle as they reached the bottom of the slope. Above them loomed the massive stone archway straddling the road and the stream. Ned slowed the car to a crawl. "You know what happened here?" Kyle said, turning to Abby.

"Yeah, I saw it, remember?"

"No, I mean before that. Long time ago."

"What?"

"My sister killed herself. Jumped off the top of the fuckin' arch."

Breathe, Abby told herself. "I'm sorry."

"Yeah, me, too. Fucked up my whole life. Go on through and then pull off to the side, Ned. I think we'll leave Mr. Jud Frederick right in the middle of the road, about where Kayla landed. What do you think?"

Ned looked in the mirror and said, "We got a little complication."

"What's that?"

"Somebody's been following us."

Kyle twisted violently to look out the back window. "No shit."

"No shit. I noticed him when I parked at the motel. He pulled over a block behind us. He pulled out again when we took off and he just stopped at the top of the hill back there and cut his lights."

"Why, that sly bastard. Who the fuck?"

"No idea. What do you want me to do?"

Kyle peered out the back for a moment. "Like I said, go on through and pull over. There's a place by the stream where the bushes'll screen you. We'll see what he does."

Ned accelerated gently through the tunnel. Abby was finding that it was possible to go on thinking even at searing levels of stress. Was this the police behind them? If there was going to be a confrontation, she had to be hyperaware of that gun two feet from her. With the car stopped, with Kyle distracted, there could be a chance to run, but at point-blank range there was no margin for error.

A few yards beyond the arch, just before the road started to rise out of the hollow, Ned braked and pulled off onto a patch of grass bordered by brush. Beyond it the land fell away to the stream. Branches clawed at the windows as Ned parked. Looking out the back, Kyle said, "OK, what you gonna do, smart-ass?"

Everyone waited. Abby closed her eyes, opened them again. It was very dark and very quiet. After a time headlights shone on the road and a car came creeping through the tunnel. It went past them and climbed the slope out of the hollow. At the top of the hill was a single lamp high on a pole. As the car passed it, they could see that it was a dark-gray sedan, maybe a Honda. "Who the fuck is that?" said Kyle.

Nobody answered him. The car disappeared around the bend at the top of the hill. "Go do your business and let's hit the road," said Ned.

"Gimme the keys," said Kyle. Ned shut off the engine and handed the keys back. Kyle took them and pulled on the door handle, releasing the latch.

"Hang on," said Ned. "He's coming back."

They watched as the dark-gray car crept back down the hill. It slowed as it approached and then it stopped, fifty feet away, and after a moment turned so that its headlights shone directly into their eyes. "Shit," said Ned.

Kyle butted the door open. "OK, fucker. You want to play, we'll play." He jumped out of the car, thrashed through bushes, and strode past the front of Ned's car toward the newcomer. His right hand, holding the gun, was behind his back.

Abby's hand was already on the door handle when Ned said in a low voice, "Abby, go. Take off. Now." She pulled on the handle and shoved, and then she was out of the car and sprinting back toward the arch, in the adrenaline rush of her life. Behind her she heard Kyle say, "Well, fuck." She ran into the black tunnel, knowing she couldn't outrun a bullet but knowing he would have to be lucky to hit her. Kyle was yelling, but she couldn't make out what he was saying, and then as she came out of the tunnel there were shots behind her, a flurry from what sounded like two weapons, *snap-snap-crack*, sharp and loud. She veered to the right toward the end of the bridge where the stream ducked under the road, and as she did she cast a look over her shoulder and saw Kyle reel away from the dark car and fall to the pavement.

Abby jumped off the road and down into the streambed. She stumbled and fell, bashing a knee and bruising the heels of her hands, but she was up and running in a second, away from the light, on the muddy fringe of the stream. She went a hundred feet into darkness, splashing in shallow water and slipping on rocks, tripped and fell again, and lay panting, half in the stream and half out, craning around to look back at the arch.

The dark car came roaring through the arch and braked on the bridge with a squeal. Abby lay motionless. The car paused there for a moment and then took off again, burning rubber, and climbed the hill back toward town.

Abby waited until the sound of the car had died away and then got to her feet. She was panting, her knee hurt, and she was wet and covered with mud, but she was alive. She floundered into a low-hanging branch and realized that her best bet was to stick to the middle of the stream. The slip-on sneakers she had been too preoccupied to shuck off when she got home were a blessing now. She was walking in a few inches of water, on what felt like a bed of pebbles. There was very little light but the water glimmered faintly, guiding her. The stream narrowed and went around a bend under a cut-out bank. She ducked under a tree that had fallen across it. The bed grew rough again and Abby slipped and fell to her knees in the water, skinning her hands on the rocks. She got up and went on.

She could not even approach the task of processing everything she had seen and heard in the last half hour. All she wanted was to get help. Lights had begun to show above her through the trees, distant windows, the backs of houses. She approached the bank on her right, found it too steep to climb, went on. The streambed seemed to open out on her left onto a low bank and a gentle slope beyond it. Abby slogged out of the water and began to climb.

The slope got steeper and the underbrush thicker; Abby was accumulating injuries, scratches on her arms. She pushed on and then suddenly there were lighted windows above her and she came out of the woods and clambered up a grassy bank to the edge of a gravel parking lot behind a large house, a few cars haphazardly clustered near the back door. Abby could see through uncurtained windows: the corner of a bunk bed, two boys peering into a refrigerator in a big kitchen. It took her a moment to realize where she was: she was looking at the Tau Kappa Zeta house where she and Graham Gill had had lunch weeks before.

Abby trotted across the gravel to the back steps, took them two at a time, and started pounding on the back door.

29 |||||||

"Detective Ruffner's on his way," said the Lewisburg police chief, gazing down at Abby. He was a man in late middle age, heavy around the middle and the jowls, black browed and buzz-cut. "He was called out to a crime scene, but he seems to think maybe you had something to do with it. 'Don't let her go,' he said."

"I just saw a man get shot," Abby said. She was wrapped in a blanket, shivering in her wet clothes, her knee aching, blood running down her leg. "He was the man who killed Jud Frederick and Rex Lyman. He had Frederick's head in a plastic bag. I don't know who shot him, but whoever it is, he's driving a dark-gray Honda. He's probably the same one who shot Lisa Beth Quinton this afternoon." Abby was pleased that she was able to speak calmly. Her rage had subsided, leaving an arctic cold.

The chief just looked at her for a moment, frowning. Then he turned to the sergeant who had driven Abby to the station from the Tau Kappa Zeta house, siren on and lights flashing, leaving behind a fraternity house in an uproar where not much homework was going to get done tonight. "Did Ruffner say anything about a head?"

The sergeant shook his head. "He's got an ID on the body and he's bringing the witness back here."

"OK." The chief turned back to Abby. "You're shivering."

"It's the air-conditioning."

"You're probably in shock. That's a nasty cut on your knee."

"I'm fine."

"If you need medical attention, I can have somebody run you out to the hospital. Ruffner can interview you there."

Abby scowled at him. "I'll live. I need to talk to Detective Ruffner."

The chief shrugged and made for the door. To the sergeant he said, "I'll be in my office, talking to the ISP guys again. Call me if there's a riot or Al-Qaeda invades."

Abby accepted a cup of vending-machine coffee and tried to drink without spilling it, not an easy proposition with shaking hands. She sat with her eyes closed, thinking about what she had seen, what she had heard, what she had read in Lisa Beth's notes. Voices sounded in the hallway and she looked up to see Ruffner and Ned in the doorway.

The bottom fell out of Abby's stomach. Ned called her name and came across the office, knelt in front of her, put his hands on her arms. "Are you all right?"

Abby stared at him. "Get your hands off me."

She watched as his face fell. He released her and said, "Abby, I didn't know you were home."

The chill in Abby had deepened; she remembered talking to Ruffner about leads, about Everett Elford's secretary. She remembered Ned telling her about his old friend Mitch. She remembered Lisa Beth saying, "In a place like this they all know each other." Ned and Ruffner were staring at her. "I think I would like the chief to be here, too," Abby said.

Ruffner looked only slightly more haggard than he had the last time he had talked to Abby, four hours before. He said, "What do you think is going on here?"

"I don't know. All I know is, this man here was helping the man who killed Lyman and Frederick to escape."

Ruffner nodded once. "This man here was the one who called me to tell me the killer was sitting in his kitchen. If he'd done what I said and stayed clear of the house, we'd have had a nice quiet arrest."

Ned scowled at him. "More likely a shoot-out. And if I'd stayed clear of the house God knows what Kyle would have done to her." He turned to Abby. "I had no idea you were home. When Kyle showed up I told him to make himself at home and I'd go out and get some beer. Instead I called Mitch. I knew Kyle was the guy they were looking for. Mitch told me to get clear and wait for him but I was afraid Kyle would split if I didn't come back, so I grabbed the beer and went back. And there you were."

Abby looked from Ned to Ruffner and back. Was this something she could believe? "OK. Talk to me. Who the fuck was Kyle?"

Ned exhaled, shoulders sagging. "It's a long story."

The desk sergeant appeared in the doorway and beckoned to Ruffner, who went out into the hall. A few words were exchanged in a low murmur and then Abby heard Ruffner say, "OK, put her in the interview room." He leaned into the room, frowning, and said, "All right, just sit tight for a while. I gotta talk to someone." He pulled the door shut, leaving Abby and Ned alone in the office.

Ned pulled a chair out from behind a desk and sat down opposite Abby. He rubbed his face for a moment with both hands and Abby saw that he was having his own issues with stress. "Kyle was a kid I knew in grade school."

"You and Everett."

"Yeah, we were all in the same class. Kyle had a twin sister named Kayla. They were hardscrabble kids. I think their father was a drunk. They'd come to school with holes in their clothes, dirty faces, that kind of thing. Kids made fun of them, but I felt sorry for them. Kyle and I were playground buddies for a little while in like, fourth grade. After that I'd see him around, say hi sometimes, but he grew into kind of a hoodlum, started getting in trouble, and I steered clear of him. And Kayla was one of those girls my mother used to say grew up too fast."

Abby watched Ned stare at the floor for a while. "What happened?"

"I was off at college, up at Purdue. I came home one weekend and there was a party. I went with Everett. I don't even know whose house it was, out by the creek somewhere. A bunch of people I didn't know. Kayla was there, getting drunk. It wasn't really my kind of thing, but at the time I was really into rebelling, flouting that strict morality I'd been raised with. So there I was, drinking and scheming to pick somebody up, get laid, like the teenage dope I was, and then the word went around that Kayla was upstairs pulling a train."

Abby could see something naked and pleading in Ned's face. "Pulling a train."

"Yeah. Having sex with a bunch of guys one after the other. That's what they called it. Now we'd probably call it a gang rape."

"Oh, God."

"And to my eternal shame, my first thought was, wow, that's exciting, maybe I can get in on that. But Everett and I kind of looked at one another, and that brought me back to earth. So we left. I dropped Everett off and I went to find Kyle. Yeah, you don't need to say it. I should have gone to the police. But I was just thinking, her brother should know about this. So I found him and I told him about it. But it was too late. By the time he got there it was over. The next day Kayla went to the cops and said she'd been raped, and she named names. A guy named Duane Schipp, Jud Frederick, and Everett Elford."

"Everett? Wasn't he with you?"

"Yeah. I think Kayla was too drunk to know who they were after a while. Other people told the cops Everett never went upstairs, so he wasn't charged. Schipp and Frederick were charged, but Rex Lyman got them acquitted at trial. Kayla had a reputation, she was pretty promiscuous, and he used that to the max. So they skated. And then a few days after that, Kayla jumped off the arch and killed herself."

Abby put a hand to her face.

"A week later, Kyle went into the bowling alley out on Lafayette Road and broke up league night by beating Duane Schipp to death with a bowling ball. He didn't skate. He went up to Michigan City for twenty years."

"My God."

"When Lyman and Frederick got killed, I thought of Kyle. Right away, and I told Mitch about it. He remembered the case. But Lyman and Frederick were into so many things, the other theories seemed to make as much sense as anything. Mitch showed me the video from Frederick's house and it didn't look like Kyle to me. Twenty years inside changes you. But I went and talked to his mom, at the trailer park."

"That's who he was there to see that night when I saw him."

"Yeah. He was laying low there, and moving around town at night in the streambed. His mother told me she hadn't heard from him since he got out of prison, but I could tell she was lying. I told Mitch about that, so he was aware. But nobody else had seen Kyle, or at least was willing to say so. And then he came to my house tonight."

"Why?"

"His mom had told him I'd talked to her. And he wanted to ask me about Everett, to make sure he was guilty, before he killed Everett like he killed the other three. He trusted his old playground buddy to give him the straight dope, I guess. I had no idea you were downstairs or I never would have left. Why didn't you come in through the house like before?"

Abby didn't answer him right away; she was too busy looking at everything she had spent the evening working out and wondering if it could be wrong. Finally she said, "I came in through the back because I was too pissed off to be scared anymore. I thought your pal Everett and that guy, Ingstrom, were behind Lisa Beth getting killed."

"Ah, Jesus. No. Everett wouldn't be in on anything like that. Never."

"I didn't make this up. It's all about the scandal Lisa Beth dug up. I can show you her notes."

"Mitch is aware. He's looking at her computer."

"Then he'll see. Everett and Ingstrom had a plan to make a killing on a piece of land in the south part of the county by selling the state government an easement so they could put the new interstate extension through. But Everett sold the land to Frederick before the payment was made. Lyman and Frederick were blackmailing Everett, forcing him to cut them in on the deal. Everett must have told Ingstrom. And how do you react to blackmail if you happen to know a bunch of outlaw bikers? I thought Kyle was the guy they got to do the dirty work for them. I'm still not convinced he wasn't. Who was that that shot him? Whoever shot Lisa Beth was in a dark-gray Honda, too. I think Ingstrom sent somebody to clean up after he realized what a loose cannon Kyle was."

"I don't think Kyle was involved in that," said Ned. "But you're partly right. Lyman and Frederick were blackmailing Everett."

Abby gaped at him. "You knew about it?"

"Everett told me about it a couple of days ago. Frederick found out about the deal from Everett's secretary. But when Frederick and Lyman came to put the arm on Everett, he just bailed and sold them the land. He didn't want any part of it anymore. It was Ingstrom's idea from the start. And the word going around Indianapolis is that Ingstrom's about to be indicted for it. So Everett withdrew his candidacy for the House seat today. He's decided he doesn't want to get into politics after all."

Abby felt things slipping out of her grasp. The door opened and Ruffner came back in. Rage stirring again, Abby said, "So what about Lisa Beth? She didn't kill herself."

Ruffner said, "Kyle didn't shoot her. At least not with the gun he had on him tonight. That was Jud Frederick's forty caliber. Lisa Beth was shot with a nine millimeter. And so was Kyle, it looks like."

"By whoever it was who set Lisa Beth up. Her source."

"It wasn't her source," said Ruffner, shaking his head.

"How do you know?"

"I just talked to the source."

"Who is it?"

Ruffner walked to his desk and sat down heavily, sighing. "All I'm gonna tell you is, it's someone close to Elford. She knew the land deal was crooked and she had agreed to talk to Lisa Beth about it. But she showed up late for the meet and our guys were already there, looking at a crime scene. So she panicked and drove off. Then she realized she had to talk to us. That was her just now."

Abby and Ned traded a look. Ned said, "So where does that leave us?"

Ruffner exhaled, a long weary sigh. "Well, we got plenty of suspects."

"Like who?"

"Like Jerry Collins, to start with."

There was a silence. Abby said, "No. That's impossible."

"Is it? According to the doctor in Lafayette, he left the office up there in plenty of time to drive down here, shoot his wife, and then get home in time to be there when our officer showed up."

Abby glared at him. "No. Why would he do that?"

"Who knows? She cheated on him, more than once. For years. That might get to a man after a while. Anyway, he's the first guy we gotta look at."

Abby shook her head, not finding the words to refute it.

Ruffner went on. "Seems to me, if she wasn't set up, Lisa Beth had to have been followed to the Azteca. So who was sitting on her house, watching it? Who knew where she lived?"

"All kinds of people," said Ned. "I'm not buying Jerry."

Ruffner shrugged. "OK. There's no shortage of people who didn't like Lisa Beth in this town, if you want to know the truth."

Abby said, "And what about Kyle? Why the hell would Jerry shoot Kyle?"

Ruffner shot her a look. "You're assuming the same person did both shootings. We're not."

The silence had a certain stunned quality this time. Ruffner said, "Here's another question for you. Tonight, where did this dark-gray Honda pick you up, when he followed you out to the arch? At the Tarkington?"

Abby leaned forward and put her face in her hands. She was exhausted and light-headed and her head was full of nightmare images, but she knew there was nothing more important than to think it all through. She thought about everything and after a time she said softly, "Oh, my God." She took her hands away from her face and opened her eyes to find Ruffner and Ned staring at her.

"I know who killed Lisa Beth," Abby said. "And Kyle. And I'm pretty sure he's not finished."

"A doctor will be with you right away." The nurse backed out and tugged at the curtain, closing off the alcove where she had led Abby and Ned. Abby's knee was throbbing and she had been grateful to be delivered to the hospital in a squad car. Ned pulled a chair to the side of the gurney where Abby lay. She put a hand over her eyes to shield them from the fluorescent light. "I had it all wrong. There was never any reason to think the person who killed Lisa Beth was the same one who killed the other two. As soon as I started thinking about Lisa Beth in isolation I saw it. I should have seen it sooner."

"Give yourself a break. Nobody saw it."

"But it was obvious. If Lisa Beth's source didn't set her up, then the killer followed Lisa Beth from her house. Specifically from the front of her house, where my car was parked. Not from the alley in back, where her garage was, where any competent stalker would watch. So he wasn't there to watch her. He was there to watch me. He followed me from the campus, from behind the library."

"And then he saw Lisa Beth come out and get in your car."

"And that set him off. And tonight, he didn't pick us up at the Tarkington. You said he was already behind us when we got there. So it was somebody who was interested in me. He must have been watching my house. But where was his car?"

Ned gave it a moment's thought, brow wrinkled. "Across the stream, on that gravel patch by the shed at the corner of the soccer field. He saw us leave, he ran across the stream and got in his car and waited for us to go by on Jackson."

Abby shuddered. "He's been following people all day, and we never saw him."

"You had no reason to look for him."

Abby took her hand away from her face. "Now I'll be looking for him everywhere."

"They'll get him. If you're right about him and the frat house, they'll get him."

Footsteps sounded beyond the curtain and they looked to see it pulled aside. A man in a doctor's white lab coat came into the alcove. It took Abby a second to recognize him and then she went cold with horror. "Hello, Abby," said Ben Larch.

30 |||||||

"What are you doing here?" Abby said, stupidly.

"I'm stalking you, what do you think?" Ben's voice held just a bit of an edge. A nice-looking boy, almost pretty, dark-eyed with a faintly Asian cast. "You thought you could ditch me, huh? Where else am I going to wait for you to show up except the police station? I guess I'm smarter than you think. Smarter than that dumb-fuck cop who drove you here, for sure."

"Hey, kid." Ned had risen and was moving around the foot of the gurney. "Let's take this outside."

"I know who you are," said Ben. He was reaching inside the unbuttoned lab coat. "You've been trying to get in Abby's pants, haven't you?" Ben brought out the black 9mm automatic and pointed it at Ned. "And that's why you have to die."

The gun went off as Ned whipped the chair at him. It went off again as Ned sprang, knocking him back against the counter, and then Ned was staggering back, saying, "You little shit," in a ragged hollow voice and Abby was off the gurney and clawing at Ben's eyes.

Ben clubbed her with the butt of the pistol, stunning her with a flash of pain, and then he was dragging her by the hair, through the curtain and out into the hall, and people were shouting. Ben squeezed off another shot, there were more screams, and then Ben jerked her upright and jammed the muzzle of the gun under her jaw. "Freeze or I'll blow her head off!" His voice cracked as he yelled it, the first time Abby had ever heard him raise his voice. Abby caught a glimpse of shocked faces, nurses in scrubs, another doctor in a white coat running away, and then Ben was crashing through doors, pulling her down a hallway and pushing through an exit door out into the night.

They were in a parking lot, well lit, nearly full. Ben had her neck in the crook of his arm, the gun to her temple, hauling her along a row of cars in an awkward embrace. Warm blood was trickling down her face. "Ben," Abby gasped. "Talk to me."

"Now you want to talk to me?" He halted at the rear of a dark-gray Honda and forced her to her knees. "That's a switch." He had keys in his hand, the gun at her temple. The trunk popped open. "Get in the trunk," he said.

"Where are we going?"

"Where do you think?" Ben grabbed her by the hair again and pulled, making her cry out. "Get in."

Abby went limp, sinking back onto the pavement, grimacing against the pain in her scalp. "Not till you tell me where we're going." All Abby could think to do was to make him keep talking.

"We're going back to the Tau Kap house and I'm gonna light those dumb jocks up. You sicced those assholes on me, now you're gonna see how tough they are when I've got the equalizer. Now get in the fucking trunk."

Eyes squeezed shut, Abby sagged back against the fender of the car. She heard a door open somewhere, urgent voices emerging from the building. "Let go of my hair."

To her surprise, he obeyed. Ben stepped back, raised the gun toward the building, and squeezed off a shot. Somebody swore loudly and there was a rapid scuffling of feet. Ben leveled the gun at Abby and said, "Get in the trunk, Abby. Or I'll shoot you right here."

Abby raised her hands. "Ben. First of all, I didn't sic anybody on you." She knew she was talking for her life; she was on the high wire in a high wind, teetering over the abyss.

He drew himself erect, the gun aimed at her face, "You can stop lying any time, Abby. I know what you did. All I wanted was for you to be nice to me. And you laughed at me."

"I never laughed at you."

"I saved you from that old dyke. I saved you from that creep tonight. I saved you from that guy inside. But you don't care. You laughed at me, you snitched on me to Spassky, you set those gorillas on me. All you are is a cold heartless bitch. Well, bitch, now you're gonna have to watch what happens when people get pushed too far."

Abby stared into the dark eyes, seeing nothing but the void. "All right, I'll watch. But don't make me get in the trunk. I won't give you any trouble."

"No, sure you won't. Get in the trunk or I'll shoot you right here."

In the distance a siren sounded, faintly. Abby looked past the muzzle of the gun into Ben's eyes and tried to read how many seconds of life she had left. "OK, Ben. You're the boss."

"God damn right I am."

Abby climbed into the trunk.

As far as Abby could tell Ben was driving carefully, smoothly and not too fast. She was in total darkness, in a fetal position on her side, face to the rear, but there was just enough room for her to move her limbs, shift position slightly.

A detached part of her was amazed that she was so calm. The police will save you, she thought. They will have evacuated the fraternity house and they will be waiting, watching for a dark-gray Honda with a couple of bullet holes in it. They will arrest Ben and they will set you free.

That, Abby thought, is a desperate mind at work.

There is a tire iron in here somewhere, she thought. If this car is like mine, it is next to the spare tire in its well and I am lying on top of it. In despair, she began to feel around her. Something was digging into her shoulder; she squirmed, twisted, grunted with the effort, and managed to close her hand around it. She pulled a metal cylinder to her chest, explored it with her fingers, identified a spray can with a nozzle. She turned the nozzle away from her face and pressed the button once. There was the hiss of a powerful spray and an oily, pungent odor, and after a moment she blinked, her eyes stinging.

Not without a fight, Abby thought.

Ben drove for what seemed a very long time. Abby lay in the dark thinking about her mother, her father, about New York and Cambridge and people she loved, Samantha and Evan and all the sweet wasted life she had not enjoyed enough. The car stopped and she tensed, but nothing happened, and after a long time it began to move again. Abby began to cry, weeping for everything she had lost, for Lisa Beth and Ned massacred, for the stupid lizard brutality that was about to stamp out her life. The car stopped again.

Abby wiped tears from her face and took a deep breath.

A door opened and then slammed, shaking the car. Footsteps sounded, coming around to the rear. A latch clicked and the trunk lid popped open, a line of dim light appearing. Then the trunk lid was rising, Ben standing there with the gun in his right hand. Abby reared up, supporting her weight with her left hand as she pushed up on the lid with her right, the spray can hidden by the curve of the lid.

"You double-crossing cunt," said Ben, dimly visible in the light from a streetlamp on a tree-lined street. He had shed the white coat and was just a slender figure in the dark. "There are cops everywhere. You set me up."

"Please just do me one favor," Abby said, squirming to stabilize her position with her knees under her, looking at the muzzle of the gun a yard from her chest. "Please don't shoot me in the face. If you ever loved me, please just do me that favor. Shoot me in the heart instead." Slowly she reached for the pistol with her left hand, looking Ben in the eye. "Shoot me here," she said, gently grasping his wrist and pulling his hand toward her chest. Ben's eyes were wide, riveted to hers.

Abby swept the gun away from her as she brought the spray can down from under the trunk lid and gave him a face full of lubricant from a foot away. Ben snarled, pitching backward, and a shot deafened Abby as he tore his wrist out of her grasp. She dived headfirst out of the trunk and caught Ben square in the chest with both hands, knocking him backward, landing hard on the pavement and rolling, coming up against the curb. She was on her feet in an instant as another shot cracked, whistling by her head, and then she was running in the dark again, alive. "Police!" she screamed. "Somebody please call the police!" Abby ran with death at her heels, not feeling her injured knee or her blistered feet, trusting her well-trained muscles to save her life. Behind her, steps slapped on the pavement, too close.

Tires squealed, a siren blared impossibly loud, impossibly close, a bright light hit her in the eyes. "Over here!" somebody yelled. Men were coming out of the shadows, into her path. She ran into the arms of a uniformed policeman as behind her a man shouted, "Drop the fucking gun!" The cop steadied her, pulled her upright, said, "It's OK, honey, we got you."

Abby wheeled, struggling in his grasp, and looked behind her. A searchlight on a police car had caught a figure kneeling in the middle of the street, a boy with one hand to his face and a gun in the other. He was waving the gun back and forth, his head bowed. "God damn you, Abby!" the boy screamed.

"Drop the gun!" Policemen were at the edge of the pool of light, guns leveled at the boy.

Ben raised his head, eyes squeezed shut, and put the gun to the underside of his jaw. "Abby!" he shouted, hoarsely now.

Abby closed her eyes and was spared the sight as he pulled the trigger.

31 |||||||

"If you have to get shot, the emergency room of a hospital is about the best place to do it," said Ruffner, tie loosened and shoulders slumping. "They had him on the table in about three minutes. They stopped the bleeding and were able to repair the intestine, and the prognosis is good. He'll be in intensive care for a while but he's going to make it."

"Thank God." Abby was drained; her capacity for emotional reaction was exhausted. She was lying on a gurney again, perhaps the same one, but this time instead of Ned she was sharing a curtained alcove with Ruffner and a uniformed police officer. There seemed to be somewhat more commotion outside the alcove than there had been on her previous visit an hour before. "Don't leave me, please," she said.

"Don't worry," said Ruffner. "We're not letting you out of our sight. When you get stitched up we'll put you in a room and Officer Thornton here's going to camp outside. When you've had a rest I'll be back to take your statement." He hesitated. "I believe you have set a world record tonight for abductions by separate offenders. I can't remember anything like what you've been through, ever."

"Lisa Beth said it was the cluster effect. That makes me nervous because I don't know how many make a cluster."

Ruffner rested his hand on her arm for a moment. "You saved lives tonight. It would have been real ugly. You came up with the right answer just in time."

"I don't feel like I won. I feel like I lost. My friend's dead."

"And you're alive. From my point of view, you just won two of the toughest fights anybody's ever had to face. In one night. I don't know how you did it."

Abby closed her eyes, her head spinning, enormously, fathomlessly tired. Her mind shied from the grieving she knew lay ahead but at the same time she felt herself soaring in wonder at the immensity of the life she had come close to losing. "It didn't kill me," she said. "I don't know what it did to me."

"Be careful on the steps," Abby said. "They're icy."

"I'm good. See you next time." Natalia waved and disappeared around the corner of the house, stepping carefully on the snowy ground. Abby lingered for a moment at the door, looking through the bare trees across to the chapel on the campus, the centerpiece of a postcard view. She shivered and went back inside, closing the door. She walked to the steps at the rear of the room and went up to tap on the door at the top and open it.

Ned was at the table in the kitchen, frowning at his laptop. "How's the prize pupil doing?" he said.

Abby shrugged. "She's getting there. I don't know that she's going to ace the SAT, but she should score high enough to get into school somewhere. She's come a long way." Abby sat at the table and rested her chin on her hand. She gazed at Ned until he looked up from the computer. "So have you."

"Me?"

"You're putting the weight back on, starting to look . . ." She hesitated.

"Less like a corpse?"

"I was looking for a more tactful way to put it."

"I feel good. I feel like the innards are finally healed. Eating is fun again."

"Well, you'll have to manage dinner without me tonight. I've got a session in Lafayette."

Ned shrugged. "I've been cooking for myself for twenty-five years. So this thing is working for you?"

Abby nodded. "Yeah, it's good. If you'd told me a year ago I'd be in group therapy I'd have run the other way fast. But I wish I'd done it sooner."

"You need people sometimes."

Abby's gaze went away out the window. "They're my new best friends. You cry on my shoulder, I'll cry on yours."

"They say it helps."

"It's the only thing that helps. We've got a couple of vets of course, guys that got worn down by too many trips to Iraq and Afghanistan. Tough guys, salt of the earth, but suffering. And we've got a woman who stayed with her husband for twenty years, till the kids were raised, despite the beatings. Talk about tough. And then there are the rape survivors. I had no idea there were so many people with PTSD out there."

"There's a lot of trauma out there."

Abby stared out the window. It had begun to snow again. "I'll tell you one thing. I'm done with the guilt. That's gone."

"Glad to hear it." Ned shoved the laptop away. "I'll be gone soon, too," he said.

Abby stared. "What?"

"I got a job."

"You're kidding me."

He shook his head. "Passing that physical last week was the last step. I'm cleared to go."

"Go where?"

"Africa."

"You're serious."

He nodded. "I'll be doing logistics for Doctors Without Borders. In the Central African Republic. Where there's a civil war on and a hell of a lot of suffering right now. Minimum one-year commitment. I leave in a month."

They looked at each other for a while. Ned's expression was grave. Abby found she was not really surprised. "Well. It was good while it lasted. Who's going to be my landlord?"

"A nephew of mine just got married. He works in Lafayette. He and his wife are going to take the house. You'll like them. They're good people."

"I hope so."

He frowned out the window, then turned back and reached across the table for her hand. "I never was much for social conventions, but I think starting a romantic relationship while recovering from a serious gunshot wound is kind of out there, even for me."

"I can't say I have much experience in this regard, either. It just kind of happened. But it's been good. I think we needed it."

"Yeah. Anyway, we said there were no strings attached and we would just kind of roll with it."

"We did."

"I don't know how long I'll be out there. You don't know where you'll be in two years, either. If this is worth it, we'll know."

Abby nodded. "I suppose we will."

"No strings attached, but I'm starting to feel like Humphrey Bogart at the end of *Casablanca*."

"Excuse me?"

"I think this could be the beginning of a beautiful friendship."

Abby considered that, frowning faintly. "I'd say that's romantic, but I think that makes me Captain Renault."

The laugh was good; the tears came and went quickly. Outside, the snow went on falling.

ACKNOWLEDGMENTS

The author wishes to thank Andrew Salter, Bob Rivers, Adriana Deck, Jessie Salter and Nick Salter for the professional, sociological and mathematical information they were kind enough to share.

ABOUT THE AUTHOR

Photo © 2015 Kevin Valentine

Sam Reaves was raised in small towns in Indiana and Illinois but gravitated to Chicago upon graduating from college and has been there ever since, when on US soil. He has lived and traveled widely in Europe and the Middle East and has worked as a teacher and a translator. He has published fiction and nonfiction as Sam Reaves; under the pen name Dominic Martell, he has written a European-based suspense trilogy. He is married and has two adult children.